Do I Love You?

To Manai

with very best wishes

from

Paul
McDonald.

X.

Do I Love You?

Paul McDonald

**Tindal
Street
Press**

First published in May 2008
by Tindal Street Press Ltd
217 The Custard Factory, Gibb Street, Birmingham, B9 4AA
www.tindalstreet.co.uk

A CIP catalogue reference for this book is available
from the British Library

ISBN: 978 0 9551 384 8 5

Typeset by Country Setting, Kingsdown, Kent
Printed and bound in Great Britain by Clays Ltd, St Ives PLC

FSC
Mixed Sources
Product group from well-managed
forests and other controlled sources
Cert no. SGS - COC - 2061
www.fsc.org
© 1996 Forest Stewardship Council

In memory of Debbie Ball

Do I Love You?

love (*n*). 1 very strong affection. 2 very strong affection and sexual attraction. 3 great liking. 4 a person or thing that you love. 5 a score of zero.

Oxford English Mini Dictionary

BIRMINGHAM UNIVERSITY
1985

A Naked Billy Goat

It was 2 a.m. and Warren was busy burgling the research laboratories of Birmingham University. He was looking for drugs, amphetamines preferably, and he'd already filled three carrier bags with stuff: powders, capsules, pills; anything that looked promising in the orange flare of his fag lighter. He'd never burgled a university laboratory before. He'd burgled everywhere else – chemists, doctor and dentist's surgeries, the houses of fat ladies who he knew were prescribed amphetamine for slimming purposes. But this was his first laboratory – and it was full of chemicals. Thousands of them.

But he hadn't expected a billy goat, let alone a naked one. And yet there it was, standing alone in a pen made of plywood and chicken wire. Naked. Nude. Bare-beamed and obscenely starkers.

In the ordinary course of things the word naked isn't one you associate with billy goats. They're always naked, aren't they? Except for the ones that dress up as mascots for marching bands. But few words could better describe the billy goat that Warren Clackett observed.

Warren screamed.

It was a proper scream too: almost prepubescent in its shrillness. He hadn't screamed that way since the day he saw his pet pit-bull terrier, Panzer, lose a fight with a squirrel. His assumptions about how the universe works were undermined that day and it was happening again.

Another scream welled within him, but this time, having dropped his carrier bags, he managed to get his hand over his mouth. Saliva sprayed through the grill of his fingers and his lighter went out. Moonbeams from the skylight kept the spectacle illuminated, however, and, despite himself, Warren remained transfixed. *The billy goat is naked. They're always naked. But this billy goat seems particularly naked. Why? How?*

This billy goat seemed *particularly* naked because this billy goat was hairless. Hideously hairless. Its skin hung pink and wrinkled from its dithering, pitiable body. Even Warren, generally a self-centred fellow, couldn't help feeling that the beast had been wronged in a fundamental, ungodly way. It was ugly too. Perhaps the ugliest thing he'd ever seen. And given that Warren lived in Walsall, that's saying something.

The animal made a kind of bleating noise as it gazed wide-eyed at the burglar. Warren wanted to look away but was unable. He could do nothing but gape as, abruptly, the goat sat down. This too was an unexpected and somewhat unnatural thing for a goat to do. Goats don't sit down, do they? At least not on their bottoms. This one did: its hind legs buckling as if someone had shot it in the rear.

The bleating became more high-pitched and agonized and the air began to thicken with the foulest of odours. Had the word dysentery featured in Warren's vocabulary, he would have used it to describe the scene he now witnessed: goat dysentery. Naked goat dysentery.

Warren panicked. What had he stumbled upon? Was the animal diseased? Was its condition catching? He scooped up his bags and made for the door, the rubber soles of his Dunlops squeaking on the floor tiles. He was leaving prematurely as there were thousands more bottles to inspect, more cupboards to open and he had another three carrier bags in his pocket. But the goat had spooked him and his half-haul would have to do. It wasn't just the racket it made, or the stench: it was the look of the thing. Naked.

Warren's exit took him through two adjoining labs, along a corridor, past an office in which a security guard was watching *Miami Vice* and out into the campus grounds. Here he began retching. Nothing came. This wasn't a surprise as all that Warren had eaten in three days was two licks at the lid of a Marmite jar. The sight of a young man retching at three in the morning is nothing new for a university campus and it was nothing new for Warren, whose drug-scorched innards spasmed hourly. But he wanted to be as quiet as possible as he made his way to his car. The last thing he needed was to get nicked, despite the fact that, in his experience, the gear in prison is cheaper than that on the outside.

Warren retched again and, again, only managed to produce a squirt of sour wind. Perhaps ridding himself of the smell would help kill the nausea? He sucked at the cool night air with his mouth and exhaled through his nostrils. He repeated this a dozen times and, by the time he reached the side street in which he'd parked his Austin Metro, he felt a little less queasy.

Once in the car he switched on the courtesy light by punching it twice and began inspecting his swag. He knew this was reckless but he was hungry for a hit. He tore through the bags scrutinizing labels as he went. Two bottles that he thought were amphetamine sulphate turned out to be ammonium sulphate and he tossed these angrily aside.

The next three jars he retrieved were the same and Warren was half-hysterical with panic by the time he found a bottle whose label he'd read correctly. He unscrewed the top and took a healthy pinch in each nostril.

The buzz didn't come immediately; it never did, but it *would* come and just knowing this made Warren relax. In minutes his yelping nerves would be muzzled for a while.

As the fierce powder burned exquisitely beneath his eyes, it chased away the stench of goat dysentery and he became calm – or as calm as the wired, twitchy twenty-two-year-old ever got. Still, Warren was able to sort through his booty in a slightly more focused way.

It was disappointing. Most of the sulphate jars were half empty and a large carton of red and grey capsules that looked exactly like the amphetamine-based slimming drug, Duromine, turned out not to be. Still, he might be able to flog these later: untrained eyes would never tell the difference. Five years ago, when the Northern Soul scene was still flourishing, it would have been easy. You could sell any old shite to the freaks who flocked to the big all-night discos like Wigan Casino. Happy days. Now no one seemed interested in speed. Warren himself was an exception. But maybe he could pass it on to one of his country bumpkin contacts in Shrewsbury or Hereford. Those hay-nibblers were a push-over. And at least that way he would salvage something from a break-in that would doubtless give him nightmares. What with the goat. And the bleating. And the stench.

Warren popped off his courtesy light and, after nine goes, managed to start the car. The engine vibrations shook the knitting needle from the hole where the aerial should have been and the windscreen-wipers came on of their own accord. The door to the glove compartment flopped open and the volume knob dropped off the radio. Easing the rattling Metro down the side street, Warren headed for the A34 and it occurred to him, as the exhaust pipe began dragging on the tarmac, that perhaps he should have stolen a better car.

EIGHTEEN YEARS LATER

I

'Very Ape'

Nirvana, *In Utero* (Geffen)

TREBBO

Most people would blame me for what happened to our family. Personally I blame Colonel Sanders. You'll see why.

This is how it started. Me and my girlfriend, Tiffany Milton, were chilling in my bedroom. We were watching a documentary about how the stroppy minger, Courtney Love, killed Kurt Cobain by depressing him to death. There was an ad break and I was slipping my hand experimentally up Tiff's shirt when the door burst open. My father – aka the Div – tumbled in.

'Stroll on, Tom!' he went.

This is the kind of irritating thing the Div says. I don't know what 'stroll on' means or who Tom is. I think it seems like a fitting combination of words to him simply because they nearly rhyme. Such is the way with numpties.

'Oi!' I said, snatching my hand from beneath Tiff's shirt. 'What do you think you're doing?'

'Stroll on, sweet Thomas!' he went, then half fell and half staggered to the left, and half fell and half staggered to the right. This half falling and half staggering the Div likes to call dancing.

'What do you think you're doing . . . *in my room*?'

'I haven't heard this for years,' he cried, fall-staggering to the left again, clapping twice and then fall-staggering to the right.

'What?'

'This,' he said, pointing at the telly. He was referring to an advert for Kentucky Fried Chicken, which ended as he spoke. 'That,' he said, panting a little. He was wide-eyed and flushed and his wiry, salt and pepper hair seemed to hum with gratuitous perkiness.

'What about it?' I'd seen the ad before a couple of times. It appeared to be part of a new advertising campaign in which KFC promoted itself as 'soul food'. The ad was set at a party and showed people dancing around buckets of bird-bits to the accompaniment of an uptempo soul song. They were scoffing Chicken Nuggets and banging on that 'You don't need forks, plates or tables, you just need soul.' To me this sounded like a fast track to salmonella. The central dancer was an athletic black dude with a big Afro who, unlike the Div, moved in time with the beat. The fashions and the feel of the scene implied that it was set in the old days, but I couldn't say when. Victorian? Elizabethan? Palaeolithic? The Div's youth? The tune itself had pounding snare drums and a wailing vocal of the kind your average saddo might find stimulating.

'That's classic Northern Soul,' went the Div. 'Frank Wilson's "Do I Love You". It was one of the most sought-after sounds when I was on the Northern scene. Stroll, stroll on, it's brillo, absolutely brillo. Are Chicken Nuggets the same as Chicken Dippers, by the way?'

Ever since I can remember the Div has enjoyed boring the breasts off me with tales about his days on something called the 'Northern Soul scene'. I don't know much about it because I make a point of not listening to him, but I *do* know that whenever Northern Soul becomes a topic of conversation he starts using words like 'brillo' and things nosedive from there. Generally it ends with him making a glorious, rosy-nippled nork of himself.

'Sit down, take some deep breaths and think this through,' I told him. 'Knead your temples if you have to, but think: *why would we be interested*?'

Tiffany elbowed me hard in the ribs; 'Trebbo,' she hissed. She didn't like it when I was rude to my parents. Her old man bolted when she was a nipper and she was forever telling me I was lucky to have a dad. But it was difficult not to be rude. My folks had, after all, named me Nigel. Kids have become serial killers over less; or worse, train-spotters. This is my beef with the name Nigel: it's a ming-ing name! People who have friends *can't be called* Nigel. At least not people with cool friends. Cool people can't publicly speak the name Nigel, obviously, and it's impos-sible to shorten. Nig? Gel? *Nige?* And it gets worse. My middle name is Pookie. The Div insisted on naming me after one of his Northern Soul heroes, some freak called Pookie Hudson. Have you ever heard of him? No one has, at least no one you'd feel comfortable sharing a cell with. I never tell anyone what the P stands for. Luckily I have a surname, Trebor, which can be adapted in a relatively cool way. Trebbo I can live with. But I am pissed that the Div collared the coolest Trebor-related nickname before I was born. Minty is wasted on the sad gimmer.

'It's all right, chick,' went the Div, his eyes twinkling with crackpot joviality, 'I'm used to it.'

'What's a "Northern Soul scene", Mr Trebor?' she asked.

I could list a gazillion things you just don't do in life: tie the laces of your trainers in a bow, say, or pass up the chance of punching Richard Madeley. Yet at the top of the list is: you don't ask the Div about Northern Soul. The result is like being barfed over by someone who's eaten the most boring book in the world.

'Ah, Tiffany,' he said. 'You can call me Minty. The Northern Soul scene . . . Where do I begin? It was the biggest thing in my life when I was your age.' And off he went.

My age indeed! Surely the wobble-gutted git had never been my age. He'd never been sixteen, on a bed with a bra-less, sixteen-year-old Tiffany. If he had he'd know that I needed to be fondling her tits, getting her worked up enough to let me go all the way. Or at the very least I needed to be watching the Nirvana documentary, which had now resumed. What I *didn't* need was to be listening to him reminiscing about the good old days when he used to dance all night to music no one in their right minds had ever heard of. But that's what the Northern Soul scene's all about.

'We travelled all over the country, Tiffany: Cleethorpes, Blackpool and, particularly, Wigan. Wigan Casino was the place to be. It was our Ibiza.' He annoyed me, as he always did, by pronouncing it Ibit*sah*. Who did he think he was, a freaking Vengaboy?

'You went to Wigan to gamble?' asked Tiffany, who was now sitting up on the bed with her legs folded beneath her. My girlfriend is what you'd have to call the 'earnest' type and she asked her question as if she was interviewing Desmond Tutu.

'Oh no, chick,' he went, 'God bless you. We went to hear rare soul: it was music that you couldn't buy in the shops or hear on the radio. Old, deleted, forgotten soul from America.'

16

'Like the song in that chicken advert?'

'Exactly. There were only two original copies of that record in the country.' He then began singing it and fall-staggering again. To the left, clap, clap; to the right clap, clap.

Tiffany nodded thoughtfully. Inexplicably, she seemed to like the Div. I would have liked him better if he'd been roasting on a spit with his nads where the apple should be.

My fear was that next he'd start bragging about his 'moves'. It's when he starts bragging about his 'moves' that he makes the biggest Spam-javelin out of himself. I wouldn't mind so much if his uncoolness didn't taint me by association. But how can it not? The useless twerp seemed to be motivated by a perverse need to humiliate me; that's probably why he decided to take a job as a lollipop man. *Lollipop man!* What kind of career choice is that? It would have been less embarrassing if my father had been a rent boy. I'm a sixteen-year-old called Nigel, whose father is a lollipop man. Gee thanks, Daddy.

'"Do I Love You" was an ace tune, Tiffany,' he said. 'They were all ace tunes; and they called for a very athletic style of dancing.'

'Minty, you'd better not,' I warned.

'The best dancers, and I count myself among that number, had our own floor moves years before these break-dancers started doing it.'

Tiffany raised her eyebrows and he needed no more encouragement. He promptly dropped backwards on to his hands, clapping them twice before they touched the floor. About two quid's worth of change dropped out of his pocket and his Fruit of the Loom T-shirt rode up to reveal a lardy white gut. He managed, after two or three wheezes, to push himself back up.

'Not bad, eh? Wicked, eh?'

Tiffany nodded her appreciation.

'Minty,' I pleaded, 'could you not?'

Without bothering to retrieve his change, he popped another backdrop. This time, instead of pushing himself upright, he twisted into a semi-splits: his left leg was straight out in front, while his right fell into an L-shape behind him. He winced but, somehow, managed to pull it off.

'Eh? Eh?' went the Div, scrambling to his feet. 'It's better to the music of course.'

It was inevitable by now that he'd demonstrate his spinning technique. It was the next rung on the humiliation ladder. Spinning around on the spot is another Northern Soul dance 'move' at which he reckoned himself adept in his increasingly distant youth. I imagine that, ideally, it should be executed on a polished dancefloor by an athletic eighteen-year-old in leather-bottomed shoes. I'm guessing, in other words, that Northern Soul spins shouldn't be performed on bedroom carpets by pot-bellied, middle-aged mingers in slippers. My guess proved to be spot on because it was the spin that did for him.

'And spinning,' he went, 'was my forte.'

'*Minty!*'

He positioned his palms on his bitch-tits, placed his left leg over his right and, elbows out, span himself round on the ball of his right foot. For an instant he became an impressive blur but, on the third or fourth revolution his slipper, meeting too much resistance on the carpet, buckled. It seemed to knot itself into the shagpile. He twirled from the slipper, lost his balance and, still spinning, careened across the bedroom.

Tiffany put her hand to her mouth as she watched the wild-eyed forty-year-old fly. Certainly it was something to behold. The old bloater couldn't have cut a more spectacular arc through the air had he been bowled by Shane Warne. Tiffany winced as he hit the shelving unit which supported my telly. His collision with the 14-inch portable was so precise you'd have thought he'd been aiming for it. Yet the fact that his head passed so neatly through the wire loop of the indoor aerial was obviously a fluke. You couldn't have slam-dunked a basketball into it had you taken fifty goes. But there he suddenly was, corkscrewed into the antenna of a Sony.

He tried to stand upright but the set hung like a yoke at his throat. Its weight dragged him down as Cobain growled a live version of 'Come as You Are'. The shelving unit hit the floor, the telly hit the shelving unit and the Div hit the telly, skew-whiffing his head, perky hair and all.

It was Tiffany who leapt to his aid. I refused to indulge him. I just sat on the bed observing as my girlfriend eased the aerial wire over his fag-ash frizz and rolled him on to his back. His eyes were wide and watery and his nose oozed blood.

'Trebbo, go and get a towel,' went Tiffany.

'Behave,' I said.

She glared her guilt-glare. I tutted but, with my mind on future privileges, I made for the bathroom. Can all women make you feel guilty? I hadn't met *that* many yet but I had the impression there's always a part of them that could be your mom, particularly Tiff, who could best be described as a bit of a Poppins (as in Mary). She's the type who buys fair-trade coffee and worries about where her trainers are made. Once she didn't speak to me for an hour after I chucked my McDonald's McFlurry pot in the 'Glass' hole at the bottle bank. I thought I'd been pretty conscientious taking the time to deposit it in any kind of hole! Don't get me wrong: I liked the fact that she was considerate, I just wished she wasn't quite so worthy all the time. Or do I mean boring? Actually I probably mean virginal.

When I returned the Div was sitting upright with his hand on his nose. Blood spiralled down his wrist. I tossed him the towel and it landed in his lap. The telly had been knocked out of tune and was hissing white noise and flickering into the carpet. I turned it upright and noticed the screen was cracked.

'You dozy old gimmer!' I told him. 'Have you seen what you've done to my telly?'

Tiffany looked at me with disgust.

'I can't move my head,' said the Div.

'Never mind,' I said.

Tiffany looked at me with disgust again.

'Do you want to go to the hospital, Mr Trebor?' she asked.

'No, no, I'll be OK, chick.' He tried to stand but groaned, grimaced and sat back down.

'Should we phone your mom, Trebbo? She's a nurse, after all.'

Actually, though my mother trained as a nurse she was now, technically speaking, a health visitor. Tiffany knew this because in just over a week's time she'd be working alongside her. Tiffany had chosen my mom's clinic as a work experience placement. It's something I'd tried to discourage, obviously. You don't want your mom and your woman getting too chummy, after all. I'd failed.

'The old girl's out with her mate,' I said.

'Doesn't she have a mobile?'

I shrugged. 'I s'pose.'

'Don't phone Hazel,' went the Div as, once more, he tried to stand. This time he managed to raise himself fully upright.

He swallowed queasily and pressed the towel to his nose. His hair had lost its perkiness and the jovial sparkle had dimmed in his eyes. It was clear he wouldn't be upright very long. The Div managed to utter the words 'Stroll on' once more before fall-staggering to his left. I couldn't be sure, but I guessed that this time he wasn't dancing. He tumbled drunkenly in the direction of my bed, clipping the corner of it as he fell. The impact turned him a complete revolution and he hit the floor with the towel turbaned around his head like a curl of ice cream.

Tiffany dashed to his side again and began unwrapping him. His eyes flickered open for a second but they were as blank as boiled egg whites.

'He's fainted, Trebbo. We're going to have to phone someone.'

She gazed at me expectantly. Strands of her raven hair fell sexily across her face. I loved it when she wore her hair down. She looked much better than when she wore it tucked up on her head with slides, as she did for school, or for anything formal. The latter was the 'conformist' style she adopted out of what she called 'respect for other people's expectations'. I preferred the non-conformist style she adopted, I assume, to reveal tantalizing glimpses of the sex kitten that purred beneath her Poppins exterior. Unfortunately, wearing baggy T-shirts with her hair down was as far as her non-conformity ever went. She never let her hair – or anything else – down in the fullest sense of the phrase.

Tiffany breathed heavily and, as her chest rose and fell, I found myself distracted by the nipple bumps in the fabric of her Nirvana *In Utero* top. Its colours complemented her eyes and complexion. I should've been easing that shirt over her milk-white shoulders.

'Trebbo! Your dad's in a bad way!'

She wanted me to say or do something useful; she wanted me to care. On one remote level I suppose I *did* care. But an invisible Evil Puppeteer must have been manipulating my limbs, making me shrug my shoulders. He must have been a ventriloquist too because I found myself saying: 'And your point is?'

The Div *was* in a pretty bad way and, before this story is over, he'll be in a much worse way. But it isn't my fault; at least it isn't *all* my fault. The Colonel is mostly to blame.

2

Husband (*n*)

HAZEL

It all started for me that night in the lounge bar of the Lyndon Hotel. I was enjoying a drink and a chat with my friend, Suze. It was rare for me to be enjoying anything very much at the time. Our topic was humiliation, which is a subject I felt I understood too, too well.

'My husband is a lollipop man,' I said. '*This* is humiliation.'

'Someone's got to do it,' said Suze.

'But you expect it to be someone with liver spots and tweed knickers, not a forty-year-old in the prime of his life.'

Suze chuckled into her Hooch.

When I tell people what my husband does for a living they assume I am married to a geriatric. And you *do* have to come clean. It's a waste of time saying he works for the council, for instance, because people ask, 'In what capacity?' You can counter this with his official title of 'School Crossing Patrol', but this only elicits a quizzical look. You may as well get it over with.

'Didn't he give up a full-time job when Nigel was born?'

'Yes, as an accident investigator with British Rail. He was earning a little less than me at the time, though, so he opted for the role of house-husband.'

'That's quite a sacrifice.'

'Accident investigator isn't the most desirable occupation in the world. Whenever someone got run over by a train it was Minty's job to measure the distance between the accident site and the victim's final resting place.'

'That's gruesome.'

'He didn't mind the gore, it was the exercise he resented.' Suze chuckled.

I was exaggerating – it *was* something of a sacrifice for him. And it was useful having him at home when Nigel was little. But it had been *twelve years* and Minty was still the twat in the luminous hat. He'd seemed to have such a lot of promise when I met him. Mind you, my previous boyfriends hadn't been stunningly impressive by comparison. My most substantial relationship before Minty was with a guy called Davie Whales. We dated for seven months, two weeks and four days. I chucked him after he received a police caution for sending 'lewd' letters to Janet Street-Porter. When I told this story at an NHS self-esteem study day the facilitator said I was lucky it hadn't precipitated a 'spiral of self-loathing'.

'I could have done worse, I suppose.'

Suze nodded, her eyes resting briefly on a ginger-haired bloke in a lime-green nylon suit.

I knew there *were* worse things than being married to a lollipop man. And I *did* love my husband, but I think I'd have preferred it if he'd worked as the arse end of a pantomime horse – at least then no one could see him. He had his reasons for wanting to be a lollipop man, however, just as he'd had his reasons for wanting to be an accident investigator. As they say on *Oprah Winfrey*, my husband has 'issues'.

Suze noticed I'd emptied my glass so, after quickly

draining hers, she nodded towards it: 'Orange and passion fruit J_2O?'

'Go on, I'll risk another.'

While Suze was at the bar, I looked up the word 'humiliation' in my *Oxford English Mini Dictionary*. I carry this book everywhere and I've christened it Mo. I have other dictionaries at home, most given as Christmas presents by people who think I need a better dictionary, but I prefer Mo despite her being 'mini'. I expect this has something to do with the fact that I've had her so long (she superseded the *Bunty Book of Facts* as my Bible). I also like that her definitions are so succinct – it gives me more of a sense that I'm pinning meaning down.

I noticed a bloke near the bar eyeing the book so I closed it. Its tatty blue cover is something of an embarrassment: it is creased and stained from age and from the number of times it has been in the bin at home. Whenever I argue with Minty I end up reading him definitions of insulting adjectives and he responds by tossing Mo in the bin. Sometimes this routine is performed comically, sometimes seriously. If I had a penny for every time my dictionary has been in thebin, I'd have enough to buy the complete *OED*.

The bloke who'd been eyeing Mo was now eyeing Suze at the bar. This was usual. She's ten years younger than me and, at ten stone, eight pounds, two stone and two pounds lighter; she could carry off her combat trousers and the skin-tight T-shirt that bore the words: FAKE IT SO HE'LL BUY YOU STUFF. Men ogle her the way I ogle white chocolate Cornettos. Before I could look up the word 'bitch' she returned with the drinks.

She nodded at the little book as I slipped it into my bag. 'What were you looking up? Don't tell me: "drink", "glass"?'

'"Passion".'

'Aha!'

'And "orange".'

'Ah. You're the only person I've met who looks up words they already know.'

'Some people collect stamps, some people basket-weave.' We'd already had the 'Why do you do it?' conversation. It's a question I can't answer, except to say that I enjoy reading definitions. Stamp collectors and basket weavers can't explain their hobbies either: I know because I've asked.

'It probably explains why you're the brainiest mate I have,' said Suze.

I cooled my lips in juice to conceal my pleasure. Suze is a tonic. I'd been her health visitor when her youngest, Chloe-Jo, was born last year (six pounds, nine ounces). She falls into what I call the 'Worry Mother' category. This is a type who needs constant reassurance: you have to count their kids' toes for them every thirty minutes. As a result I tended to see a lot of her, so much so that we became mates. I tell her almost everything.

'Fancy a barbecue?' asked Suze.

'We already have one: I use it as a planter for my geraniums.'

'At our house? A week on Wednesday? You could bring Minty. I'd love to meet him.'

We were forever saying that we should meet each other's husbands, but the prospect made me uncomfortable. Like colonic irrigation, it was a potentially positive experience, but I couldn't help feeling it might reveal too much of something that should be kept hidden.

'I'd like to meet your Mike too of course but –'

'It's for Chloe-Jo's first birthday.'

My mind raced for excuses not to go but, as Suze well knew, my social calendar wasn't overly asterisked. Last Wednesday, for instance, I'd spent half the evening watching telly, while Minty read the Argos catalogue. The other half I'd spent trying to talk him out of buying an electric guitar. The word 'Argos' refers to a city in ancient Greece.

'Er, OK.'

'Really? You'll come? And you'll bring Minty?' She said this as though I'd promised to introduce her to the world's biggest strawberry cheesecake.

'I have to warn you that the last time we went to a barbecue Minty put his head through the roof of a Wendy house.'

'Okaaay.'

'One of the kids slipped a frog down his jogger bottoms.'

Suze giggled and took another sip of her Hooch. 'Was he hurt?'

'He burst and this horrible white foam started oozing from his body.'

'I mean Minty.'

'No, the Wendy house was only made of plywood – and he *was* wearing a foam-rubber Mickey Mouse helmet.'

'The frog?'

'Minty. It was from our Orlando holiday. You have to buy them, don't you?'

Suze was laughing, and now so was I. These things are always funnier in retrospect. At the time I'd had a dickie-fit. The kids tumbled screaming from the Wendy house while Minty thrashed about inside. My cousin, Toby, helped untangle him from the splintered wood, felt and offcut carpet and curtains that decorated the interior. A bull-elephant with a badger up its arse couldn't have done a

27

better job of demolishing it. When we finally retrieved the frog someone joked about it looking like it had been in a blender. The grown-ups ushered the tearful kids indoors while I wrote a cheque for £249.99 – which is how much Wendy houses cost apparently. Minty is still paying me back at the excessively reasonable rate of ten pounds per month. Yes, I know all about humiliation. My juvenile husband – a man whose lollipop behaviour so often serves to complement his occupation – taught me everything I know.

'I have to meet this bloke,' said Suze, still tittering.

One thing you *could* say for Minty is that there's generally some comic mileage in his daftness. Over the years I've tried to make a virtue out of this. Socially I tend to adopt the role of his long-suffering carer. There are times when I feel like his mother. Luckily I'm the motherly type. I fall into what I term the 'Universal Mother' category: my maternal instincts cover everything from husbands to Jelly Babies.

Babies.

The average weight of a baby is seven pounds. I weigh them a lot in my line of work. The easiest way is to pop them naked into a plastic bucket and then hang them on a spring scale. I love weighing babies and do it even when I don't need to. This is one of my guilty secrets. It wouldn't be so bad if it was my only guilty secret, but it's not. My other guilty secret is called Kelvin.

We were interrupted by the sound of my mobile's ringtone: a slightly off-key, synthesized rendering of 'Isn't She Lovely?'

'Sorry, Suze. Minty's probably tried to take his boxers off over his head again.'

But it wasn't Minty. The screen told me it was my son calling on *his* mobile. This was so unusual as to be terrifying and I experienced an unsettling weightlessness reminiscent of a sensation I had on the last two occasions I've travelled by air: Birmingham International to Orlando and Orlando to Birmingham International. I call it take-off terror and it had become a familiar feeling over the past few months.

'It's me.'

The morose, world-weary tone was a giveaway even without the caller ID: 'Hello, Nigel. What's wrong, love?'

He tutted and sighed. I'd forgotten to use his nickname.

'Trebbo?'

'Thank you. *God.*'

There was another pause before I prompted, 'What is it, love?'

'Me and Tiffany are at the hospital.'

'Are you all right?'

'It's the old man. He's seen that advert.'

'Advert?'

'The one for KFC – with the Northern Soul rubbish.'

'I need more information, son.'

'Well, he was dancing about like a numpty and he managed to throttle himself on my telly. He's totally wrecked it.'

'Is he hurt?'

'Dahaa. I'm phoning from a *hos-pit-al.*'

'Is he *badly* hurt?'

'Er . . .' I heard him mumble a question to someone and it was several seconds before he replied, 'Er, nah.'

'Are you in A&E or has he been admitted?' I asked, my weightlessness diminishing slightly.

'He's on er . . .' I could hear him mumble another question before announcing, 'Penguin Ward.'

'I'm coming.'

'Yeah? Well, please yourself. Me and Tiff are off back to hers for an hour anyhow. We'll have to watch *her* telly seeing as mine's gone west.'

I heard some more talking in the background. 'Wha?' asked Nigel. Then I heard some rustling and bumping and then a more emphatic '*Wha?*' There was yet more rustling, then another voice.

'Mrs Trebor?' It was Tiffany.

'Yes, love?'

'There's no need to worry. Mr Trebor had a bit of an accident with the telly but he's OK. He has slight concussion, whiplash and a sprained ankle. But he's not in any danger.'

'Thanks, love.' I was back on the ground. Glancing at my watch I saw that it was 9.30. 'Could you let Minty know I'll be there in half an hour?'

I clicked off.

'Shame Minty wasn't wearing the Mickey Mouse helmet tonight,' I said to Suze.

'Pardon?'

I filled her in.

In the days to come Minty would need more than a Mickey Mouse helmet to protect him and I would spend less and less time on *terra firma*. We're all to blame, I suppose: Nigel, Minty and, perhaps most of all, me. But maybe it depends on how you define the word 'blame'.

3

'Mr Bang Bang Man'

Little Hank (Sound Stage 7)

MINTY

I was lying in Wesley with my head on backwards. The quack said I was lucky the TV aerial hadn't severed my windpipe or broken my neck. I assumed that Hazel would take care of that for me. My accident was certain to give her one of her dickie-fits. She'd probably go for my neck first then tackle my windpipe if I still happened to be breathing. You'd imagine she'd have more sympathy, what with her nursing background. Nope. The NHS train their staff to be callous – they have puppy-drowning workshops to desensitize them to suffering. If I had tuberculosis she'd call it 'man flu'. And don't talk to her about accidents: Hazel doesn't believe in them. She says I have so many accidents because I like drawing attention to myself. I'm probably the only bloke in Walsall who knows the *Oxford Mini Dictionary* definition of the words 'hypochondria' and 'liability' off by heart.

I was busy worrying how to explain my current dalliance with masochistic self-promotion when a nurse appeared at my bedside. 'All right, Mr Trebor,' she said, 'I've come to fit your neck-brace.'

'Go ahead, chick.'

She was in her late teens and her lean figure, pale skin and broad mouth made her look a bit like Geena Davis. She had a nice way with her: she smiled easily and her breath whiffed, not unpleasantly, of Bovril.

'They tell me you've had an accident with a television?'

'I was dancing, chick.'

'With a television?'

'There was a song I haven't heard for years on an advert for Kentucky Fried Chicken. I went a bit twizzler.'

'"Do I Love You?"'

'You know it?' She was fastening the brace at the back of my neck and in my excitement I instinctively turned my face up to hers. A sharp pain fired into the base of my skull. I didn't manage to keep a lid on my yelp.

'You need to keep your head still, Mr Trebor. Yes, I'm a Northern Soul fan, big time.' She took a step back to check the alignment of my collar.

'*Really?* How did a youngster like you get interested in old-timer's music?'

'It's not "old-timer's music" as far as I'm concerned! I've been going to all-nighters ever since I persuaded my mom to let me stay out all night. I love them!'

'All-nighters? Blimey, I used to go to them all the time when I was young. I was pretty hot on my pins and barmy about record collecting. But I jacked it in when Wigan Casino closed in eighty-one.'

Wigan Casino shut shortly after I met Hazel. She hadn't been a fan of the music or the scene so it didn't bother her. It filleted me. When we married in 1982 I was nineteen and Hazel was eighteen. I sold all my soul sides to help raise the deposit for our mortgage. Hazel took the piss when I cried – see, insensitive.

I continued chatting with the young nurse – whose

name, I learned, was Kylie – as she filled in my obser-
vation chart. She was a soul fanatic and it was easy to
imagine her at a Northern Soul all-nighter. She had the
look of a dancer: slim and straight-backed, unlike the
majority of kids these days who walk around like question
marks. Some people suit certain environments and she
seemed born for the scene. She was also a nutter. I mean
that in a good way. During our talk she listed all the all-
nighters she'd ever been to in order of the springiness of
their dancefloors. She drinks Bovril and eats Curly Wurlies
to keep her going through the night and, the morning
after, she soaks her feet in Mazola Corn Oil.

'You should come to a modern all-nighter,' she said,
hanging the clipboard at the end of my bed.

'I'm a bit long in the tooth these days, chick.'

'Hardly.'

I liked Kylie; she cheered me up. Clearly she was yet to
attend her puppy-drowning workshop. Despite having
finished my chart she sat on the bed and continued chatting. I had the impression she'd have chatted all night. She
widened her eyes when something interested her and
laughed unselfconsciously, filling the air with Bovril fumes.
When she told me her name, she saluted! It's great when
kids are that way. I can't help wishing our Nigel was a bit
more sociable, instead of so obsessed with being cool. Even
Tiffany – who is at least polite – seems far too serious to
me.

My conversation with Kylie was cut short when a colleague shouted for her assistance. A patient called Droppy
had swallowed the lid off an Ovaltine tin and my new soul
chum, after saluting once more, departed in a hurry.

*

I suppose I should've been wishing I'd never seen that chicken advert. My head felt like it was trapped in a drainpipe. And I'd shown myself up again. I'd shown Nigel up too. He hadn't uttered a word in the ambulance, choosing to spend the time playing Snake on his mobile. But I'm glad I heard that song because, if nothing else, it returned me briefly to my 'real' body: the one I'll get back in heaven. It's not the one I have now, with the love handles and the man-dingers, but the one with the slinky hips and the trim, vest-friendly torso. It sent me back to the first time I heard 'Do I Love You' – February 1978. I remember it because it was my first trip to Wigan Casino. Me and my mate Dave McVane were fifteen at the time. Our mothers thought we were camping in Upton-on-Severn. We travelled up from Walsall in a coach that smelt of Benson & Hedges and we shared sarnies Mac's mom had made that were covered in Yorkshire Terrier hairs. The bloke in the seat behind asked us if we were sorted for gear and we exchanged some sarnies for a couple of slimming pills. That bloke was Muncher Preene. He was fifteen, too, and an apprentice peddler in illicit substances. Muncher also lived in Walsall and introduced us to a couple of other blokes on the coach: Liam (Nipper) Kid and Petey (the Coiffure) Fleetwood. Muncher sorted them both for gear. He sorted everyone with chalkies, blueys, bombers, Dexies, red and greys, and sulphate powder. He could get anything. It seemed like no time at all before we reached the Casino. The queue was a hundred yards long and everyone had *Coronation Street* accents and chewed gum. It was freezing cold and I felt young, vulnerable and a long way from home. But that feeling vanished in the damp heat of the dance hall. Ultraviolet tubes hung from the ceiling on chains but barely illuminated the massive room.

Here and there dancers wore luminous bands on their wrists which seemed to float in the air like fireflies. The main hall was surrounded on three sides by a balcony and people peered down, white-faced in the violet glow. It was as hot as a Turkish bath, with the musty smell of old buildings mingling with the odour of sweat, talc, deodorant and aftershave: Brut, Old Spice, and Blue Stratos. The dancefloor was crowded but occasionally spaces would open around displays of acrobatics: lightning fast combinations of floor movements and blurred spins where dancers seemed set to drill theirselves into the sprung maple floor.

The first tune I danced to was 'Mr Bang Bang Man' by Little Hank. Water was dripping on my head throughout and it took me a while to realize that this was condensation from the ceiling. Mac, dancing like a maniac, knackered the zip of his ten-button high-waisters and spent the rest of the night trying to conceal his *Six Million Dollar Man* Y-fronts. It was a brillo, brillo night and, thanks to Muncher Preene, we grooved non-stop till 8 a.m.

Whatever happened to Northern Soul? I hadn't given it serious thought for donkeys'. Frank Wilson sounded as good as he did twenty years ago. *Was* I too long in the tooth? 'Hardly,' Kylie had said. *Hardly*.

I noticed a staff nurse doing her rounds with the drugs trolley. They'd promised me a shot of something for my discomfort and I was looking forward to it. Experimentally, I clenched the toes of my right foot and a pain punched up my shin. The X-ray said it was just a sprain, but I'd need the week off work. That was bad news. Despite my embarrassing status as a lolliman, I hated missing my shifts.

People often ask me how I ended up as a lollipop man. It was an accident. I'd been at the town council offices with a child benefit query one morning and I accidentally knocked over the carousel holding their information flyers. As I replaced them I noticed a leaflet recruiting stand-by patrols to cover sick leave. I did it for a month and when a permanent spot came up near Wurlington Infants School I took it. As Nigel was to start at Wurlington himself it meant I could take him to school and work at the same time. I wasn't embarrassed by it because, when I was still looking after Nigel, I could call myself a lollipop man *and* a house-husband. Somehow the latter mitigated the former. Over the last few years, though, I've become less comfortable. I never mention this to Haze, of course: it would hardly be fair of me to moan while she works full time. And there is always the option of looking for something else. But I don't. Hazel says it's because – accident prone as I am – I have a subconscious need to prevent accidents. Apparently it's the same need that drew me to my first job as an accident investigator for BR and it has its roots in my past.

Picture the scene: I'm five years old and a passenger in my dad's Ford Anglia. He asks me if I want to change gear for him and I jump at the chance. He dips the clutch and says: 'Go ahead, son.' Instead of shifting the gearstick from third to fourth, however, I pull on the handbrake. I have no idea what makes me do that but, hey: I'm only five. We skid, screaming and revolving to a halt and, a half-second later, the car travelling behind us – a Hillman Imp – smashes into our rear. The latter also contains a father and son: Ernest Peebles and his seven-year-old off-spring, Billy, who lived next-door-but-one to us.

It was a very bad day for Billy. He burst through the windscreen of his dad's motor like a diver breaking water.

And he flew. I can remember watching him through the triangle of the Anglia's side window. He was wearing a Batman outfit and he was flying – his arms were stretched in front of him and his cape was a perfect delta on his back. It was as though he'd consciously struck a superhero-style flying pose. But I knew that Batman *couldn't* fly. In fact, Adam West (Batman) and Burt Ward (Robin) had recorded a public safety film making that very point. They'd screen it before the show in the sixties: 'Holy broken bones,' Robin would say, driving his gloved fist into the palm of his hand. However, Billy Peebles *could* fly – the only problem was he couldn't land. He ended up sandwiched between two crates of ice-cream soda in the back of an Alpine pop delivery van. The driver travelled for two hundred yards without realizing he was there. The real harm came when the van stopped. Billy rolled off the back and the driver reversed over both his feet, crushing every bone in them. But even *that* wouldn't have been such a problem if Walsall's Wesley-in-Tame Hospital hadn't compounded the damage. They reset the bones incorrectly so they re-fused misaligned. Billy Peebles was unable to walk, or even stand for long periods, from then on. Everyone else was fine: me, my dad, Billy's dad. But not Billy.

Holy broken bones.

Wesley-in-Tame settled out of court for an undisclosed sum, but that wasn't much use to Billy. Lord only knows what became of the poor kid – after the local kids had called him 'Weeble' for three or four months, his family moved away.

It wasn't my fault. Ernie Peebles had been speeding, the kid wasn't wearing a seatbelt and I was only five! I don't feel guilty about it and *there's absolutely no relationship between my jobs and my accident*. But Hazel says I'm 'in denial'. One of her problems is that she's too easily taken in by tuppenny-ha'penny psychology. A few years back she attended a workshop called 'Accidents, the NHS and the Non-Judgemental Allocation of Blame', which, she said, confirmed her suspicion that there's no such thing as accidents. She claims that 'subconsciously' I agree with her and fear that I'm responsible for Billy's ruined life. She says my lolly is 'the weapon with which I ward off my guilt'. That's bollocks: sometimes a lolly is just a lolly! Hazel also claims that Billy's accident is the reason I've never learned to drive. That's bollocks too. It's not guilt, it's apathy.

I've always intended to drop the lolly for something better, one day, when I can get round to it. Indeed, despite being a passionate and committed lolliman, I was becoming more and more conscious of a gap in my life. That night in the hospital was the first inkling I'd had that the gap might be seven inches wide.

Then I saw her – the familiar figure chatting at the nurses' station in her 'going-out' clothes. Haze. It was ten o'clock so I suppose they shouldn't really have let her visit, but my wife knows the right things to say. She's one of them.

As she approached I braced myself for a dickie-fit.

'Haze,' I said.

'Minty,' she said, 'the staff nurse tells me you garrotted yourself with a television.'

'Sorry, love, it was an acci– . . . It couldn't be helped. I know I'm a liability.'

'You look as if they've planted your head in a pisspot.'

Hazel was in a good mood – relieved that I wasn't badly hurt. She loves me really; or at least I'm pretty sure she does. She took a seat by the bed and produced her dictionary.

Chuckling, she read me a definition of the word 'burden', which, I was informed, means 'a cause of hardship or distress'. She then searched for a definition of 'tosser', but, as I'm sure she already knew, it didn't feature in her little book. Nor did 'pillock'.

4

'Big Cheese'

Nirvana, *Bleach* (Geffen)

TREBBO

It was Wednesday morning, a week and two days after the Div danced my telly to death, and I was with the gimmers at the breakfast table. I scooped the last Coco Pops from the bowl and then examined my goatee in the back of the spoon: it was still a bit wispy but it looked pretty cool.

The gimmers were getting ready for work. The Divette was in her navy-blue health visitor's rig-out; the Div was spraying deodorant into his lollipop man's hat. It was his first day back on duty. He could have milked his injury for much more skive time if he'd felt inclined, but the numpty actually *wanted* to go to work.

'I was on the phone to Nipper again last night,' he went. 'He invited me to a Northern all-nighter. What do you think?'

I saw the Divette's eyes roll and I'm not surprised. He'd been banging on about Northern Soul for days now. Nipper was an old buddy who was still 'on the scene'. *Nipper!* I mean, what kind of name's that for anything other than a Jack Russell? The Div hadn't seen him for years but called him the morning after being sprung from Wesley. He'd phoned Nipper almost every day since. The guy would probably go ex-directory; either that or buy a whistle. After seeing that KFC ad, the Div had even started eating his Chicken Dippers with his fingers: 'Don't need no forks, just soul,' he would say, much to the Divette's annoyance.

'Aren't you a bit old for all-night discos?' she went.

'Hardly.'

The Divette sighed. 'Then I suppose it's a good idea to go if it makes you happy.' I knew she was lying.

His eyes glittered. 'Yeah? Nipper says there's one in Wolverhampton on Friday. They're reopening Fanny's for a one-off do.'

'This Friday coming?'

'Yeah. Nipper emailed the flyer to me yesterday. He didn't mention it before because he assumed I'd be too ill to go, with my injury.' He put his hand to his neck-brace.

'*Fanny's?*' I couldn't help saying.

'Yeah: it's what we used to call the Fantasy Rooms back in the seventies. Great place. It closed the same time Wigan did in the early eighties. Now they're knocking the building down and the owners have agreed to turn it over to a Northern Soul promoter for one last night.'

The Div spread a flyer out on the table. It read:

FANNY'S: THE PLACE TO COME!
JOIN US FOR A NIGHT OF NORTHERN SOUL
NOSTALGIA AT THIS LEGENDARY
WOLVERHAMPTON SOUL CLUB

DJs include: Soul Steve; Harry the Wag;
Chopper Floss; Many Bellies; Whizzer Tilsley;
Pops; and Chris Kite.

'Eh? Eh?' he said. 'Brillo, eh?' It's weird but when the Div gets excited about something his hair seems to get bigger.

'Coo,' I said. I wouldn't ordinarily have been having a conversation with the gimmers but the battery was out on my MP3. As a rule I like to keep my utterances to a minimum. It's uncool to talk too much, particularly to parents. They'd be staggered if they knew I had so much yap inside me.

'I thought I'd try and get a few of the old gang together,' went the Div. 'I know where to find some of the lads: Mac's at the Leather Museum, of course, and I think Petey Fleetwood still lives with his mom. I've left a message on her answerphone. I'm not sure what happened to Muncher, though.'

'Muncher?' asked the Divette, just to be polite. She was checking through her bible-thick diary to see which school-girl mothers she was due to visit. I wondered if there was a note in there reminding her it was the first day of Tiffany's work experience. I felt sure there would be.

'I'm not certain if you ever met him, Haze. Square-headed bloke with freckles? You've heard me talk about him loads of times, though, surely: Muncher. Muncher. Mun-*cherr*.'

The Divette shrugged.

'Stroll on, don't you ever listen to me! *Muncher Preene!* He was the main dealer in these parts.'

The Divette gave him a glare that could've poached his nads.

'In cars . . . In cars,' spluttered the Div.

He'd meant drugs obviously.

The gimmers were silent for a bit. She was pissed because he'd nearly mentioned drugs in front of me. I wonder how dumb they think I am? I don't know much about seventies Northern Soul clubs but I know this: you couldn't move for flared trousers, shite music and speed. I read an article in the *NME* called 'A Brief History of Club Drugs'.

I read everything connected with drugs. I'm a fan of them – or at least I was until they landed me in the shit. The shit that drugs landed me in is a subject that I'll have to come back to.

'I bet Minty was off his tits every night back in the twentieth century,' I quipped, just to make the point that I'm not one of those kids that the Divette refers to as 'developmentally delayed'.

'Nigel, do you mind!' went the Divette.

'Who?' I asked her.

'Don't use expressions like that in this house.'

'OK,' I said, 'I bet Minty was off his tits every night back in the *nineteen hundreds*.' I don't know where I get it from.

She clammed again and I picked at a hole in my over-shirt. I was wearing this unbuttoned above a Pearl Jam T-shirt. I don't really like Pearl Jam, but it was only £1.99 in the Virgin sale. It advertises *No Code*, their worst album.

It was the Divette who eventually broke the silence: 'Don't forget we've been invited to a barbecue tonight.'

I knew this was a strategy on her part. A barbecue is the kind of thing the Div would usually whine about having to go to. His drug talk had put him in the doghouse, though, so he needed to tread carefully.

'A *barbecue*?' His hair seemed to droop slightly.

'I told you last week, so don't look surprised.'

'But what about my neck?'

'If you're well enough to go to work, then you're well enough to go to a barbecue.' She looked in my direction and seemed about to ask me to go too. Apparently she came to her senses and this saved her from my sarcasm.

The Div thought for a while. You could tell he was thinking because he hadn't taken a bite of his Pop-Tart for a minute and a half. Eventually he uttered the following stroke of genius: 'I'll go to your mate's barbecue, *if* you come to my Northern Soul reunion on Friday.'

This *was* fiendish stuff from Minty. I knew the Divette thought the Fanny's gig would be a wanker-fest, but she'd look like a bitch if she turned him down.

'Er . . . I suppose,' she said.

Normally I'd be made up at this news. I'd be getting the house to myself and that could only mean one thing: me versus Tiffany's virtue. But I had more important things on my mind. Like I said, drugs had landed me in the shit. You could fertilize all the periwinkles in Walsall with the shit I was in.

The Divette began collecting her things together ready to leave for work. With some difficulty she forced her diary and mobile into her work-bag. It was already straining at the seams with everything from baby milk samples to pubic lice cream. She struggled to her feet with her bag under one arm (the handle's snapped) and a set of scales for weighing kids under the other. Well, I say kids. A month ago I got up early and caught her in the living room weighing her make-up mirror. She got very flustered and told me she was testing the scales (though I hadn't asked). Then just last week I caught her in the kitchen weighing a punnet of gooseberries. She got flustered again and claimed she was checking to see if the scales at Morrisons were accurate (though I hadn't asked that time either). Go figure.

'Don't worry, I don't need any help,' she said, in my direction. 'My endorphins are numbing the pain.'

And I'm supposed to be the sarcastic one.

The Div was adjusting his neck-brace in the mirror. 'Mind how you go, love,' he said.

'Don't say anything stupid about me to Tiffany,' I told the Divette as she trundled down the hall. She muttered

44

something that seemed to rhyme with streaky runt. I felt a slight pang of guilt for not helping her with her bag, but I managed to suppress it.

Her exit left me alone with the Div. For the next half-hour he blew his twaddle-horn as he readied himself for lolly duty. On and on he went: Northern Soul. Fanny's. Wigan Casino. Fanny's again. His numpty mates from 'the scene': Mac, Muncher, Petey, Nipper. They sounded like characters from the *Beano*. I spent the time slow-chewing a Juicy Fruit. Eventually, when my twaddle-resistance finally gave out, I split for school.

We both have to travel to roughly the same place in the mornings: I'm at Wurlington Barnett Community College, while the Div does lolly duty just round the corner near Wurlington Infants. Obviously we can't go together. I'd rather French kiss Gary Glitter than be seen walking the streets with the Div, so I leave home ten minutes before him. And I walk a different route, with my hood up.

The Div was still yapping as I adjusted my beanie, picked up my canvas backpack and shouldered it with a practised, insolent shrug. He interrupted an anecdote about the time he'd seen 'Junior Walker' live on stage to ask: 'What's that badge say on your bag, Nigel?'

I ignored him and headed for the door.

'Trebbo,' he said, 'what's the badge say?'

I turned the bag round so he could read it.

'"NOTHING SUCKS LIKE SUCCESS",' he read aloud. 'Funny slogan.'

'Yeah,' I said. 'Hardee har.'

'I used to have an Adidas holdall covered with badges from the all-nighters I'd been to.'

'Coo,' I said, and walked.

'Isn't grunge music out of fashion?' he asked, as I opened the front door.

'Only if you're into fashion,' I said, and left him to his Divness.

Of course grunge was out of fashion. Grunge, after all, is anti-fashion; it defines itself against fashion. When, to the dismay of true grungers, the grunge and slacker look actually became fashionable in the early nineties, I'd been four years old. Fashion is for rat-racers. While all the kids at school listen to the Ministry of Shite, or anything that's 'in', I'm proud to be above that: proud to be neo-grunge; a slacker for the twenty-first century. But it is more than just the identity – it's impossible to hear Nirvana and not worship them. When I listen to Cobain I hear a man who knew what it was like to be snubbed by his peers, even though he was the coolest of them all. I love that. The man had 'teen spirit' and he never lost it – you can hear it in his furious wail. I can't always work out what he meant but, whatever it was, I know he really meant it.

I walked down the drive, switching on my mobile. It beeped straight away to tell me I had an answerphone message. Seven messages, all from my mate, Dicey Price. I listened to the first, received 8.30 a.m.

'[Sound of Dicey panting] Trebbo. Things have gone mental. Blubber-T's looking for us. I saw him coming up Layton Road so I legged it down Petty Street and I think I gave him the slip, but watch out.'

The next was received at 8.34.

'[Speaking in a hissed, urgent whisper] Trebbo? Switch your phone on. He's still after me. I'm hiding behind some bins in Moss Street. What should I tell him if he . . . hang on . . . shit [sound of Dicey running].'

I was just about to check the next message when my phone began ringing in my hand. It was Dicey.

'Trebbo! BASTARDING HELL! Where are you? [I

heard someone shout 'Yow tell im, bitch' at Dicey.] I'M TELLING HIM, Blubbs.'

'Where are you, Dice,' I asked, 'and what's going on?' But as soon as I turned into Kilbourn Road both of these questions were answered.

Dicey had clambered on to the roof of a bus shelter and Blubber-T, who is too enormous and lumbering to follow, was standing beneath. With his right hand he was pulling rubbish from a bin and slinging it at Dice: a crushed Fanta can followed by a half-empty bottle of Waggle Dance beer. With his left hand he was eating a Twirl. A queue of people waited for the bus, pretending to ignore the spectacle.

'Dow fuck wi me, yow mutha,' screamed Blubber-T, fragments of Twirl spraying from his lips. 'Just dow fuck wi me.'

Remember me saying that drugs had landed me in the shit? This is the shit.

Blubber-T is a nasty bastard. Worse, he's a gigantic nasty bastard. Blubber-T isn't his real name, of course: it's his street name. His real name is Trevor. He doesn't have much going for him in many ways. For one thing he was named Trevor; for another he looks like Rick Waller. Or, I should say, like a hard version of Rick Waller. He looks the way Rick Waller might if he'd been raised by wolves. He is the same age as me but, where I've spent my sixteen years sitting about watching telly, he spent his making contacts with every drug dealer in the Midlands. He doesn't go to my school: he's a pupil at Newbolt College, perhaps their most respected pupil – respected in the way only large ugly criminals can be. My ambition was to become more respected at *my* school through my association with him.

As everyone who's ever been to school knows, respect is important. Prior to my move into the drugs business I didn't have any. If I was lucky the cool kids called me Scrag-arse (because of my grunge look); if I was unlucky, they called me Wankrag (which also had to do with what one teacher called my 'courageous sartorial transgressions'.) To improve my status I'd been acquiring cream-of-the-crop skunk from Blubber-T and supplying my fellow Wurlington Barnett students. Since then they'd adjusted their name-calling in line with the prices I charged. When at first I tried to make a profit on the transactions I was still Scrag-arse and Wankrag (although they tagged the term 'the Weedman' on the end). Wankrag-the-Weedman is a slight improvement but I was still unhappy. Then I began scaling down my profit and became Trebor, Slackerman, and Nirvana-Dude. Better. As soon as I started giving them the skunk for less than it cost me, I became Trebbo, Trebbs and the Beard. Better still. Selling skunk at a loss might not seem very entrepreneurial but, hey, as Dicey is always saying, it's a mistake to be hung up on economic self-advancement. That's for rat-racers. Respect is more important than money. Money can't buy you cool. Two words: Richard Madeley. Cool kicks in ways that coins can't. But how, you ask, can I afford to make a loss on the skunk? Well, when I buy my drugs from Blubber-T, I don't use money.

Blubber-T is the world's biggest fan of gangsta porn. The majority of 'normal' people may not know what this is and, come to think of it, the majority of perverts might not either. I'm no expert myself but, from what I've seen, gangsta porn refers to a genre of films in which women are ordered about by blokes who wear too much jewellery. It does nothing for me personally, but I'm not a fat freak who yearns to be a gangster. The rumour is that Blubber-T wants to get into the porn business himself and uses the films as research material. Go figure. You can find good gangsta porn on the internet but Blubbs doesn't own a computer because his dad is some kind of fascist who doesn't believe in them. This is where I came in. I had a top of the range desktop with a Celeron processor and state-of-the-art movie-burning software. I could ride the net like the Silver Surfer and, what's more, I could access paysites with the Div's credit card details. The Div had a Visa card he never used – he only signed up for it to get the free ear-hair trimmers they offered as an incentive. He didn't even know what a statement looked like because I intercepted them and paid them by return of post. Dicey contributed some cash towards this in return for a little draw. Given the 'exploitative and degrading' nature of the films, Dicey had trouble squaring this with his conscience, but Blubber-T's gear was so good he always managed it. I rarely smoke the stuff myself as it tends to leave me feeling a bit random, not to mention the fact that – surprise surprise – Tiffany disapproves.

It had been working pretty well, until now.

The problem was this: the Adult Verification System that allowed me to access the websites had cut me off. Apparently I was out of credit. When I phoned Visa they told me that the Div's card was maxed out. Impossible, I thought, because the AVS only costs fifteen American dollars a month. But it turned out that the Div himself had recently used his card for a generous purchase from someone called Scarce Soul Supplies. Generous to the tune of nine hundred and ninety notes.

'Films,' went Blubber-T, 'I want me cowing films. Die vie die quality, yow said.' He fired a Minute Maid Orange can at Dicey and it ricocheted off the shelter, missing a bloke in the queue by a gnat's. The bloke was a weedy, trainspotter type who wisely kept his squeal-hole closed. He, like the rest of the queue, continued to pretend nothing was happening.

Blubber-T was pissed because he'd given me a bag full of skunk as an advance on a score of high-quality flicks that I hadn't yet delivered. I'd made the mistake of trying to palm him off with some of the short, low-quality MPEG clips the porn sites offer as free samples. I thought they'd buy me some time until I could get the credit card business sorted. They hadn't.

'Blubbs, dude,' I said, alerting the sixteen-year-old monster to my presence, 'is there a problem?'

Blubber-T turned on me. '*Yow!*' he thundered. 'Tremolo, yoam fucking wi me, bitch. Yow owe me some films, and cowing quick!' At this point the 404 to West Bromwich turned up and the people in the queue scrambled to board – even those who didn't even want to go to West Brom (which one can only assume is all of them).

'My name's Trebbo, Blubbs.'

'Just answer mi cowing question, bitch. And dow diss me.' He popped the last of the Twirl into his mouth, tossed the wrapper over his shoulder, then added, 'Yow muthafucker.'

Another thing about Blubbs is that he can't seem to grasp that Walsall isn't South Central LA. Though this town is probably just as dangerous, Blubber-T's lingo – peppered as it is with 'bitches' and 'muthafuckers' – is out of place. Being a muthafucker in many parts of Walsall simply means you're sleeping with any girl over the age of fourteen. His speech is like a cross between Ali G and Noddy Holder. It would perhaps be less incongruous if he was black, but he doesn't have that going for him either. He is white; worse, he's white with acne. He's red and white: surely the least cool colour for complexions. And yet, bizarrely, Blubber-T seems to contravene the laws of cool by being, in spite of everything, pretty cool.

'Didn't you like the last collection, dude?' I asked.

'It ay the proper stuff, bitch, so dow try to fuck wi me.'

Blubber-T walked towards me. He was conspicuous in his orange tracksuit, mirrored Ray-Bans and what appeared to be five hundred quid's worth of gold. Had the latter been *real* gold he'd've been wearing five hundred grand's worth, but still the boy was bling. For reasons best known to himself he also sported a raccoon-skin hat.

The Div is always saying how teenagers seem to be getting bigger these days and Blubber-T bears this out. He really is *massive*: six four and a bull-elephant's worth of kilos. Though, admittedly, most of this is lard, I still had to choose my words very carefully.

'Blubbs, the last disc was just to tide you over, dude. It was a goodwill gesture in lieu of the real thing. I'm having problems with my computer.'

'What cowing kind?'

'Nothing that can't be sorted, bro.' I noticed that Dicey had begun to ease himself down from the bus-shelter roof. The crack of his arse was showing above the waistband of his Wranglers.

'I want mi skunk back, bitch.'

Sadly this had long since been distributed around Wurlington Barnett's key faces. I raised my hands and then pushed them slowly downwards in what I hoped was a calming gesture.

'The skunk's gone, dude,' I said, trying to keep my voice soft, level and, above all, respectful. This is the way you're supposed to address psychotics, terrorists and people with small cocks. Apparently they're less likely to go off on one.

Blubber-T punched me in the face.

The blow caught the bottom of my chin, snapping my head backwards.

'I want mi cowing films, two hundred bones worth of

cowing skunk, or two hundred cowing bones, by tomorra, bitch!'

'Blubbs,' I groaned, praying that his rings hadn't scraped any of my goatee off, 'could you give us a week?'

'Denied,' he said, taking a four-finger Kit Kat from his tracksuit pocket.

I thought hard. 'It's my brother, dude, he's ill. He's dying. He's almost dead.'

'What's up wi im?'

'Diluvian skitts. It's touch and go, Blubbs.'

Blubber-T pondered this for a moment, his fat fingers working deftly on the wrapper of his chocolate. 'Kay,' he said at last, 'but,' he added, using a finger of Kit Kat for emphasis, 'yow'd berra not be fucking wi me.'

With that he sword-swallowed the Kit Kat finger and left. We watched him walk away, the tail of his raccoon-skin hat swinging in response to his lumbering swagger.

'What a mentalist,' went Dicey, as soon as Blubber-T was well out of earshot, 'although I guess he's a victim of the system and the illusory promise of capitalism.'

I straightened my beanie. 'How's my goatee?' I asked, offering Dicey my chin for inspection.

'Mental.'

I'd known Dicey for years. We started at Wurlington Barnett together in the days when it was still a school. Five years later it was a 'community college' and we were in the final year of our GSCEs. We were both tipped for A-grades across the board. Dicey was into the Seattle sound, too, and that day he was dressed pretty much the same as me, except that he sported threadbare baseball boots where I wore trainers. He also had an NYC baseball cap, worn catcher-style, and a T-shirt that said: IF AT FIRST YOU DON'T SUCCEED, REDEFINE SUCCESS. Neither of us joined in the competitive dressing that, to use the Divette's words, was 'an inevitable consequence of Wurlington Barnett's unwillingness to implement their policy on school uniforms'.

'Where are you going to find two hundred quid?' he asked.

I gave him a 'who-gives-a-shit' shrug to imply that Blubbs hadn't fazed me.

'Safe,' went Dicey.

But Blubbs *had* fazed me: I was clueless. The Div's card was maxed and I didn't really have much I could flog now that he'd choked himself on my telly. There was the computer, of course, but this was the goose that laid the golden porn-eggs. Besides, the Div was always reminding me that it was a 'family' computer. By far my most valuable possessions were my rare Nirvana records. I owned about a dozen collectables including original vinyl copies of the heart-rending 'Molly's Lips', the bewitching 'Sliver' and, wait for it, their dazzling, raw first album, *Bleach*. I bought the lot from a Wednesbury charity shop for five quid! Can you believe it? They're worth hundreds. I kept it between me, Dice and Tiffany, though, because if the Divette ever found out she'd have me stump up compensation money to the charity shop. The woman is a Poppins. Flogging these sacred discs to pay Blubbs was out of the question. I'd do *anything* rather than flog them – they are rare cuts from a rare man. I play them over and over and the force and torment in them never fail to give me goosebumps.

But this meant that finding two hundred quid would be a big, big problem.

'No problem, Dice,' I said, 'I have it covered.'

5

Lucky (*adj*)

HAZEL

As I drove to Tiffany's house that Wednesday morning I couldn't take my mind off my husband. There'd been something odd about him at breakfast. It reminded me of the way he acts when he's trying to cover something up, like having taped *Star Trek* over *Holby City*, which has happened twice, or having soiled my curling tongs by trying to cook a sausage with them which, bizarrely, has also happened twice.

I thought I'd heard the last of Northern Soul. I'd been relieved when he grew out of it. It was a ridiculous hobby: travelling all over the country, spending fortunes on useless bits of plastic, throwing himself around like a demented break-dancer. Since seeing that KFC advert he'd barely spoken about anything else. The crack on his head must've knocked the last bit of sense out of him. If I caught him eating his Chicken Dippers with his fingers again I'd brain him.

I knew I'd made a mistake agreeing to go to the Fanny's reunion. I didn't like the music and I was dubious about the crowd he hung around with in those days. Minty dragged me along to a couple of Northern Soul all-nighters when we first met. The first was at Derby swimming baths and, if there hadn't been a dancefloor over the pool, I'd have gladly drowned myself. I've never been so bored. Every record was the same: like Tamla Motown but not as catchy. And everybody was speeding on amphetamines – even Minty, though he'd tried to hide it. They talked like they were in a words-per-minute contest and death was the second prize. And it was all rubbish: they'd list their 'current top five sounds'; they'd discuss the 'most collectable US record labels; the most collectable non-US labels; the best clubs north of Nottingham; the best clubs south of Nottingham; the best clubs *in* Nottingham; the best motorway service stations on the way to Nottingham'; and they'd say things like, 'Has anyone seen Wozza since Nottingham?' 'Podger was off his shed at Nottingham;' 'Dodger was off his neighbour's shed at Nottingham.' Christ almighty! I spent four hours wrapped in a pile of coats pretending to be asleep. The only occasion I'd been more bored was the one time I'd gone with him to Wigan Casino: there everyone talked the same rubbish but with Lancashire accents.

It wasn't much of a trade: eight hours of sleepless, terminal boredom in return for a barbecue. But this seemed pretty typical – it felt like I contributed the lion's share of everything except buffoonery.

I arrived at Tiffany's and sounded the horn. The curtain twitched and, two seconds later, she stepped out of the front door. I knew she'd be keen; she's a good, sensible girl. What she was doing with Nigel is beyond me. I can't see the attraction and I'm his mother! He used to be lovely but now it is hard to think of him as the product of my genes. What upsets me most is that he seems to loathe me. *Me?* Aren't you supposed to love your mom? I loved mine – that's part of the deal, isn't it? But it had been at least ten years since Nigel told me he loved me.

Tiffany climbed into the passenger seat. 'Good morning, Mrs Trebor,' she said, in a tone that most people would reserve for an audience with the Pope.

'Morning, Tiff,' I said, wondering if Nigel ever used the word 'love' with her. I found it difficult imagining him ever saying anything nice to anyone.

I often speculated about whether my decision to continue my career affected my relationship with Nigel. I'd struggled to keep the bond strong, but he always seemed to gravitate towards Minty when he was little. I remember one time – he must've been about two – he'd wanted Minty to bath him, but I insisted *I* did it. I lifted him out of the bath, held him trophy-like above my head and the little bugger shat in my face! A startling, reeking blast of hot diarrhoea sprayed my eyes, mouth and hair; *everywhere*. It wasn't his fault, obviously: it turned out he had a tummy bug. But it's difficult not to think of it as a comment on our relationship. He could have shat in my face all day long and I'd still have loved him, of course. You couldn't help it, then: he was so wide-eyed, top-heavy and helpless. Now it isn't so easy.

I eased my car into the busy traffic of the Broadway ring road. 'So tell me again, Tiffany,' I said, 'why do you want to do your work experience at our clinic?'

She wrinkled her brow in thought. Had it been any other sixteen-year-old I wouldn't have bothered asking because the answer would be obvious. The clinic is convenient because I happen to be her boyfriend's mother; either that or, 'Der . . . I just fought it'd be cool.'

'I thought it would be cool,' said Tiffany.

'Ah.'

But then she redeemed herself with, 'It looks as if it could be a rewarding job. When I leave school, I want a career that will allow me to serve the community.'

Blimey, I thought, she sounds as if she means it!

Nigel had done his work experience at my clinic too – 'working' with the manager in a 'clerical' capacity. It had been an embarrassing disaster. My son spent an entire fortnight surfing the internet. I had no such worries about Tiffany. That morning she looked the part in her white blouse and blue skirt. I hadn't often seen her in a skirt – she usually opts for the T-shirt and jeans style that Nigel favours, though somehow she never manages to look quite as scruffy as him. Her outfit was slimming too. I'd guess Tiffany is nine stone, but her clothes gave the impression of eight five to eight seven.

It wasn't a very exciting morning for Tiffany. She watched me give two dozen MMR injections and explain to two dozen mothers that the jabs weren't going to give their kids autism. This is something I've had to do since some twit appeared on GMTV and claimed there is a link between the two. The entire scientific community poured scorn on the theory, but the media ignored the less newsworthy science and went with the twit. The people of Walsall don't listen to scientists, obviously: they listen to Lorraine Kelly. It would probably lead to an epidemic of mumps and measles.

After I'd despatched the two dozen screaming toddlers, Tiffany sat politely and listened to me deal with a phone call from a woman whose three-year-old had bitten the head off a terrapin. There was a threat of salmonella so I referred her to her GP. Then she watched me write up the case notes from a visit I'd made the day before to a potentially at risk two-year-old called Mateus Rose Nobbs (two stone, three pounds).

I'm sure none of the morning's activities left Tiffany frantic to join my profession. Indeed, she spent most of her time cooing over the clinic's pet degus: the weird and aggressive South American rodents that we purchased to entertain the children. We keep them in reception as a distraction for fractious kids. Turns out the degus are more fractious than the kids.

'Don't put your fingers through the bars for goodness' sake, Tiffany,' I said.

'Do they have names?'

'Ant and Dec.'

'Hello, Ant. Hello, Dec.'

Both rodents hissed at her and revealed a centimetre of yellow fang.

'I wanted us to get a lop-eared rabbit,' I said.

Then Eunice arrived – two hours late because of a dental appointment. If anything was guaranteed to make Tiffany question her work experience choice it was my garrulous co-worker. She is the only other full-time health visitor at the Walsall clinic but she does the talking of forty people. She is more sociable than the degus but a thousand times more annoying. I've never seen anyone talk with as little regard for other people's sanity – not even Minty's whizzing Northern Soul mates. What makes her even more annoying is that she's too nice a person to say bugger off to.

Sadly Eunice's trip to the dentist had merely involved a scrape and polish, not, as I'd hoped, a mandible-immobilizing local anaesthetic. She treated us both to a protracted account of her conversation with the dentist, his nurse, his receptionist and two unfortunates she'd met in the waiting room (a waiting room that, incidentally, has powder-blue walls, sky-blue curtains and royal-blue carpet tiles). Then, as I pretended to distract myself with my case notes, Eunice filled Tiffany in on the minutiae of her recent trip to Lincoln Market. She explained the exact route she and her husband had taken, including such details as the hair colour of the lady who sold them their travel sweets in a newsagent's two miles south of Knobbers' Bonk. Tiffany's face took on the appearance of a girl who's realized that life is cruel as well as pointless.

'I have some visits to do this afternoon,' I told Tiffany, as Eunice motored full-throttle into another insanely trivial digression. 'Do you want to come?'

You'd have thought I'd offered her Richard Madeley on a baguette. 'Oh, yes! *Yes, please,* Mrs Trebor.'

Strictly speaking I suppose I shouldn't have taken a work-experience kid on a home visit – there's an issue of confidentiality – but I hadn't the heart to leave her with Eunice. Looking back, it was a mistake, but not the worst one I made that day.

'How long have you lived in Walsall, love?' I asked, as we drove towards the Jerome K. Jerome estate.

'All my life.'

'So you know that some areas can be a bit . . . colourful?'

Tiffany nodded. 'I think I'm prepared.'

'I'm pleased to hear it. It suggests you're made of the right stuff; either that or you're crazy.'

Tiffany smiled uncertainly and it occurred to me that, though she is a nice girl, she doesn't have much of a sense of humour. Mind you, my last comment was in bad taste – as someone who'd picked my son for a boyfriend her mental stability might not be an absolute given. About six months back Minty told me that looking at Nigel made him think about having a vasectomy and putting pluto-nium down his pants just to be on the safe side! He said the only thing stopping him having the chop was the thought of strangers messing with his 'plums'. This caused a huge row which ended with Minty trying to force my dictionary into the paper shredder.

The Jerome estate is the worst in the area. The most desperate places usually qualify as social group V but, among themselves, Walsall social services came up with a new rating for Jerome: 666. Minty calls it Darwin's waiting room. He is wrong. His joke assumes a relationship between evolution and progress and there isn't one. The future belongs to the type of people who have the most kids. In my experience that tends not to be career women, sadly.

There *are* a lot of decent people in Jerome, but the estate has big problems. In the six years since I'd been at the clinic I'd seen it all: from a house with nineteen Alsatians, to one with a pigeon coop in the kitchen. I knew of twelve children on the estate, living at eight different addresses, who all called the same man Dad. Or they would if they ever saw him. The average age for a first pregnancy is seventeen; the average age for a second is eighteen; the average age for a sixth is twenty-five. Drugs are a problem too. The kids get into them early because there's nothing else for them to do. And along with drugs comes crime. Burglary, prostitution. Jerome is a wonderful place to visit if you're a fence or a pimp; not so good if you're a health visitor.

'If I shout run,' I told Tiffany as we climbed out of the car, 'don't ask any questions, just run. OK?'

My first visit was to a young woman called Clover Soul. I needed to do some development checks on her two-year-old daughter. For this we had to make the perilous journey to Jerome View Towers, a large and, to my mind, inexcusable tower block.

Before we'd even left the car park I was forced to give a couple of truanting ten-year-olds a pound each to mind the car. They were well trained in the art of extortion and even offered me a receipt just in case I wanted to claim tax back against the charge. I chose to assume they were joking and ushered Tiffany towards the flats.

'Don't bother with the lift,' I told her. 'Even if it's working you wouldn't eat for a week if you used it.'

After four flights of stairs Tiffany was probably wishing she hadn't offered to carry my scales, but she didn't complain. I know they are heavy. Two stone, two pounds to be exact. I weighed them on the bathroom scales at home. I know that weighing scales is a bit like painting a paint tin, but I hadn't been able to help myself.

'For a visit of this kind,' I said, 'we're interested in the child's language skills, their social and cognitive development, their pre-school education and their nutrition. We like to ensure that they're not sleeping in a shoebox and living on dog biscuits.'

The door to Clover's flat had wires hanging where the doorbell should've been, so I knocked. A pale, lean boy who looked about Tiffany's age answered. This, I happened to know, was the father. He wore tracksuit bottoms without shoes or socks, no shirt and a Burberry baseball cap.

'Hello, David, I've come to see Clover and . . .' I clenched my jaw into straight-faced mode, 'little Patsie-Creole.'

Without a word of greeting he turned his back on us and walked into the flat, leaving the door open behind him. We followed his razor-sharp shoulder blades into the living room where he placed himself cross-legged in front of a 50-inch flat-screen TV and his game of *Tomb Raider II*. David was what we in the trade call 'pumpkin positive' – shine a torch into his mouth and the lack of brain matter will allow his head to illuminate like a Halloween lantern.

'Won't be a sec,' shouted his enormous wife, 'I've just got to get Manson out.' She was in the process of wrestling a pony-sized Dobermann on to the flat's balcony. Manson, who to his credit hadn't barked or growled, was reluctant to leave. Clover, however, was a woman of considerable substance and things were apt to go in the direction she felt they should. I've noticed it's often the case that weedy blokes like David Soul go for obese partners. Although obese wasn't really the clinically accurate word for Clover. She was *morbidly* obese. Her velour tracksuit bottoms throttled her waist like a tourniquet. I was impressed they made such garments in a size 40. Sadly, Mrs Soul needed a 46.

Tiffany's eyes widened at the voluminous spectacle and, sweating, she set down the scales.

'How is everything, Clover?' I asked.

'Wicked,' she said, and continued to urge the dog towards the balcony.

'And how's Patsie-Creole?'

'Wicked. We've just had her ears pierced. Weem thinking about her belly button next, ay we, Dave?'

Dave was mute.

'I think she might be a bit young for that, Clover,' I said.

'Oh ar?' She trapped Manson's snout in the door, forcing the dog to yowk and skitter backwards on to the balcony. Seizing her opportunity, Clover snapped the door shut. 'Serves you right, you little fucker!'

'Yes, Clover,' I continued, 'a belly-button ring is a choice a girl needs to make for herself. Preferably when she's an adult.'

'Is that right?' said Clover, placing her hands where her hips should have been. I could see she was bristling. Clover fell into what I call the 'Right Mother' category. This type aggressively assert their 'right' to bring up their children *their* way. One thing you can't do is let them think you're telling them how to raise their kids. It's the first thing you learn in 'Conflict Resolution' workshops.

'It's a shame, isn't it? I know Patsie-Creole would look lovely with a belly-button ring, it's just that social services wouldn't like it.'

'They can kiss my arse.'

'And they'd take her away.'

'They could fucking try!'

'And that would be a pity because you're such a good mother.'

'Damn right.'

'And of course you'd lose your child benefit.'

'They could fucking try!'

'So you see, it's best to play their game.'

'Whatever's best for the kid, like.'

'Absolutely. Speaking of your daughter . . . ?'

'Wha?'

'Could I see her? I just need to weigh her and do some development checks.'

'Oh, yeah, course,' she said, and then addressed her husband: 'Dave?'

Dave didn't answer – he was still cross-legged and goggle-eyed in front of his game, easing Lara Croft up what appeared to be a sheer rock face.

Clover persisted, 'Oi, saft cunt!'

Saft cunt didn't respond.

Clover waddled over to her husband, thighs quivering, and booted his joystick out of his hand.

'Clooooveeeeeer,' he whined, 'you aaaaa me mom, you know.'

'Where's Princess?'

David Soul gaped at his wife. The last time I'd seen an expression like his it was on a geriatric stroke patient who'd been stung on the tongue by a wasp.

'WHERE'S PRINCESS!' she thundered.

'I aaaaa saying unless you ask propeeeer. You aaaaa me mom.'

She grabbed him by some of the straggly bits of hair that hung out beneath his cap and jerked his head back.

Seizing his bare nipple between her thumb and forefinger she squeezed and twisted.

'EEEEEAAAAAA, geeeeerroff, Cloooveeeeer.'

'I wo ask you again, saft cunt, WHERE'S PRINCESS!'

'Aaaa she next dooooor?'

Clover stamped off in the direction of the front door and then out on to the landing. I followed her.

The door to her next-door neighbour's flat was ajar and Clover entered without knocking. Once more I followed, albeit tentatively. Tiffany trotted behind.

'*Princess! PRINCESS*,' Clover bellowed. 'Where am yow?'

Patsie-Creole did actually look a little like a princess when we found her. At least she was wearing a tiara, together with what appeared to be a miniature ball gown. Sitting opposite her was a boy of around four years old and the two were busy throwing red and grey capsules at each other. A brown-glass pill jar lay upturned and lidless on the grime-encrusted carpet.

Oh dear.

I ran into the living room, scooped up both children and placed them on the black plastic sofa that sat along one wall of the flat. I then began collecting the capsules.

'Why are these children unsupervised?' I asked, furious. 'This could be a matter for social services, possibly the police.'

'Cunting ell,' said Clover, 'I'll do for that slapper if she a ere. SHAZ? *SHAZ!*'

Clover stamped into the kitchen while I inspected the capsule jar. The contents had been prescribed to a Mrs Layla Clackett in 1985. There must've been a hundred 30mg gelatine capsules in all. The jar's label said Duromine and I was pretty sure this was a slimming drug. I'm no expert but I guessed there were enough capsules to turn Luciano Pavarotti into Lena Zavaroni.

'SHAZ! *SHAZ?* Where the fuck am yow?' Clover continued to stamp around the flat, in and out of bedrooms, randomly kicking at things as she travelled. It was as obvious as her broad backside that the kids were home alone. Eventually, breathless, the twenty-five-stone woman turned to the little boy.

'Hunter, where's Mommy?'

Hunter sucked hard on his dummy and began tugging on his crucifix earring. His head was shaved to the skin apart from a circle on top which was about half an inch long. It was like an inverted monk's hairdo. He wore a red Nike sweatshirt, blue pyjama bottoms and white football boots. He made no attempt to speak but, as I watched, he pressed a red and grey capsule into his right nostril. I moved swiftly to remove it and this was his cue to cry. His mouth opened, the dummy dropped out and he began to wail like a two-year-old. I began to suspect Hunter was developmentally delayed. With his mouth open I also observed that the boy had begun to develop 'dummy teeth': angled incisors that would leave him looking like a beaver in later life.

'What am yow doing with mar babby?' screamed a female voice. I turned to see a whippet-faced, ginger-haired woman glaring, yellow-eyed, at me. Weight-wise, she couldn't have been more different from Clover. I'd put her at six stone two to six three: she'd be six stone exactly if she took the trouble to brush her teeth.

'Shaz, where you bin?' asked Clover. 'The kids have bin in your medicine cupboard.'

'Who's er?' screamed Shaz, meaning me.

Clover's voice dropped to a near whisper. 'She's a fucking ealth visitor,' she hissed. 'Where the fuck you bin?'

By now I had taken my mobile out and I was making a big show of punching in a number.

'Who you phoning?' asked Shaz, a little more subdued.

'The police,' I lied. I wasn't going to do anything until I'd heard what she had to say, but I wanted to frighten her.

'No, no, dow do that,' said Shaz.

'Could you tell me why these children have been left alone in a flat with access to dangerous prescription drugs?' I noticed Tiffany standing in the doorway and wondered if any of her mates would be getting work experience as interesting as this. Not a chance, and for good reason. I was suddenly very conscious of the fact that she shouldn't be here at all.

'I just nipped round me mom's,' said Shaz. 'I was only gone five minutes. She phoned to tell me there was a dia-mondique sale on the shopping channel – I ay got satellite meself.'

'And you left two toddlers to fend for themselves? That's grossly irresponsible; in fact, it's criminal. I'm going to have to report it.'

Tears streamed down the woman's pasty face. 'Dow report me,' she blubbed, 'they'll tek Hunter away.'

I felt sorry for her; I always do, but I couldn't let her see that I was softening. It was clear she fell into the 'Dumb Mother' category. This has a number of sub-categories from 'benignly dumb' to 'dangerously dumb', and I feared Shaz might be close enough to the latter to warrant intervention.

'What about these capsules? They should've been dis-posed of years ago, not stored where a young child can get at them!'

'Them's me mom's not mine; theym left over from when she used to live here, before she moved in with Tommo the Chink. Tek em away, throw em away. Dow tell the coppers or me social worker.'

I glanced again at Tiffany. If I were to make this official I might be obliged to explain the presence of a work experience schoolgirl and that would be difficult. Besides, the kids no longer seemed to be in any immediate danger; certainly I'd seen worse on this estate.

'Who's Hunter's health visitor?' I asked Shaz.

'A woman called Eunice – never stops yapping.'

'OK. The police don't need to know but I'll inform Eunice and make sure she keeps an eye. And get rid of those capsules.'

'Thanks, love,' said Shaz. 'It wow appen again. Yow can tek the pills away. Yowm right, theym dangerous: I remember me mother's Rottweiler, Fist, ad one by accident and it killed him. All his fur fell out and his back legs went to pot. He kept shitting himself too. Tommo the Chink had to tek a spade to his yed to put him out of his misery. It was tragic, me mother was closer to Fist than to any dog she's ad. They'd been together for months.'

I didn't bother telling Shaz that Fist's symptoms were unlikely to have been caused by amphetamines. But confiscating the capsules *did* seem like a good idea. At least I'd be sure they were disposed of properly. I picked up the bottle and led the way out of the flat.

Before she left, Clover turned on Shaz: 'Later me and yow am going to have words, lady.'

If it was possible Shaz's skin became even paler. I don't blame her. Clover could have used Shaz as a ginger G-string.

Thankfully, the remainder of the Jerome visits were uneventful. I had to admonish one young mother for trying to feed her two-month-old son a Twix and I was a bit worried about one of my asylum-seeker families who was getting hassled by the Jerome Fascist Brotherhood. For this estate, however, it was a relatively trouble-free afternoon.

'Did you enjoy yourself, Tiffany?' Eunice asked, when we returned to the clinic at about three. She didn't give the girl a chance to answer before embarking on a lengthy tale about *her* first day as a health visitor on the mean streets of Walsall.

I decided to store the confiscated capsules in our dangerous drugs cabinet. I was going to have to consult Joe, the clinic manager, about how to dispose of them. He was attending a creative management course called 'Painting the Box Sky Blue' and wouldn't be in clinic till tomorrow. I felt I had to be careful because, strictly speaking, I'd no right to confiscate them. Also, as an amphetamine-based substance, they were a potentially sought-after commodity. I didn't want to be accused of stealing them for my own use, or anything silly like that. I wanted my line manager to know *exactly* why I'd taken them and, more importantly, get his advice on how to ditch them. One thing I've learned in this game is that you've got to cover your back.

As dangerous drugs cabinets go, ours isn't up to much. In fact it isn't a cabinet: it's an old fridge with a Victorian flat-iron wedged against its loose door. The lack of hi-tech security is largely due to the fact that we don't keep any dangerous drugs on the premises. We only use it to store adrenaline, together with the degus' salad. The latter is the reason we've a Victorian flat-iron wedged against it. Several times they've escaped and managed to squeeze under the office door, get into the fridge and gorge themselves on their feed.

Sliding the ancient iron away from the fridge, I asked Eunice what she knew about Sharon Clackett.

'A ginger piece with a crypt pallor? That's Hunter Clackett's mom. She's a bit half-soaked but I've seen worse. That flat's her mom's, if I recall. Sharon stayed in it when her mother moved out – I'm not sure the council know.'

'Her mother's name is Layla?'

'Yes, Layla Clackett. She looks nothing like the daughter. She's a big woman – forty stone if she's an ounce; uses a rag on a stick to wipe her arse. Her husband, Sharon's dad, was a drug addict. Killed himself in the mid-eighties after eating thirty-six nasal inhalers.'

'Pardon?' asked Tiffany, agape. 'Why would anyone want to do that?'

'Good question,' said Eunice. 'There was a time when inhalers had benzedrine in them – a kind of speed or upper. But these didn't. He was just too dumb to realize. He choked to death when some of the inhalers' cotton cores expanded in his throat. His name was Warren. Warren Clackett.'

'Eunice,' I said, holding up the bottle I'd confiscated, 'we just found about a hundred slimming pills belonging to Layla Clackett, with a prescription date of 1985.'

'Well, she probably got them for him, on prescription,' said Eunice. 'One thing's for sure, she wasn't taking them herself. The woman's a brontosaurus and she's been that way for as long as I can remember.'

'Why didn't her husband *take* the capsules, then, if he was a speed addict? Why did he bother eating nasal inhalers?'

'You've been visiting Jerome long enough to know not to ask those kind of questions. Why do they wear Burberry boxer shorts? Why do they have TVs the size of barn doors in rooms the size of wardrobes? Why do they buy their kids mobile phones before they're old enough to talk? Why do they . . .' And off she went, detailing numerous baffling Jerome eccentricities. I'd heard her rant a million times, so I made an excuse and slipped into an empty consulting room.

I noticed that my hands were trembling slightly as I fitted a dish on to a set of Salter desk scales. I felt a bit light-headed too, which I blamed on the fact that I'd only had a Cox's orange pippin for lunch.

I weighed a tin of baby milk formula, followed by a paper punch and a stapler. The paper punch was the heaviest, although it was smaller in size than the tin. Denser, I thought. I removed the punch, zeroed the scales, then weighed it once more. No change. I removed it again and pulled off the plastic cap that allows you to discard the surplus discs of punched paper. I tipped a load of little circles into the wastepaper basket and popped the punch back on the scales. The weight didn't change and, inexplicably, this pleased me.

I had a date with Kelvin at five. I wished it was sooner. I'd told Tiffany I had a late visit and that she'd have to make her own way home. She didn't mind.

I felt guilty about seeing Kelvin because visits to Jerome always made me feel lucky about everything I had. I moaned about Nigel and Minty but, as I said before, I knew I could have done worse. Minty acts the goat sometimes and embarrasses me, but next to some Jerome men he's a prince. He'd never hurt me and, though he could be a pillock, I was sure he'd never do anything really stupid. I mean *Jerome* stupid. What right did I have to feel hard done by?

I replaced the punch on the scales and added a box of incontinence pants: four pounds, three ounces. Heavier. I set my diary on top of the box of pants. Heavier still.

I felt a bit better, although my hands still shook slightly as I tidied the desk and packed away the scales.

My watch said 4.10 p.m. Fifty minutes to go before I'd see Kelvin.

I *was* lucky, wasn't I? Unlike many of the wives and mothers I visited, I never had to worry about being abandoned, or beaten up. I never had to worry about the police ringing our doorbell.

6

'Baby Boy'

Fred Hughes (Brunswick)

TREBBO

When the police rang the doorbell I was in the middle of the washing up and I answered in my Marigolds. I immediately expected the worst. Maybe Hazel had had a crash in her Micra or Nigel had been tossed into a dustcart? What I didn't expect was 'gangsta porn'. Well, you don't, do you?

'Pornography?' I realized I was semi-screaming but couldn't help myself. 'I don't know anything about pornography! I'm a school crossing patrol!'

The copper eyed my Marigolds with distaste. 'Do you mean you're a lollipop man?' he asked, although I knew he knew perfectly well.

He was a sarcastic bastard and so was what I assumed was his lesser-ranked sidekick who did nothing but titter at his superior's smart-arse comments. They were both plain clothes but, for some reason, had seen fit to advertise their presence with a marked police car. They'd parked this on our drive at what I felt was a rather insolent angle. When curtains began to twitch I was compelled to invite them in. Then, after allowing me to relinquish my Marigolds, they'd produced some sheets of paper listing the details of a computer's internet history – a series of web addresses – including www.pimpsinthehoodgetwood.com and www.mafiamuffmen.com.

'They're paysites accessed via a computer at this address,' said the non-titterer, 'and that access has been funded by *your* credit card.'

'What? *What?*'

He handed me an A4 photograph of what appeared to be a still from a porn movie. It was the image of a woman fellating the barrel of an Uzi. She had white, inch-long fingernails cut into squares at the end and collagen-implanted lips.

'What am I supposed to be looking at?'

'The evidence would seem to suggest that you've been paying to view speciality pornography,' said the non-titterer.

They observed my reaction carefully as I let this sink in. A large lorry rumbled past outside and rattled the plates on Hazel's Welsh dresser – a row of purple and white Royal Albert, arranged like shooting-gallery targets.

'I didn't authorize any payments.'

The non-titterer grinned. There was something cold about him: despite his sarcasm he seemed completely humourless. His grin was fixed and forced, like something carved into a pumpkin.

'I think there's been some kind of mistake,' I continued. 'Someone must've stolen my credit card number. I've only ever used that card once, last week. To buy some records.'

'From Scarce Soul Supplies?'

'Er, yes. But how –'

'We have a record of that. Nine hundred ninety pounds. Must have been a good collection of records for that much. Gangsta rap?'

'Look, I've had enough of this, officer . . . ?'

'Smiles. Detective Inspector Smiles.'

'Whatever. Credit card transactions are private, or so I'd always assumed.'

'You can assume whatever you feel happy assuming, Mr Trebor, it doesn't concern me. What does concern me is my investigation into the trafficking of illegal pornographic images. Images of children.'

Suddenly I was acutely conscious of my innards. I experienced a sensation that Hazel calls 'peristalsis', but which I refer to as 'thinking I might shit myself'. What was going on?

'I don't . . . I've never . . . I'm a school crossing patrol.'

'So you keep saying. In some circles the phrase "lollipop man" is code for nonce, you know.'

'No, I do not! As I say, *someone must've been using my card without my knowledge.*'

'And have they been sneaking into your house to use your computer too?' He could see I was on the verge of incontinence and, though his manner remained menacing, his voice softened a little. He leaned towards me. 'Listen, Mr Trebor, we have no evidence that you're accessing paedophile sites. If we had we'd be kicking the shit out of you. But the AVS that you fund with your card *does* act as a portal for numerous such sites, as well as the "legal" ones you enjoy –'

'I don't enjoy gangsta porn, I –'

Smiles raised his hand. 'I'm not here to argue with you about that. With your permission we'd like to take a copy of your hard drive, just for our research, you understand, and we can leave it at that. But we'd prefer it if you didn't continue to fund that AVS.'

'I don't even know what an AVS is!'

'Adult Verification System. Yours is called the Golden Key.'

'I . . . I . . .'

Smiles thought for a moment. The plates on the Welsh dresser rattled again. 'Where do you keep your computer, Mr Trebor?'

'In the spare bedroom at the top of the stairs.'

'And does anyone else have access to it?'

'My son, Nigel.'

Smiles showed his teeth. 'Ah. You might want to have a word with him.'

'Could he have stolen my – ?'

Smiles raised his hand again. 'My advice would be to speak to him. Contact your credit card company too. Any possible theft from your card isn't something *we* want to get involved with: we're vice not fraud, but you could pursue it with our colleagues if you choose. In my experience, though, it's best to sort out domestic problems domestically, so to speak.'

'I'll kill the little bastard!'

'I agree that children need a firm hand. That's always been my policy with my own boy. You don't want him to grow up a pervert, do you?'

I didn't know how to respond to this and I searched his eyes for the implication. They seemed to have had the colour boiled out of them. 'Well, I –'

'I hate perverts personally, I really do. I suppose it's because I have to deal with them every day. I meet some repulsive fuckers in my line of work (Lord forgive me for swearing), some *really obnoxious* fuckers: kiddy fiddlers, beast botherers and such like.'

Was he supposed to swear? His words had a belligerence that made me shudder. Even his sidekick shifted uneasily in his seat.

Smiles turned to the latter and said, 'Go and get the hard drive out of the car, Jenkins. We'll copy this gentleman's files then be on our way.'

As soon as we were alone the inspector moved closer to me. He was a bulky, powerfully built bloke and for a second I was worried he was going to punch me. Instead he put his hand on my arm and said, 'Have you considered parenting classes?'

Parenting classes! I hadn't even wanted to be a parent. I'd been gutted when Hazel told me she was up the duff. Nigel had been another accident in my calamity-littered life. We'd only been married five years and I'd wanted it to be just us for a bit longer. I wanted to carry on enjoying myself in all the ways we had been up till then: meals out at the Korma Sutra, holidays in Tenerife. Sex. Nigel fitted into Hazel's plans for self-fulfilment, but not mine. For months while she was carrying him I'd been unsure if I'd be able to love him. I did, immediately, and always will; but I couldn't help resenting him too. I'd be a *senior* accident investigator by now if I'd stayed with BR. But I had nothing to show for my life except him and I was coming to feel that the stork had delivered us a pig in a poke! Don't get me wrong: if he needed a blood transfusion I'd cut my throat to give him one, but I couldn't help wondering what had happened to my baby boy. These days the sight of him makes me want to have my tubes knotted. I would too if Hazel would let me (and if I wasn't so touchy about strangers fiddling with my plums).

The second the police left I scaled the stairs to my son's room with the phrase 'gangsta porn' flapping in my head like a mad bat.

As I entered his lair, the biscuit stink of socks hit me. I could barely see where I was going because of his blackout curtains so I opened them, letting the afternoon sunlight illuminate the black walls and ceiling. The room seemed simultaneously cleaner and dirtier: cleaner because of the light, but dirtier because that light betrayed just how squalid the place was.

There was a giant picture of Kurt Cobain on one wall and, over the bed, a poster for a film called *Slackers*. I held my breath and started searching through the drawers of his dressing table. His clothes were scrunched rather than folded and it was as if they'd been attacked by moths the size of pterodactyls: my fingers occasionally slipped through deliberate tears. Finding nothing in the drawers, I turned to the bookshelves, fanning the pages of any books which looked large enough to conceal something. There were a couple of graphic novels, *The Watchmen* and *Batman: The Dark Knight Returns*, and several volumes about Kurt Cobain, Nirvana and the Seattle sound. I don't know what he sees in that tripe. To me Kurt Cobain was just a whining ragbag. It may be hypocritical, but I can't help disliking people who take drugs to excess. I'm irrationally hostile to folks who commit suicide too, particularly when they have kids. To my mind they're getting off too easily.

I began pulling the storage drawers out from under the bed, still not really knowing what I expected to find. Anything seemed possible. I'm not a prude, but I didn't like the idea of Nigel accessing *specialist* porn sites. The word 'specialist' somehow smacked of perversion. I supposed if he *was* some kind of pervert he'd have a lot of photographs. Perverts always do. Whenever they're reported on the news the coppers don't just find two or three photos, or even two or three hundred; it's always two or three *hundred thousand*. They're like obsessive-compulsives or stamp collectors. All I found under Nigel's bed, however, was a decrepit pair of trainers and half a Jammie Dodger.

I glanced at my watch: 2.30. I needed to be back on duty at 3.15, before the infants started coming out, so I moved quickly to the MFI flat-pack wardrobe we bought when Nigel was three. In its mirror I saw that my neck-brace made me resemble a dark-haired version of that talentless ginger twat off *Bo' Selecta!*

The biscuit smell hit me again when I opened the wardrobe. There were no clothes actually hanging in it, just loads piled up at the bottom: an old lumberjack coat, a denim jacket with the pockets ripped off, a couple of thick cotton overshirts, a variety of woolly hats and heaps of T-shirts, jeans and hooded sweatshirts. It was the kind of gear destitute farmers dress their scarecrows in. Holding my nose with my right hand I pushed my left arm amongst the rags and moved it about experimentally. It happened upon a cardboard shoebox and I eased this out, fearing the worst.

The box contained a packet of giant, joint-sized Rizla papers, six dozen condoms, and a sheaf of credit card statements. The pot papers didn't worry me too much: I was aware he'd tried it at least once because I'd smelt it on his rags. I'd considered speaking to him about it but couldn't see the point. Having experimented myself when I was young, I knew it wasn't the end of the world. Like me, he'd grow out of it. I wasn't bothered about the condoms either; in fact, they reassured me. I was infinitely more concerned about the Visa statements.

The bastard had been using my credit card.

I leafed through them. They were all addressed to me and went back to December 2002. No wonder the sod was always first to the post. Each statement had roughly the same monthly amount deducted: sometimes ten quid something, sometimes eleven quid something. It was credited to Golden Key Internet Access Services, Nassau, Bahamas. All of the debts had been settled apart from the most recent and that was *my* debt: the sum of nine hundred and ninety pounds paid to Scarce Soul Supplies. This particular statement was one that I'd been looking to intercept myself, but I hadn't expected it to arrive so quickly. The purchase was made just four days earlier! My heart fluttered slightly as I was reminded of my recent extravagance. Six months' wages for ten 7-inch singles . . .

It sounds excessive, it *is* excessive, but it was worth it. In fact, the records had arrived in the post that very morning. When I got home from the early lollishift there was a card from Royal Mail to say that they'd tried to deliver a package. Because it had to be signed for, they'd taken it to the central post office in town. If I'd not been forced to spend time answering questions about porn I could've picked it up. Now it would have to wait till tomorrow.

The main problem was that Nigel now knew about my recent extravagance too, and that complicated everything. He could tell Haze and if there was one thing Haze didn't need to know it was that I'd blown nigh on a grand on what she'd see as ten pieces of worthless plastic. She'd have the dickiest of dickie-fits. I knew this because a few days earlier I'd tentatively suggested beginning to collect rare soul records again and she hadn't given me much encouragement. In fact, she threatened to smash them over my 'stupid, sodding, cretinous, immature head'. As is her way, she took the trouble to read me definitions of the words 'cretin' and 'immature' from her *Mini Oxford*. Actually she only managed 'cretin' – I'd already tossed her dictionary in the bin before she could get to 'immature'.

The only good news was that I didn't find any gangsta porn.

Forty minutes later, I took my place at the kerb, fuming. I was all set to disembowel Nigel and I needed to calm down – I had to try and concentrate on the job.

Being a lolliman might be a slightly humiliating occupation, but it's not as easy as you think. There's a pretty rigorous training programme in Walsall. You learn the formula used to determine whether an area qualifies for a patrol. I still remember it: $P \times V^2 > 4,000,000$ (where P = pedestrians and V = vehicles). In other words the number of pedestrians times the number of vehicles squared must be greater than four million for a stretch of road to qualify for a lolliman. They teach you important stuff too, of course. Lolly positions, for instance: holding your sign upside down means you're not crossing pedestrians (so cars can pass); holding your lolly across the body, parallel to the ground signals that pedestrians must stop on the kerb; holding the lolly at 45 degrees to the body signals to cars that you're about to cross someone; holding the pole with your arms at full span means all vehicles must stop. OK, it isn't quantum physics, but people *do* fail the course. It's a job you have to take seriously. Yet that day – for obvious reasons – I was finding it difficult to concentrate; I couldn't get my mind off Oxfam Charlie's gangsta porn.

The impossible happened, however: something *did* take my mind off it.

It was ten past three and I was anticipating the first wave of kids from Wurlington Infants when a Ford Mondeo made its way around the mini-island about twenty yards from where I stood. The driver struck me as familiar. I knew the face, I thought, but at first I couldn't place it. You get to know the regulars in a job like mine – the folks who pass by at the same time every day. But this guy wasn't a regular, I was certain of that. So where had I seen him? On telly? It wouldn't be the first time. I've seen quite a few celebs driving past my spot: when the traffic's blocked on the M6 people get off at Junction 7, take the Walsall ring road and rejoin at Junction 9. When the ring road itself is packed they're often forced on to the side roads. Folks who wouldn't normally so much as fart in the direction of Walsall get to glimpse its delights. I've seen Jade Goody, Christopher Timothy and Dom (from Dick and Dom). I've even seen that chunky woman who does the late-afternoon chat shows. I lowered my lolly to stop her, just to make sure it *was* her. She was a bit annoyed at having to stop when there was no one crossing so I'd tried to win her over by saying that she didn't look quite as chubby in real life as she does on the box. She gave me the bird and said I was lucky she didn't put a knot in my lolly. Bloody prima donna.

The Mondeo slowed to a stop and the driver was grinning at me. When he cracked his window the breeze delivered a powerful blast of hair lacquer to my nose. Such an odour could only emanate from one man's head: my old Northern Soul mate, Petey (the Coiffure) Fleetwood. He must have got the message I left on his mom's answerphone.

'Minty Trebor!' he said.

'Petey Fleetwood, stroll on: I'd know that scent of Silvikrin anywhere!' Petey had sported exactly the same layered, centre-parted hairstyle since the seventies, and he always used a monsoon of hair lacquer to keep it in place.

'What happened to your neck?' he asked, regarding me through his open window.

'I inadvertently headbutted Kurt Cobain.'

Petey snapped on his hazard lights, climbed out of the motor and began shaking my hand. He pumped it as we moved to the kerbside and the line of drivers that had built up behind him began easing their motors around his.

'I got the message,' said Petey. 'I remembered you worked on this road so I thought I'd try and catch you.'

'What are *you* up to these days, Petey?'

Petey is someone I'd bumped into maybe three or four times since my youth. When I'd last seen him, about five years before, he'd been working in Taylor's music shop cleaning the spit out of second-hand trumpets. He was one of the few people I was confident I'd out-achieved.

'I have my own business,' he said.

Stroll fucking on, I thought. 'Well done, mate,' I said. 'What's your line?'

'I sell cleaning materials, personal hygiene products; all kinds of things.'

'Working for yourself?'

'Yep.'

'Great.' On the back seat of his car I was pleased to notice a large box full of Amway products.

'You're flogging Amway?'

'Er, yep. You've heard of them?'

'I know the name.' There'd been an Amway representative on a consumer rights programme recently denying that Amway's business practices involved illegal pyramid selling. I should've known there was no way a Charlie like Petey would be running a real business.

'They offer great opportunities for people who are keen to get on,' said Petey, handing me a business card. 'If you like we could arrange a time and I'll give you a presentation.'

'I'm not sure about that, Petey, but it would be good to get together and, would you believe it, I've got just the occasion for us to –'

A Hyundai Coupe came belting down the road at full pelt so I broke with Petey to yell at the driver: 'SLOW DOWN! SLOW DOWN! SLOW DOWN!' I was appeased when I saw his brake lights come on.

'Sorry, Petey,' I said, 'that bloke was an accident waiting to happen. But listen: how do you fancy going to a Northern Soul all-nighter!? They're having a one-off closing-down night at Fanny's this Friday!'

'I've seen that KFC advert. Memories, eh?' Petey patted his coiffure with his palm, revealing a rugby ball-sized sweat stain in the armpit of his suit.

'Stroll on, you're not wrong.' Rummaging in my back pocket I found one of the flyers. 'Can you make it? A bunch of us are going for old times' sake.'

A Vauxhall Corsa came roaring from the opposite direction, exceeding the limit by at least 10 m.p.h., so I broke with Petey again: 'SLOW DOWN! SLOW DOWN! SLOW DOWN!' When no brake lights came on I shouted, 'SLOW DOWN!' again, but it was clear I'd been ignored. Bloody maniac – if Petey hadn't been there I'd have taken his number.

'Sorry, Petey,' I said, composing myself. 'I know I'm a bit zealous but I don't want any accidents on my patch.'

'Same old Minty,' said Petey, folding the flyer and placing it behind a row of pens in his breast pocket, 'still shouting at traffic.'

'It's part of the job, mate. Anyway, forget that, what about the nighter, are you up for it?'

Petey Fleetwood gave me an odd look as the cars continued to trundle past and his lacquered hair shimmered in the sun. Perhaps my bawling at the traffic had unsettled him. Had I gone OTT? I had to admit that my nerves were still on edge after my encounter with the coppers.

'Well?' I pressed.

'It's short notice, Minty,' he said, 'but . . . OK, OK, I'll be there. I could do with a night out. It's all work and no play with me at the minute – what with the new business and everything.'

'Nice one, Petey,' I said, stepping back into the road to stop the traffic for Nardeep, one of the regular mothers, who was looking to cross with her six-year-old son. 'See you Friday.'

Petey gave me the thumbs-up and then headed for his motor.

'Did that bloke have his hair cut at Disneyland?' asked Nardeep, as she ushered her kid across.

'Never Never Land,' I said, winking.

By this time Petey was back in his Mondeo and he didn't hear. He'd always been proud of his hairstyle. It was his 'feature' and he carried it around like Carmen Miranda's hat. Actually, apart from his taste in music, Petey was a bit of a no-hoper. But he was a nice bloke. In the Northern days we'd all call him 'the Coiffure' and touch his hair for luck. It was like touching a raffia lampshade. The guy used so much lacquer that I recall at least two occasions when his hair caught fire: once at Wigan and once at Blackpool Mecca. The former was caused by a fag-end dropped carelessly from the balcony, but the latter was a mystery. At the time Petey suggested static and, given his penchant for manmade fibres, this seemed possible.

I gave him a wave as I stepped back to the kerb and he drove away. It was nice to see him and great that he was up for Friday. At last something exciting was happening in my life. One thing's for sure, it took my mind off Nigel. Until, that is, I saw him.

7

'Milk It'

Nirvana, *In Utero* (Geffen)

TREBBO

It'd been a bad day. I'd been slammed in the face by Biggie Small's albino brother, then I'd spent the rest of it failing to raise enough cash to avoid having him slam me again. Not only had I not raised enough, I hadn't raised any. My first thought had been to approach some of the people I'd supplied with cut-price skunk – I figured they owed me something. Just a tenner here and there would have been a start. I drew blank after blank. It's not as if I'd asked them to *give* me the money. I'd promised to re-imburse them two-fold with skunk as soon as my source was re-established. No chance. They'd started calling me Wankrag again; well, four Wankrags and a Scrag-arse to be precise. Bummer.

I had so much on my mind that I decided to slack off school early. I was nervous about Blubber-T. I don't like fighting. I'm not a coward but I avoid mixes whenever I can. To be honest I don't really like hurting people. Generally, if I can't avoid the fight, I let myself get beaten up. I usually put my hands up and say: 'Hey, man, relax'; or, 'It's not worth it, dude'; or, 'Stay cool, bro, life's too short.' Mostly it works. I'm not the type people pick on.

They'll call me Wankrag, but they'll usually stop short of violence. This has to do with my cool. Bullies are wary of cool. Whenever my cool holds out I'm safe. Think about all the people in the world who are punchable: Richard Madeley, Darius Danesh, Peter André, etc. None of them are cool. Now think of some people it would be impossible to punch: Jim Morrison, Jimi Hendrix, James Dean, John Travolta's character in *Pulp Fiction*, Samuel L. Jackson in anything, Cobain. Even if you don't like them you'd be reluctant to punch them. They have an aura; they are self-possessed in a way that makes folks instinctively wary. And this is what I was trying to cultivate.

Here are some tips for being cool. First, and most important, is you shouldn't laugh. You can be funny, but you should avoid laughing. The only kind of laughing that's acceptable for cool people is ironic laughing; in other words, laughing in quotation marks: 'tee hee', for instance, or 'hardee har'. Enthusiasm is also something you should avoid. For instance, I love my rare grunge vinyl as much as the Div loves Northern Soul, but you won't hear me flapping my mouth about it. If you ask the Div about his music he'll yak at you until you take an axe to him. Try asking me about mine and I'll just shrug and yawn. There's the difference. Another thing you shouldn't do is argue. Just state your opinion and then zip it. If people want to disagree with you that's merely a reflection of their lack of cool. Cool people don't bandy words with numpties and the definition of a numpty is anyone who wants to bandy words with *you*. Perfect your shrug and the tone of voice with which you utter the word, 'whatever'. You should also dress like you don't give a shit. This is optional if you're black but crucial if you're white. Black people can be bling and designer-conscious and still be cool; white people who are bling and designer-conscious are almost always wankers.

I was pondering these key tactics when I became aware of someone screaming: 'Nigel!'

It was the Div.

I'd been so preoccupied I hadn't noticed where I was going. With my mind wandering I'd mistakenly taken the direct route home instead of the Div-free route. He was the last thing I needed, particularly as he seemed to be even more off his cake than usual. I didn't acknowledge him, obviously: after all, who is Nigel? But he wasn't about to be ignored.

He sprinted towards me bearing his lolly like a pikestaff and, despite his neck-brace, luminous green jacket and dancing bitch-tits, he looked dangerous.

When it comes to cool, being seen running away from someone who wants to beat you up is much less cool than actually being beaten up. And being seen running away from your dad – particularly if your dad happens to be a lollipop man – is the least cool thing in the history of uncool. So staying put was an easy decision. It was also easy because the Div had never laid a finger on me. He dislikes violence as much as I do.

I yawned and tried to shoulder past him but he blocked my way with the lolly and forced me back against a set of railings. The school traffic droned past – an endless line of people carriers and 4 × 4s – and every face in every car seemed turned towards me. If only I'd been wearing my hoodie!

'I've had the coppers round our house all morning, you fucking bag of rags. You've got some explaining to do.'

'Relax, dude, relax,' I told him. 'Stay cool.'

'Relax? *Relax?* They accused me of downloading "gangsta porn" from the internet and paying for it with my bleeding credit card!'

I'd anticipated getting caught one day and I'd rehearsed my response: '*You* never used your credit card, so I thought

I would.' I took the time to smooth my goatee with my thumb and forefinger. 'I paid off the balance every month.'

'To watch gangsta porn! What kind of freak are you? If your mother found out there aren't enough words in her dictionary for what she'd do to you.'

'The porn wasn't for me.'

'And drugs! I know what pot-smoking gear looks like. I found your funny fag papers, son.'

I shrugged. I wish he wouldn't call skunk 'pot'. He makes it sound like powdered terracotta. 'It's virtually legal,' I said. 'Relax.'

'If you tell me to relax one more time I'll relax you for good. Got me?'

'Excuse me . . . Mr Lollipop Man?' said a prehistoric gimmer who'd just appeared at the kerb. 'Ronan needs to cross.' She was accompanied by what I assume was her grandson and she was carrying a giant Toblerone in a Morrisons shopping bag. She had an 'I might be a loveable old duck but I know my rights' air about her.

'I'll be with you in a sec, love,' he shouted.

I made to move but again he stopped me with his lolly. More people carriers; more 4 × 4s. I thought about deliberately distorting my face so that people wouldn't recognize me, but I figured it was useless: my grunge threads were a placard to the world.

'So, come on: why gangsta porn? I'm all ears.'

Again I knew exactly how to respond to this. 'Does Mom know you've spent nine hundred and ninety quid on that credit card you never use?'

'What?'

'Nine hundred and ninety quid has gone off the card. You've used it to buy soul shite, haven't you? Does Mom know?'

'Mr Lollipop Man, Ronan needs to cross, *please*!' persisted the gimmer.

The Div turned on her. 'Look, you daft bint, I'm having a bit of a family crisis at the moment. *All right?*'

'Listen, Nigel,' he went, turning back to me, 'your mother doesn't need to be told anything about that because it would only upset her.' I wasn't really paying attention as I could see something that he couldn't, namely the gimmer bearing down on him. With the kind of venom only an outraged geriatric can muster, she began poking the back of his head with her finger, tipping his Day-Glo hat over his eyes.

'Don't you dare talk to me like that!' she said, poking. 'You're a public servant!' Ronan clapped his hands seal-flipper style and, for reasons best known to himself, began chanting, 'Postman Pat is a twat.'

As soon as the gimmer noticed the Div was wearing a neck-brace, however, she was all apologies. 'Goodness me,' she said, 'I didn't realize you had a spinal injury: I'm so, so sorry . . . My husband had a herniated disc, you know, and my son-in-law has spondylitis.'

'Don't worry, love,' he went, composing himself, 'I apologize for snapping.' He straightened his hat and made for the kerb.

'I'll be off then, Daddy,' I said, ice as the iceman.

'We've not finished, mate,' he told my departing shoulder blades. My reply was to fire my spent gum into the gutter.

I reckoned the Div and me *had* finished. I'd got something on him with the credit card purchase and I was going to milk it. I'd seen a spark of fear in his eyes. Crisis averted.

The Simpsons was on when, later that day, the Divette returned from work. Me and the Div were both watching in

silence – we hadn't exchanged words since the kerbside fra-
cas. The Div might be a div, but he knows when he's beaten.

'All right, Haze,' he went, 'nice day?' He'd been doing
the housework and was still wearing his novelty bra and
knickers apron. I'd bought this for him at Christmas in
order to ridicule his role as house-husband but, annoyingly, he liked it.

'What's gone off?' she asked, dropping her scales and
work-bag in the hall.

'What do you mean, love?' He shot me a nervous glance.

'Nancy Valentine just collared me on the drive and told
me there was a police car round here this morning.'

The Div shot me another glance. Nancy Valentine is our
next-door neighbour. She's as mad as a cap full of crickets
and for some reason likes to keep the Divette informed
about everything. Sometimes she phones to tell her it's
raining. The Div cleared his throat while I sat back and
waited to see what the genius would come up with.

'Wha?' he said.

'The police, Minty, they were round here this morning
according to Nancy Valentine.'

'Oh, er, yeah. It was nothing.' He began fiddling with
his brace, forcing his fingers down the top as if trying to
scratch an itch. 'They were er . . . just informing us that . . .
er . . . there's a nonce in the area.'

'What?'

Despite what I said about laughter being uncool, it was
all I could do to keep a lid on mine. *A nonce in the area?*
The worrying thing is that I've inherited his genes.

'Yes, some bloke over Longwood Gardens. He's on that
Sex Offenders Register. They thought we had a right to
know as parents.' He glanced towards me again and I
showed him my contempt by opening my mouth and letting him see my chewing gum.

'That's outrageous!' said the Divette. 'I can't believe the police have been so irresponsible.' And off she went saying how she was going to contact them to express her 'misgivings' about their decision to make this guy's whereabouts known, putting him at risk from vigilantes, blah de blah. All the time the Div sank lower and lower into the settee, knowing he'd dropped a beach-ball of a nad.

'OK, OK, Haze,' he said, cutting her off in mid-rant, 'I made that up.'

'You what?'

'About the nonce, I made it up.'

'I can't believe I'm hearing this! *Why*, for God's sake?'

'I didn't want you to worry.'

'About what?'

'There've been some robberies reported in the area.'

'And you thought I'd worry less if you told me there was a paedophile in the area?'

'Bad robberies.'

'Where?'

'In the area.'

'Where *exactly*?'

'In the neighbourhood.'

'I haven't heard about any robberies. Why didn't they go round to Nancy's too?'

The Div shrugged. He's useless at this. I don't know where I get my bullshitting skills from. I decided to help him out. I wouldn't ordinarily, of course, but my own neck was at stake.

'Tell her the truth, Minty.'

'Eh?' the Div's complexion Marilyn Mansoned.

'May as well tell her the truth about the computer and the credit card.'

'Eh . . . er . . . Eh?'

'Someone is using a computer to get people's credit card

details,' I told the Divette. 'They send bogus emails pretending to be from credit card companies asking clients to update their details online. The coppers are monitoring the scam and, somehow, they know that we're on the fraudster's contact list. They wanted to warn us not to respond to any emails we might get that look fishy. Isn't that right, Minty?'

'Er, yeah, yeah.'

The Divette wasn't used to hearing me make speeches of this length, particularly on the Div's behalf, and she looked at me like I'd just offered to massage his feet after a hard day's lollipopping. 'It needs saying in plain English, cause he's not capable,' I said. This seemed to convince her.

She addressed the Div: 'No one has managed to get hold of *your* credit card details, have they?'

'No, love.'

'Are you sure, Minty?'

The Div was silent for a couple of seconds. Maybe he was thinking about blaming the nine hundred quid debt she didn't know about on hi-tech thieves. He could even touch her for the dough to pay it off. She earns thirty grand a year to his two so she wouldn't think twice about it. I suppose his reluctance had to do with 'love', 'respect' and 'morality'. The Divette had read definitions of these words out loud to me several times – usually through my locked bedroom door.

'Are you sure?' she repeated.

'I'm sure, love, no money has been nicked. There's no need to worry.'

'Well, then, OK. Now we've got that sorted, tell me this: where did that giant Toblerone come from?'

'Well, I got into an argument with this old lady and –'

'Forget it. I'll have two triangles and then you'll have to hide it from me.'

By the time *The Simpsons* finished and *Top of the Pops 2* began the Divette was in the land of zeds. She'd necked her Toblerone triangles then conked. She'd been telling us a work story about finding drugs in this flat and had fallen asleep when she twigged we weren't listening. Now she lolled with her mouth agape and her *Mini Oxford* on her lap.

When Steve Wright introduced a song called 'Sweet Soul Music' the Div started cheering (quietly, though, because he didn't want to wake the Divette). '*Yessss*, stroll on, *yessss*,' he hissed. 'Brills McGills!'

The song was by a black guy called Arthur something. I'd've split to my room if the Div hadn't killed my telly.

'You don't need to smoke pot to enjoy this kind of music, Trebbo,' he said, slapping his knees to the beat. Grudgingly I had to concede that it didn't sound too bad. The horns had an energy that was quite stirring. I wouldn't admit that to the Div, obviously, and I suppressed my unexpected appreciation of the song with a shudder.

'If *skunk* doesn't make it sound any better, then what does – a jam jar full of speed?'

The Div dropped his voice. 'Ha ha,' he said, 'and don't think you're off the hook by the way, sonny.'

'How many records did you get for *nine hundred* quid anyway?' I asked, raising my voice slightly.

His eyes went wide and panicky. '*Ssshhhhh*. Keep it down, keep it down.'

'Whatever,' I said, with a shrug. I knew it riled him when I said 'whatever', but he didn't comment. I had the impression he was so desperate to have a conversation that he was willing to tolerate my sarcasm.

'I met an old mate of mine from the Northern Soul scene today,' he said at last. 'A chap called Petey Fleetwood.'

'Fierce,' I said, in the same tone as I say 'whatever'.

'We go way back to the seventies. He's coming to Fanny's on Friday. Brillo, eh? Tomorrow I'm going to pop into town to see your uncle Dave . . .'

'Who?' On *TOTP2* they were now playing a song called 'Grandma's Party' by Paul Nicholas. Does life get any worse?

'Your godfather, Dave McVane – stop trying to be so cool or you'll freeze to death.'

My 'uncle' Dave was a prize tit who was notorious in Walsall for writing a book called *Hessian Lined* about his life as an alcoholic manufacturer of kinky leather pants. Last time I saw him he was crying on the Div's shoulder when a review in the *Walsall Reflector* referred to the book as 'mildly diverting'.

'Dave's become a bit of a recluse since he got on the wagon. It's a shame.'

'Tragic.'

'Yeah, so I'm going to persuade him to come along to this all-nighter too. I can't wait to show him the tunes I've picked up. They'll bring back some memories for him, that's for sure.'

'Is his memory that good? The drunken tit must be down on his brain cells.'

'Well, I'm sure pot-smoking isn't much of an IQ booster.'

'*Skunk!*'

'Eh?'

By this time the Div was giving me the hump so I had to think of a way of shutting him up.

'What time are you going to this barbie tonight?' I asked, with feigned innocence. My voice was loud enough to cause a break in the Divette's snoring.

The Div's face clouded and I showed him my chewing gum again.

'Shhhhhhh,' he said, 'your mom's asleep. She's doubt-less had a hard day, there's no point waking her.'

'MOM,' I bawled, 'don't forget you're going to a bar-becue tonight! Minty's starving!'

The Divette grunted and opened one eye. She brought her watch up to her face and then spluttered something incoherent.

'We're a bit late now, aren't we, love?' went the Div, hopefully. 'Didn't you say it started at half six? Besides, I've already taken a bag of Chicken Dippers out of the freezer.'

'Put em back in,' she said, rubbing her bleary eyes with the heel of her hand. 'You know I don't like that junk. The barbecue doesn't start till eight.' And with that she was off upstairs to the shower.

'Bloody buggering hell!'

'Don't go gobbling too many hot dogs, Daddy,' I said. 'At your age your digestion isn't what it used to be.'

He shook his head and, removing his apron, followed the Divette upstairs.

Nice one, I thought. Tiffany's tits were yelping to be nuzzled and, who knew, I might even get under her G-string. I zipped over to the Divette's work-bag and had a quick rummage. Straight away I found a twelve-pack of condoms. I already had six unopened twelve-packs up-stairs but I swiped them nevertheless.

8

Coincidence (*n*)

HAZEL

On the night of the barbecue Minty dressed as slowly as he could. He's worse than Nigel sometimes. Anyone would think I was taking him to have his dinkle knotted. I'd half considered telling him I'd go on my own – at least then I wouldn't have to make good my promise to go to his sad all-nighter. I wasn't letting him off, though, and as we dressed together in the bedroom I ignored his puffing and tutting.

'And Minty, please don't go showing me up,' I said.

'Don't start about that Wendy house again, Haze, it was an accident: *someone slipped a frog down my jogger bottoms*!'

'If someone slipped a frog down your jogger bottoms then it wasn't an accident, was it?'

'OK, OK, don't get your bloody dictionary out.'

I plucked a pair of black canvas trousers off the saddle of our exercise bike and put them on; from the handlebars I took pink cotton T-shirt that had a pea pod and the words 'Give Peas a Chance' printed on the front.

Minty, meanwhile, was struggling to pull a polo-neck sweater over his brace.

'Get that bloody thing off!'

'Wha? What's wrong with it?'

'For one thing it's too warm and for another *you're wearing a neck-brace.*'

'I thought the polo-neck would *hide* the brace.'

'People will think you're some kind of barrel-necked freak.'

I handed him a short-sleeved shirt from the wardrobe. Muttering, he removed the polo and began putting it on.

Whenever he doesn't want to go somewhere Minty can be pretty childish about it, but the truth is I didn't really want to go to that barbecue either: I'd been at work all day after all. But I needed to make the effort to do something different. Last year I attended an NHS workshop called 'Positive Stress Nurturing' in which we were told how much human beings need stimulation. I wasn't getting any, apart from Kelvin. Every day was the same: I came home from work, crashed on the settee and had my tea. Then I would sleep intermittently through whatever was on telly. My toilet breaks were my only distraction. Increasingly I'd find myself sitting on the loo weighing whatever was at hand: the Toilet Duck; the Listerine; the mermaid soap dish. Did you know that a wet bath towel is nine ounces heavier than a dry bath towel? What a life! Not only was it crap, it was disappearing. My days seemed to strobe-flash by with increasing frequency: dawn to dusk, da to du, d to d. All I had to look forward to was seeing Kelvin tomorrow.

'Are you fit?' I asked.

'As I'll ever be.'

I had to admit Minty now looked reasonably smart in his shirt – apart from the neck-brace which made him resemble that ginger-haired berk from *Bo' Selecta!* I'd been trying hard to ignore the brace because it irritated me so much. A neck-brace is practically a stock comedy prop, for Christsakes! It was so suggestive of the role he often performed: that of bungling clown. I prayed he wouldn't perform that role at Suze's barbecue.

As it turned out I should have prayed harder.

On the way to Suze's Minty treated me to an account of his meeting with his old friend, Petey Fleetwood.

'He was driving a Mondeo,' said Minty, 'and he told me he had his own business. I felt a bit outdone. But the motor is only a J-reg and his so-called business turned out to be flogging Amway.'

'Not exactly Richard Branson, is he?' This is what I would have expected from Petey Fleetwood. I only met him a few times when I first started going out with Minty but I recalled him as having clear pumpkin-positive status.

'Does he still have that hair?'

'Yep. And the lacquer.'

'Still single, is he?'

'Actually I didn't ask.'

This is typical of Minty. If he sees an old mate he'll ask him what he does for a living, what pub he drinks in, what his top five records are, what recent medical procedures he's undergone, but nothing that's actually worth knowing.

'Anyway,' he said, as we joined a hundred-yard queue at the Pleck traffic lights, 'what does your mate's husband do for a living?'

'I think Mike's still unemployed.'

'Really?' he said, perking up.

'Yes, he gave up his job in the SAS when his memoir of the Gulf War became a best seller.'

He managed to croak, '*Really?*' before catching on that I was pulling his leg.

'Relax, Minty,' I told him. 'He does sign on, although I don't know much about him. Suze doesn't really mention him and whenever I've visited he's been out.' But I noticed that Minty had ceased listening now that his perceived status as alpha male was no longer under threat. He was busy loading a disc into the car's CD player.

'Nipper Kid emailed me some music files and I burned them on to this disc yesterday,' he said. 'It's stuff he's taken from Northern compilation albums. I thought you might want to hear it – it'll get you in the mood for Friday.'

A beat began that sounded like every other Northern Soul record I've ever heard.

'This is an absolute classic,' Minty said, tapping out the rhythm on the dashboard. 'I flogged my copy of it for next to nothing in the eighties, now it's worth a mint. Stroll on, I could do my nut.'

One of the things that always puzzled me about Minty's Northern Soul fixation was how important the financial worth of a record seemed to be. Surely it's something only men care about. I don't know one woman who, if she liked a record, would dream of asking how much it was worth. Or if she could get an original demo of it, or a picture disc, or a copy shaped like the bollocks of the bass player.

'I remember I bought my copy of this tune off a lad from Nether Poppleton,' he continued, 'a white-haired albino chap called Midnight. Great bloke. He only charged me four quid as I recall.'

On and on he went. Eventually he asked me what I could tell was a significant question because he put on a false, jokey voice to ask it.

'Haze, love – hee hee – you didn't *mean* it when you said that if I ever purchased another rare soul record you'd break it over my "stupid, sodding, cretinous, immature head", did you? I mean – hee hee – you're not *that* against it, are you . . . as a hobby for me?'

'I think I read you definitions of the words "cretin" and "immature", didn't I? And though you rather *immaturely* threw my dictionary in the bin, again, we ended up agreeing that those words would apply to a penniless man who insisted on a hobby that costs a fortune. Didn't we?'

'I have a bit of money.'

'You're still paying me back for the Wendy house.'

'After I've finished paying you back for –'

'Get yourself a hobby you can afford.'

Minty spent the rest of the journey staring out of the passenger window, occasionally winding it down so that he could bawl at speeding cars to 'SLOW DOWN!' I spent the time trying to quell the take-off terror that, once more, was beginning to flutter in my stomach.

By the time we reached Suze's it was eight o'clock. We couldn't find a place to park outside her house so we had to go searching. This had Minty moaning about the number of cars on the roads these days and how parked vehicles are a major hazard for children and old people.

'You could park anywhere round here in the old days,' he said. 'My old Northern Soul mate Muncher Preene used to live round here, actually. *Did* you ever meet Muncher? Muncher Preene? Freckled face with a square head?'

'We went through that at breakfast, Minty: I think we established that I don't recall him.' I was beginning to wonder how Northern Soul had managed to creep into every conversation we had lately.

'I remember picking him up from a house on this very street one night when we travelled up to Wigan in Nipper's sister's boyfriend's Bedford. I'm talking seventy-nine, eighty. The house was his mom and dad's place. They were getting on a bit so they might be tits-up by now. Still, seeing as we're here, I could give the neighbours a knock and ask if they know where the family moved to. Last I heard Muncher was living in Coventry, but who knows?'

'Please yourself,' I said.

Finally we found a spot at the bottom of a steepish hill, about a hundred yards away from the house.

'Now we've got to walk all the way up that bloody hill!' Minty whined.

'It's not that far. Look out for the house with the wagon wheels under the front window.'

As we walked Minty began to pant in an unnecessarily heavy way, until he caught sight of the house.

'Is it that house, with the wagon wheels?'

'Well spotted, genius.'

'Sweet Jesus on a stick! You're not going to believe this, Haze, but I'm sure that's where Muncher lived with his mom and dad. It didn't have the wagon wheels in those days, though.'

'Suze and her family live there now. Are you certain it was that one?'

'Pozzo. What a coincidence! Stroll on.'

It *was* a coincidence and I tried to recall if Suze had ever told me the circumstances under which she acquired the place.

'Minty, what was your mate's name, the one who lived here?'

'Muncher.'

'No, his real name.'

'No idea, I – Muncher? Muncher!' Minty shouted. He was addressing a bloke in his forties who was lifting a crate of Stella from the boot of a Vauxhall Astra. Could Muncher be Suze's husband?

'Muncher, my old mucker, it's me: Minty.'

The freckle-faced, square-headed man squinted at us uncertainly. He looked vaguely familiar, probably from old photos of Minty's Wigan days.

'It's me,' said Minty, pointing at his face, 'Minty Trebor!'

'Minty?'

'The same.'

'Minteeeeeeeeee!' shouted Muncher, setting down the Stella and spreading his arms.

Minty danced over to Muncher and embraced him.

'You square-headed old cunt!' said Minty.

'You pissant! You bollock-gobbling pissant!' said Muncher.

They broke their embrace and regarded each other.

'You cunt, you absolute cunt,' said Muncher.

'*You* cunt, *you* cunt,' replied Minty.

They embraced again. Thankfully, before they started French-kissing, Muncher noticed me over Minty's shoulder.

'I'm Suze's friend, Hazel.'

'Of course, of course.' He came over and shook my hand. 'Soz for being a bit dense, Hazel. This herbert is never your husband?'

I nodded. 'I'm afraid so, Mike.'

By this time Minty was almost weeping. 'I can't believe it,' he said, '*I can't fucking believe it*. This is fate. It *has* to be fate. You'll never guess who I saw this very afternoon, Munch.'

'Go on.'

'Only Petey Fleetwood!'

'With the hair? What the fuck's he up to?'

'Selling Amway.'

'Fuck off!'

Apparently, Suze and Mike inherited the house when Mike's parents died in the late 1990s. I suppose it is one of those spectacular coincidences that make some people realize how small the world is. It made *me* realize how little Minty and I communicate. My friend's husband was an old friend of *my* husband and it had taken us a year to find out. I can be forgiven for not catching on, though:

Preene wasn't Suze's surname – she kept her family name when she married Mike. Still it was strange – unlike Minty I don't believe in fate but, in retrospect, circumstances could be seen to have conspired to enable the calamity that followed. Or should I say, *calamities*.

At the time I was pleased at this reunion. Minty hadn't wanted to go to the barbecue and meeting his old mate perked him up. And it was nice for me too. All kinds of possibilities began to present themselves. Minty and I were in a rut and maybe this could be a way out. It might be nice for us to go out with another couple once in a while: meals, pubs, theatre. Holidays, maybe.

But then I remembered something Minty mentioned about Muncher Preene – didn't he say he used to be a drug dealer?

9

'Baby Hit and Run'

The Contours (Motown)

MINTY

First the KFC ad, then Petey Fleetwood, now Muncher Preene. I was starting to think there was a divine plan at work. My Northern Soul youth would not be denied. All the months Haze had been talking about her mate, Suze, from the Alumwell Estate and I'd never made the connection. Brills McGills.

The barbie was packed. There must've been forty people there, most of them his missus' family. His father-in-law was doing all the cooking, poncing around with a giant fork and a comedy chef's hat. There were about twenty kids, dancing to an Eminem album. The songs were full of fucks, bitches and muthafuckers but no one seemed to mind except Haze, who kept scowling at the stereo. (I hoped she wouldn't show me up by getting her *Mini Oxford* out.) Me and Munch were having a great time catching up.

'I'm glad you turned up tonight, Minty,' said Muncher. 'I was all set to be bored out of me tree.'

'Likewise, Munch.' I took a swig of Stella. 'The past seems to be knocking on my door at the moment. Ever since I heard Frank Wilson on that KFC ad – do you know the one?'

'I've seen it, yeah. I was stunned. It brought it all back. Northern Soul's still got a big following, I hear.'

'I didn't know how big till I started looking on the internet last week. Even the nurse who fitted my neck-brace is a soulie.' We discussed what we knew about the current state of the scene and I gave him a Fanny's flyer. He vowed his attendance.

Muncher and I *did* talk briefly about other things: unsympathetic wives; unappreciative kids; hairy ears. But it wasn't long before we returned to the topic that was turning flik-flaks in my mind.

'So you'll definitely come on Friday, Munch?'

'Sounds like a top night.'

'Absolutely. Nipper Kid says it'll be packed with people from all over. Dozens of dealers too.'

'Dealers?' asked Muncher, a grin splitting his freckled face.

'Record dealers, Munch.'

'Ah . . . shame.'

I returned his grin. 'I know what you mean, mate. I haven't been off my tits in twenty years. You're not still in the business, are you?'

Muncher glanced in the direction of his wife and shook his square head.

'Shame. Where there's Northern Soul there's a market for good speed.' I dropped my voice. 'I was half hoping you'd be able to score something for Friday.'

Muncher gave a sly smile. 'Well, just for old time's sake perhaps. I could definitely do with a rush meself; life's not exactly exciting these days – the wife's even got me on low-fat Horlicks. How much are we looking at?'

'Well, you and me will need sorting. Nipper's coming – I haven't asked him if he still dabbles but he always did. Petey Fleetwood. And I'm popping into town to see Dave McVane tomorrow – I think he'll be up for it.'

'Mac? What's he doing these days?'

'He works at the Leather Museum demonstrating saddle-making techniques. He's a living exhibit. Count him in . . . If you *can* manage to score, that is.'

'There's not much time, but – did I ever let you down in the old days?'

He never did. He was a great bloke – someone you could trust. When people hear the phrase 'drug dealer' they're likely to jump to all kinds of negative conclusions, but the usual connotations of ruthlessness and exploitation don't apply to Munch. He was just someone who knew people and who could get things. He would only score on behalf of his mates and he would never make a profit on what he sold. Legitimate drug companies could learn a lot from him in terms of ethics. He had a brilliant sense of humour too. In the old days Muncher was great at spotting the undercover coppers that would occasionally crop up at all-nighters. He'd entertain us all by slyly slipping notes into their pockets: 'Your 7UP has been spiked with speed', or 'Check the car park. Your motor is on fire'. Sometimes in their left pocket he'd stick a note reading 'I've planted some gear in your right pocket' and in their right pocket a note saying, 'I've planted some gear in your left pocket'. Good times.

We downed half a dozen Stellas each, happily excavating memories of our youth: an intoxicating cocktail of old mates, old clubs and old songs. I was with Munch the first and only time I've seen an original copy of 'Do I Love You'. We were in the main hall of the Casino, up on the stage trying to request a track. Frank Wilson was cued to play on the second deck, right there in front of me, *in real life*. It had a simple white label with the word SOUL printed vertically down the left-hand side. The full title on the disc was 'Do I Love You (Indeed I Do)' – not a question but an affirmation. You can hear that in the way he sings it! We didn't have time to make our request before Wilson started and we both jumped down on to the dancefloor and danced right next to the stage. Up by the stage at Wigan is where the best dancers would congregate and being among them was like being at the centre of the world.

I'd got a serious buzz on by the time Muncher suggested I get my Northern CD out of the car. I gladly consented and, much to the disgust of the teenagers, we replaced Eminem with my recently downloaded selection of Northern Soul floorshakers. The older kids slouched away from the dancing area moaning and sulking, but the toddlers stayed while me and Muncher set about showing them some moves.

Muncher looked a prat dancing because he's a bit stiff and his movements are over-determined. He dances like Spotty Dog from *The Woodentops*. Also, he's too stocky to pull off any convincing athletics – though he popped a fairly neat backdrop during Judy Street's 100 m.p.h. classic, 'What' (much better than the Soft Cell version). For the most part he was leaden-footed and not really in time with the beat. I, meanwhile, was smoking. I had an agreeable lager buzz, my sprain wasn't giving me any trouble and my neck felt as sound as a pound. The kids were a bit of a nuisance, though, as they were jumping around randomly and getting under my feet. I thought about asking them to scram but, since this was a children's party, I decided against it.

When 'Do I Love You' came on Muncher and me really let rip.

My stomach teemed with butterflies at the sound of the opening bars and then, when the beat kicked in, they flew to the four corners of my body: up into my swelling chest and down into my increasingly sure-footed legs. This is what I'd felt time and again at Wigan. I could see that Muncher was experiencing similar euphoria and, as we passed one another, we high-fived. I then danced my way over to the ornamental well on which I'd placed my Stella, took another swig and waved to Haze. She regarded me with disapproval. Stroll on: the woman just can't let me enjoy myself. I tend to chalk her attitude up to jealousy: I'm still young-headed, you see. Haze, of course, would say I'm immature, but that's just a word that boring people use to describe fun-lovers like me. And there's no doubt that Haze *is* boring. Don't get me wrong, I wouldn't swap her, but she has no sense of adventure. For instance, it's a waste of time asking Haze to experiment with drugs. When I first met her and tried to get her interested in the Northern scene I pointed out that she'd enjoy herself much more at all-nighters if she dropped a few uppers. But no. She wouldn't even have a go at pot. I hardly get a chance to try anything these days. Mind you, that's probably a good thing as the last two occasions I smoked pot – on nights out with Dave McVane – didn't end well. Both times, I returned home to try and cook a sausage with Hazel's curling tongues. I'd been determined, despite the odds, to demonstrate that it could be done.

I was as loose as a goose when the stomping Frank Wilson track gave way to the slower, emotional opening of Gerri Grainger's heart-rending floater, 'I Go to Pieces'. I glanced at Muncher and he was nodding respectfully through the intro, treading water until the tempo picked up. Two little girls were waltzing around him. Three or four others had abandoned the music altogether and were playing tig around the dancing area. I wished they'd push off. They left my mind, however, as Gerri's rich and tortured vocal took me over and I began moving in time to the rhythm. It was a little difficult to adjust to the pace after the brisk Wilson track but I was soon floating nicely.

'I Go to Pieces' has a series of climaxes which peak with Gerri's voice becoming more urgent as she reiterates the chorus. I marked the first climax in the usual way with a crisp handclap, but by the time the second began to build I was feeling a bit more ambitious. Despite my neck-brace I decided to chance a backdrop.

The best backdrops are the ones that are prefaced with a kick. You kick out in front of you, clap and then drop. It's not particularly spectacular but looks good because the forward motion of the kick is balanced visually by the backward motion of the drop. It's a move for which I was often praised in my years on the scene.

As the song played, Gerri's emotion brimmed and the backdrop moment neared. I glanced at Haze who was looking on, together with her mate, Suze, and just about every adult present. Brillo. This was certainly going to impress them. Suze would wonder how her square mate managed to pull a husband with such electric moves!

Here it comes, I thought, squeezing my eyes shut. I abandoned myself to the tune and the moment.

Boom, clap, kick.

I booted a passing toddler full in the face.

The child, a little boy about three years old, didn't have time to look startled. The force of the blow lifted him two feet off the ground and sent him soaring backwards, arms crucified, on to the smoking barbecue.

Holy broken bones.

10

'Love Buzz'

Nirvana, *Bleach* (Sub Pop)

TREBBO

It had been going pretty well. My blackout curtains were drawn against the light June evening and I had Tiffany on the bed. Her T-shirt was round her neck and *Nirvana Unplugged* was on the stereo. *Nirvana Unplugged* is a good seduction album. Cobain's voice was never as tortured and haunting as here. You get a sense of the genuine quality of his vocal; much more so than *From the Muddy Banks of the Wishkah*, Nirvana's 'plugged' live album. That blows: he even manages to ruin 'Smells Like Teen Spirit'.

With *Unplugged*, though, the gentle rhythms and vocals offered a sweet soundtrack to the action I was getting. Tiffany was breathing deeply as I worked at her tits. Gently, gently. I once read in *GQ* that women enjoy sex more than men do and they particularly enjoy being complimented and talked to while you're seducing them. With this in mind I broke from kissing Tiffany and looked her in the face.

'You're beautiful,' I said, still fondling, 'you really are lovely.'

'Do you mean it?' she asked, stroking my hair with her hand in a very sexy way.

'I don't half.'

'Thanks, Trebbo,' she sighed, and she tried to pull my head down to her lips again. Seeing as I'd got her going, though, I decided to stay with the seductive chat. I know it goes against my style to be talkative, but you have to experiment.

'You've certainly got an A1 pair of tits, Tiff,' I told her, being deliberately crude for comic effect. At least that's what I think I was doing. I knew Tiff didn't respond well to crudity yet, at times, I just couldn't stop myself. Why is that? Sometimes I feel schizoid: part of me does one thing, while another part hates myself for doing it. Schizo Trebb.

I kissed her once more but this time her lips seemed drier and less responsive. I hoped I hadn't ruined things when they'd been going so well.

'What's up?'

She sighed again, not a sexy sigh this time; a pained one. 'I'm a bit distracted, Trebbo: it's the day I've had with your mom.'

'Yeah, bummer. The bitch can be a drag.'

'No, I mean the people we visited. It was a bit upsetting. We went to this one flat where two toddlers were on their own playing with drugs.'

'Needles?'

'Capsules. There were dozens of them all over the floor. Your mom said it was speed.'

'So what were they doing, training for the London Marathon? They urine-test the winners, you know.'

'It's not funny, Trebbo.'

I stretched, and stroked my goatee. 'What happened to the capsules?'

'Your mom took them back to the clinic and put them in the dangerous drugs cabinet.'

'She'll shop them to the cops I suppose, the freaking nark.'

'I wish you wouldn't talk about her like that. She's a lovely woman.'

'God, Tiff, is there anything I *can* say! It's like going out with Mother Ter*freaking*resa.'

'I just wish you wouldn't.'

'Forget it.' I knew Tiffany didn't like me talking about the Divette like that and, to be frank, I didn't even mean it. My mother *is* a lovely woman, objectively speaking. But I couldn't be objective.

'She's a boring bitch, like you,' I said, but in a comedy voice to let her know I was kidding (about *her*). I began tickling her just to make it all the more obvious.

This time she *was* sensitive to my comedy. She didn't laugh, of course, but said, 'Oh, you are comical,' in an ironic voice.

Seizing the moment, I swung over to plant one on her lips. She was responsive again. I gave her a bit of tongue and she reciprocated. Fierce. I started doing a bit of finger work on her tits again and soon she was back to the seductive sighs, poking her tongue into my mouth with more urgency. Cool as a penguin's nads, I moved my hand slowly down to the top button of her Levi's.

'No, Trebbo!' she said, grabbing my hand.

This is how it always ends: with me still a virgin.

'What's the matter?'

'I'm not ready,' she said. '*We're* not ready.'

I groaned my well-practised 'rampant-male-wronged' groan. Like my equally well-practised 'rampant-male-wronged' whine, it has never got me anywhere.

I knew it was pointless arguing with her so we lay in silence for a few minutes. Tiffany eventually broke it with the words: 'I'm sorry, Trebbo.'

'So you should be. This is going to make me ill, you know.'

Now it was her turn to groan. 'Here we go again.'

'You've got me all excited. If I can't get some kind of release anything could happen. I could have a stroke; a rupture; a spasm. Or I could go off my cake: depression is common among the sexually frustrated. You might wake up one morning and find that I've Cobained myself.'

'"Ha ha."'

'Well, just in case, is there any chance of a handjob?'

'Cheeky,' she said, but with a twinkle in her eye.

I didn't want to pressure Tiff about sex and, to be honest, I was uncertain about doing it with her unless she felt the same. But I can't be blamed for desiring my beautiful girlfriend, can I? Although, when I mentioned my frustrations to Dicey, the cheeky git called me petty. He said we should wait till it feels right for us both because that way it will be more 'spiritually fulfilling'. But that's just Dicey trying to sound like Cobain.

Tiffany unzipped me and began tossing me off. For a novice she had quite a skilful technique. There did seem to be a sex kitten beneath the Poppins exterior.

My loins were just beginning to sing the way Cobain does on the final 'hello' before the chorus of 'Teen Spirit' when the doorbell rang.

Tiffany immediately stopped.

'Wha?'

'The doorbell.'

'*Wha?*' I grabbed Tiffany's hand and tried to get her to go on.

She pulled her hand away. 'Aren't you going to answer it?'

This is something I'm beginning to learn about women: the mood has to be right for sex and if the mood changes they can stop. Trying to get me to stop was like trying to coax a gazelle's leg from a ravenous jackal. I grabbed her arm, rolled on top of it and, pressing myself against her skin, began thrusting. I could feel the underside of her forearm beneath me like a living, yielding peach. The image I had of myself in my mind's eye disgusted me, but I continued.

'Trebbo, get off!'

I pumped on, like a dog, feeling increasingly wretched with every thrust. Tiffany didn't offer any more words of complaint, though. She just lay there perfectly still, playing the stoical virgin martyr to my rampaging sex beast. Obviously this was worse than if she'd slapped my face and, inevitably, my need for sexual release was replaced by humiliation. My pumping slowed and my manhood shrank. I can't figure it when I behave this way.

'Right, right, forget it!' I said, swinging my legs off the bed and buttoning up. I was mad with myself more than with her. I hated the idea of doing something that would make her think less of me. I guess I was just frustrated with my own frustration.

The doorbell went four more times as I descended the stairs. When I reached the door I was in a black, black mood. I glanced at my Casio and it was 8.21. It couldn't be Jehovah's Witnesses at this time. Then I noticed a Betterware catalogue on the telephone table. That would be it. Round our way the local agents put them through letter boxes and then call after a couple of days to collect orders. They really annoy the Div because they always seem to come when he's halfway through a plate of Chicken Dippers. He gives them an earful but they keep sticking the catalogue through all the same.

The doorbell sounded again just as I was about to open the door. This intensified my rage so I paused for a moment to calm myself. Rage is uncool. There's no point losing it. If you're going to slag someone it has much more effect if you're not screaming. Cool, as always, is the key. Cool and irony.

I opened the door, adopting my weariest expression.

Two monster hands grabbed my T-shirt and pulled. The cloth stretched a foot from my chest and I followed it out of the house feeling, for a bizarre second, as if I was in a cartoon. I think it's what our physics teacher, Mr Mortiboys, calls the route of least resistance; although in this case it was the route of beast insistence.

'Blubber-T, what's up, dude?'

'Cowing no!' said Blubber-T.

'Dude?' His tracksuit appeared to be on the point of bursting at every seam. It was quite a distraction: things that are fluorescent orange aren't usually that large, with the possible exception of bouncy castles.

Blubber-T let one hand drop from my T-shirt and punched me in the stomach. Air forced its way up my gullet and I doubled and gagged. What did I say about being too cool to punch?

On the topic of cool, Blubber-T, as I said before, is proof that you can be an ugly, corny pervert with no fashion nous and still be pretty cool. He has no sense of irony but, in his case, he doesn't need it. His self-assurance ensures his cool status. He doesn't say much, but he doesn't have to. He just tells you what he's going to do and does it. Respect due.

Blubbs produced a Yorkie bar and went on to explain – in his unique Black Country gangsta speak – that he'd been told that I didn't have a brother. I'd 'dissed' him, and now he wanted his 'two hundred bones' by tomorrow, or he was going to put my 'pigging ass on ice'. I thought about claiming that I'd meant 'brother' in the general, kindred spirit sense, but he didn't give me a chance. He finished the Yorkie and, after bouncing the wrapper off my forehead, turned and walked down the drive. I watched him sidestep the oil slick from where the Divette parks her Micra, protecting his gold leather Airwalks. The tail of his raccoon-skin hat swung, as always, in a parodic wag.

Problems!

I sat down on the step to compose myself. Now I *was* in the shit. How was I going to pay Blubber-T? No porn and no drugs. If I'd had a week I could at least have raised *some* cash; if all else failed I could've flogged my stereo or my MP3 player on eBay. But by tomorrow? No chance. I couldn't even nick any money from the Div or Divette because they kept all cash away from me these days. A year ago I'd gone through what the Divette calls a 'dishonesty phase' during which I yoinked everything in sight and – though she less often hassled me with definitions of 'truth' and 'integrity' – she wasn't sure I was over my klepto compulsions.

I heard Tiffany descending the stairs.

'Who was at the door?'

'Just the dude for the Betterware book,' I said, getting to my feet.

'Didn't he take it?' She nodded at the Betterware catalogue, still in its protective polythene wrapper, on the carpet.

'Er, no. I gave the sad-act some sarcasm and he split without it. They're cheeky bastards disturbing people at this time of night.'

'They're just trying to make a living, Trebbo.'

'Whatever.'

Tiff shook her head. 'Why are you always pretending to be so horrible, Trebbo?'

'Wha?'

'You're always acting as if you hate everybody.'

This threw me a bit. 'Er . . .' I said, 'there are so few people worthy of my love.'

'Liar – I was talking to Bianca Clark at school last week and she said that you saved her little brother Timothy from getting beaten up. And you gave him five pounds because his dinner money was stolen.'

I yawned and shrugged, refusing to confirm or deny if this was true. I had no interest in being seen as someone who involves himself in the petty concerns of juniors, particularly when they're called Timothy. In order to change the subject I suggested we repair to the front room to take some tube.

On MTV we lucked into a vintage Beck video, 'Loser', and watched in silence till the end. Next was the Dixie Chicks, who are crap but cute, so I resisted the temptation to change channels.

'Tiff?'

'Yes?'

'Those pills the old girl found.'

'What about them?'

'Did you say she took them back to the clinic?'

'Yes. Why?'

'No reason. Did they flush them down the bog or something?'

'No, I told you. They put them in that fridge where they keep the dangerous drugs. Your mom said she wanted to check her legal position with the clinic manager before she flushed them away.'

'Yeah?'

'Why?'

'No reason.'

II

Bastard (*n*)

HAZEL

'Stand back and give me some room!' I told the concerned adults huddling around the child that my husband had just kicked in the face. Apparently it was a kid from down the road, one of Suze's middle daughter's mates. His mother was absent, having nipped home to set her video for *Big Brother*, but someone had been despatched to alert her.

Even though I'd witnessed the spectacle with my own eyes I could still barely believe it. David Beckham couldn't have planted a more accurate and powerful kick on the toddler's jaw. My stomach turned when I saw him arc on to the barbecue. Luckily he was only in contact with the hot surface for a second, glancing off the top to land on the mulch surrounding the turf area of the garden. Still, his shorts were smoking slightly as he lay unconscious on the wood chips and he had a cube of barbecued pineapple in his hair. I wanted to roll him over to check for burns but my training told me I shouldn't move him.

'An ambulance is on its way,' said someone, Suze's next-door neighbour, I think.

Minty looked on, pale and shamefaced.

'What's his name?' I asked.

'Daniel,' said Suze.

I put my mouth close to his ear and shouted: 'Daniel! Daniel!'

The toddler didn't stir. He was out cold.

I once attended an NHS workshop called 'Asserting Personal Boundaries' in which we were informed that the best way to knock someone clean out is with an uppercut to the jaw. Daniel had received the equivalent of such a blow. I knew the potential consequences of this for a child, but I tried not to dwell on them.

I spoke again into his ear. 'Daniel? Daniel?'

The lad's eyelids flickered and, after a second or two, opened. He stared at me, bewildered. I stroked his forehead and uttered what I hoped was a soothing whisper, 'You're OK, Daniel. Lay still, love.'

I was expecting him to cry but he didn't, possibly because of shock. He just gawped at me – his soft brown eyes looked massive and heartbreakingly helpless.

A dazed silence had throttled the revelry. Inevitably it reminded me of last year's Wendy house horror. My husband had done it again. The rampaging, thoughtless brat that exists inside Minty had kicked my dignity to death. *Again.* He shouldn't be carrying a fucking lollipop; he should be sucking one.

I heard a bit of a commotion and turned to see a woman with a seventies-style mullet burst through the conservatory door and out into the garden. I'd noticed her earlier on; indeed, she was difficult to miss: a big, powerfully built lady – fourteen stone to fourteen two. She looked a little like the serial killer, Aileen Wuornos, and she had a homemade tattoo across her forearm which said 'Megadeth'.

'Danny!'

This was clearly the child's mother.

'There's been a bit of an accident, Julie,' said Suze.

Minty began to blither: 'I didn't mean it, love; I didn't see him in front of me, honestly.'

The woman was oblivious to everything but the sight of her son, prostrate in the mulch.

'DANNY!' she screamed, dashing to his side and trying to bundle him up into her arms.

'No, love, he needs to lie still until the ambulance arrives. I'm a nurse.'

When he saw his mom, Danny's bottom lip began to quiver and he started to cry. I took this as a good sign. Julie was in tears too, leaning over and kissing her son's face. She was trembling.

'The ambulance has been called, Julie,' I told her, 'just as a precaution. But I think Danny's going to be all –'

'What bloody happened to him?' Her eyes darted wildly from person to person. She was clearly semi-hysterical.

'That bloke with the white tube round his neck kicked him in the face,' said a helpful little girl who'd been observing enthusiastically throughout.

'What?'

'It was an accident,' said Minty weakly. 'Honestly, love, I didn't mean –'

The woman became aware of Minty's presence for the first time.

'You kicked my son in the face?'

'Yes, but it was an acci–'

'You kicked a three-year-old boy in the face?'

'It couldn't be helped, Julie,' said Muncher.

The woman stood, plucked a discarded kebab skewer from a nearby table and went for Minty with terrifying, bestial ferocity. 'YOU BAAASTARD,' she wailed.

Minty fled and Julie made after him. 'It was an accident!' he cried, sprinting towards the house with both hands on his neck-brace. He clipped a wickerwork shelving unit with his elbow as he passed through the conservatory. It rocked but, miraculously, failed to topple; it slowed him down, though, and as Minty zoomed into the kitchen, Julie was close at his heels. The woman was that most dangerous of all things: a wronged mother.

'Do you think I should go after them?' asked Muncher. 'We don't know Danny's mother that well but she seems to be a bit of a firebrand!'

'With any luck she'll kill him,' I said. 'It will save me the trouble later.'

'They'll have to take Danny to hospital to put his head back on,' the helpful little girl announced to a cluster of children who were looking to her for a prognosis, 'it's only hanging by a thread.'

At this news one of the toddlers started screaming. This had a domino effect on the other children. One by one they burst into tears, including, eventually, the helpful little girl herself.

I wondered if this estate had ever witnessed a less successful social event. I felt myself blushing. I could imagine what they were thinking: her husband's a fool; her husband's a careless, useless tit; *her husband's a lollipop man.*

I'd have given a lot to have heard Kelvin's voice at that moment. It was only his fluent good sense that had kept me grounded over the last few days. More than anyone I'd ever met his words seemed to have weight. Just the thought of him reassured me – he seemed to know what to say to ease the take-off terror and stop me floating away. I wanted him now. I wanted him here.

I remained at the child's side as his mother hunted Minty – her muffled yells were audible inside the house. I couldn't help thinking that our roles should be reversed. The boy was still sniffling and gazing round for his mom. I could understand Julie's anger but, if I were her, I'd be with Danny. Seeking satisfaction with a kebab skewer seemed a rather self-centred response. Some parents are like that, though: their kid's problems are assessed in terms of how it affects them *personally*. They fall into what I call the 'Me Mother' category. Still, I was happy to stay with the little lad; I couldn't trust myself to be with Minty.

I stroked Danny's temple as he whimpered, my thoughts turning to when Nigel was a toddler. 'Toddler' is a word I know well from my *Mini Oxford*. I often happen upon it as I browse the letter T. It's one of those words I like to dwell on and savour. As with most words, however, Mo is inadequate for defining it. Meanings are invariably flavoured by experience. For me 'toddler' evokes images of *my* little toddler learning to walk. He'd go for two steps, then fall; three steps, then fall, as Minty cheered him on. The word is perfect to describe his unsteady, top-heavy gait. What I'd give for my son to be a toddler once more. When he was little I loved him more than anything! Had I the time over again, *I'd* want to be the one to stay home and raise him, not Minty. What a wonderful thing that would be, I thought, and suddenly, unexpectedly, I found myself yearning for it with an intensity that almost made me weep.

It was Suze's dad who broke my reverie. He'd been watching for the ambulance from a bedroom window. 'The medics are here,' he shouted, still in his oversized chef's hat, 'and that bloke, Minty, has locked himself in the toilet, if anyone's interested.'

Almost as soon as he'd announced their arrival two paramedics appeared.

'He's conscious and responsive,' I told them, 'his airways are clear and there are no obvious signs of a break.'

Danny's mom re-emerged, still carrying the kebab skewer. It didn't *seem* to be bloody. Irrationally, but, again, in keeping with the behaviour of a certain type of mother, she started screaming at the paramedics: 'Don't you hurt my baby! Don't you hurt my baby!' Did she think they were planning to stake her son to the lawn and reverse the ambulance over him?

I stood and put my arm around her powerful shoulders. 'Don't worry, Julie, Danny is in safe hands – they know what they're doing.' It was then I noticed that Minty's Northern Soul CD was still playing. The current song's chorus went, 'You hit me right where it hurt me'.

12

'I'm in a World of Trouble'

The Sweet Things (Date)

MINTY

I had my ear against the toilet door. The gloss paint was cool on my burning cheek. I heard someone climbing the stairs and the heavy, masculine footfalls suggested that it wasn't Hazel or Danny's mother.

'You can come out now, mate,' said Muncher. 'They've taken Danny to Wesley-in-Tame.'

'Has that mad mullet-haired bitch gone?'

'Relax, she went with Danny in the ambulance.'

'What have I done?'

'It wasn't your fault, mate.'

'Stroll on, Muncher, I kicked a little boy in the face!'

'It could have happened to anyone, Minty. Now, could you let me in: I need to take a slash.'

'Where's Hazel?'

'She's downstairs with Suze.'

'Is she having a dickie-fit?'

'I'd be lying if I said she was cock-a-hoop, Mint, but what do you expect?'

'I'm in a world of trouble, Munch: she's going to fucking kill me.'

'Don't be daft, Minty. Now, unlock the door, there's a good lad. I've got Lake Titicaca in me bladder.'

I was silent. I was scared to unlock the door. I was ashamed.

I listened to Muncher mutter and stamp off down the stairs then I sat down on the lidded toilet. The evening had darkened but, when I reached for the light-cord, I couldn't bring myself to pull it. If I tugged at that cord, I thought, it would probably come away in my hands. More likely, I'd bring the entire fucking ceiling down around my ears. It would be an accident, but to everyone else it would look like a ruthless plot to yank a hole in the roof for no other reason than because I'm too 'selfish' and 'immature' to open a window. Either that or I'd be accused of trying to draw attention to myself because of my pathetic, puerile narcissism.

Accidents.

Booting that nipper in the face was an accident. I didn't mean it, so it must've been. OK, I was responsible, indirectly, but you couldn't blame me. I know it wasn't the kid's fault, because he was just a kid, but it wasn't mine either. If anything it was his mother's fault for not being there to supervise him. The reckless bitch!

As I sat with my chin in my hands, my thoughts turned to the crash I'd had as a kid and to Billy Peebles. That day I'd also been responsible for a child flying through the air. Billy's accident hadn't been my fault either, of course, but . . . well, I often wondered *why* I went for the handbrake rather than the gearstick that day. I'm pretty certain I *knew* how to change gear. I even have vague memories of having done it for my dad on other occasions. The old man must've thought I could do it or he wouldn't have asked me in the first place. I sometimes replay the split second in my mind when my hand hovered between the gearstick and the brake. What was I thinking? I'd love to know what guided – or failed to guide – my hand that day.

Perhaps it would help me understand why chaos seemed to dance so persistently at my heels.

'Minty, get out of the toilet.' It was Hazel.

'Are you angry?'

'Minty, I'm furious, but the longer you stay locked in that toilet the more furious I'm becoming. Now get out here.'

'Are there many people around?'

'Almost everyone has gone home. Can you blame them? You've put the mockers on the evening.'

'How's the little boy? I haven't hurt him too much, have I? I couldn't stand it if I thought I'd hurt him, Haze.'

'He'll live.'

I began to unclench slightly.

'It wasn't my fault.'

'Just get out here, Minty.'

I thought it over.

'Minty?'

'Yeah?'

'What are you doing?'

'I'm thinking.'

'Look, Minty. I'm going home now. If you want a lift, come on out. If not, you can walk.'

I heard footsteps descend the stairs again followed by the sound of muffled conversation. I think I heard Muncher tell Haze that he'd taken a piss in the drain out in the back garden.

I switched the light on with the pull-cord and the ceiling didn't cave in. I switched it off again and, again, everything stayed in place. Encouraged, I slid the bolt on the toilet door and stepped out on to the landing.

Haze wasn't lying when she said that most people had gone. There was just Suze, her parents, Muncher and their three kids left. They were chatting but fell silent as I stepped into the living room. At times like this, and I've experienced more than my fair share, it's difficult to know what to say for the best but, once more, the onus was on me to try and smooth my reintegration into society. I gave it my best shot.

'Oooops!' I said, followed by a comedy grin.

Muncher began to laugh but stifled it when no one else joined in. Suze fired me a look that would've pickled my plums had I the courage to meet her eye.

'Come on,' said Haze, 'I think it's time we left.'

Suze and Muncher saw us to the door.

'If there's any news about Daniel could you let us know, Suze?' said Haze.

'Of course,' she said, and kissed my wife on the cheek.

'Er, are we still on for Friday?' I asked Muncher in a discreet whisper.

'No problem,' he said. 'I'll give you a bell to see where you're meeting up.'

I toyed briefly with the idea of reminding him of his promise to sort us for gear but concluded that the time probably wasn't right.

'See you then,' said Hazel, 'and, again, I'm really sorry about what happened.'

I offered Suze an apologetic grin and I shrugged my shoulders in a 'Hey, I'm just a loveable idiot' gesture. She glared back at me so I cleared my throat, mumbled, 'Bye bye then,' and shuffled awkwardly out the door.

We made the long walk to the car in stony silence but, when we were both inside, Hazel started.

'Do you want me to drive you round to my grandmother's old people's home, Minty?'

'Wha? Why?'

'Well, I thought you might want to round the night off by *murdering a few fucking pensioners*!'

'Now, now, you know it was an accident. What could I do? The kid was in the way while I was dancing.'

'Most people can share a space with others without feeling the need to kick them in the face!'

'I didn't "feel a need", Haze. *It was an accident!*'

'Accident? *Accident?* If I hear that one more time I'm going to go for your fucking throat, Minty. *When will you start to take responsibility for your actions?*'

'And do what?'

'At the very least you could have apologized.'

'I did.'

'"Oooops", you said. Sodding "oooops". What's that supposed to mean?'

'I was just trying to lighten the mood.'

'It was totally inappropriate, Minty. You ruined their evening, you injured one of their guests – possibly seriously – and all you can say is "oooops"!'

She was right, at least in a sense. Deep down I knew what I should've said but I'm not very good at . . . well, being serious. This is partly what Hazel means when she calls me immature. And yet, it *was* an accident; anyone could see that.

'Maybe everyone will see the funny side of it when it's clear the kid's OK?'

'I wouldn't bet on it, Minty.'

'He *is* going to be OK, though, isn't he, Haze? I mean, how did he look to you?'

'He looked like a three-year-old who'd been kicked unconscious.'

'Could it be serious? What sort of things could it have caused?' She had me worried now.

Haze glanced at me and, seeing my concern, softened slightly. 'Why do these things always happen to you? You're a lovely man in ways but you behave like a big kid. Why can't you act your age?'

'I'll try,' was the only thing I could think of saying. I couldn't tell her that I wasn't sure how to act my age, or what those words even meant. I didn't know, despite having said them to Nigel myself a hundred times.

Hazel sighed and shook her head.

I sensed that this might be a chance to poke my snout out of the doghouse. 'I know you're right to be angry, love. I'm sorry, I really am. Perhaps we could make it up to Muncher and Suze by inviting them round ours?'

'Mmmm. I have a feeling Suze might be too scared to come.'

As we drove home I worried about Danny. I was gutted that I'd hurt the poor little chap and, thanks to his crazy mother, I didn't even get a chance to say sorry. I'd send him a card with some money in, or a toy or something.

Eventually I was distracted by a speeding Peugeot 206 that overtook us just before the mini-island in the town centre. I shouted at him to 'SLOW DOWN!' but no brake lights appeared, and his winking tail lamps danced mockingly as he disappeared into the distance.

13

'Where Did You Sleep Last Night?'

Nirvana, *Unplugged in New York* (Geffen)

TREBBO

My Casio started beeping at 1.30 a.m. but I was awake anyway. I'd been awake since Thursday began, an hour and a half earlier. I killed the beep and slid out of bed. My black Wranglers and black 'Loser' T-shirt lay on the carpet ready to wear.

I crossed the landing and descended the stairs without switching the light on because I couldn't risk waking the gimmers. Down in the living room, though, I popped on the standard lamp while I searched the Divette's bag. I took her pencil torch, a pair of disposable rubber gloves and her keys. The key ring was an 'I Love Orlando' one from our trip there in 1996. Attached to this fob was a little yellow pouch with the words Laerdal Pocket Mask on the front. I heard her tell the Div that it contained a protection sheet just in case she ever had to perform impromptu mouth-to-mouth resuscitation. It stops you catching anything, apparently. It's the sort of thing only the Divette would carry on her key ring. That's the kind of woman she is. Nice, I suppose. Annoyingly so.

I'd already decided on my route: I'd be crossing the

fields over the back of our house which would take me to the Birmingham Road. From there I could cut along the canal all the way to the Cotterell Lane Bridge, just fifty yards or so from the Divette's clinic. It was a long walk, but doable, and the route would keep me off the street – if the cops saw me wandering about at that time they'd be too interested.

When I reached the canal I could see that it wasn't going to be as easy as I thought. There was no lighting at all along the towpath and I had to walk very carefully, using the pen torch to illuminate the way. I imagine I looked like ET with his glowing finger. It was scary and my heart punched my ribcage whenever I heard a rustle in the bushes. I'd already been in that reeking water once in my life. Last summer I'd waded in to assist a Canada goose that was tangled in a discarded fishing line. I managed to free it but in the process the beast's flapping winded me to such an extent that I vomited in the reeds. No gratitude.

When, eventually, I reached the bridge my Casio said 2.35. The road was deserted and I jogged the distance to the clinic without a single car passing me.

The clinic car park was in darkness and, when I reached the outer door, I had to use the pen torch again to locate the key in the lock. It took two complete anticlockwise turns to open it. I slipped inside and eased the door shut behind me with my arse, tensing briefly just in case the alarm sensor was active in reception. There were no warning beeps so I knew it was off. They tend to nix this sensor because of Ant and Dec, the rat-like creatures they keep to entertain the kids. They're always getting out of their cage and setting off the alarm. They've tried everything short of concrete boots to keep them in but the little gits are the Houdinis of the rodent world. The first couple of times it happened the clinic manager had to drag his arse out of bed in the middle of the night. Now he omits the sensor. The doctors' surgeries and the offices tend to be alarmed, though, including the office with the drugs fridge. Happily I knew the code: one, nine, six, six – the year England won the World Cup. I clocked it when I did my work experience. That was a nightmare two weeks I can tell you. The manager was constantly moaning because I spent so much time on the internet and didn't want to do any work. He didn't really appreciate the slacker philosophy. The screaming kids were a trial too, not to mention the yap-happy Eunice. Now it was payback time.

I balanced the torch on the receptionist's counter and removed the gloves from their wrapper: a puff of talc clouded briefly in the weak yellow light. They smelt of condoms and were so tight that even with the talc they were difficult to put on. I managed it, eventually, albeit with an inch hanging at the end of each finger.

Gloves on, I sought the alarm's keypad. My torch beam briefly illuminated the degus' cage and they instantly began scurrying about. Why they'd bought these particular animals was beyond me. Hamsters or gerbils would have been much more sensible. These bastards had long, yellow teeth that caused casualties even though their cage was kept six feet off the ground. There were plenty of kids cheeky enough to climb over reception and scale the shelving unit with its pot plants and telephone directories to ram their chav digits through the bars of the cage. Those kids had more guts than me. The degus freaked me out.

I located the keypad, swung down the cover that concealed the number keys and typed: 1966. The alarm de-activated with a long beep.

Now the building was quiet except for the degus, who were going crazy: from the noise, it could've been a couple of fitting hyenas in their cage.

I was aware that the room with the fridge might well be locked but, if necessary, I was ready to kick the door in. I knew how to do it too: one sharp kick to the lock area. That's how you break through doors when you're burgling places at night. If it doesn't break straight away you leave it ten minutes before booting it again. What you don't do is keep kicking at it. That's what draws attention. People who hear a single sharp noise will dismiss it if it's not repeated. If the noise wakes them they'll listen for a follow-up noise for a few seconds but, if they hear nothing, they'll assume all's well and go back to noddy-winkoms. Ironically, I picked up that information while surfing the net in this very clinic. I actually learned a fair bit during my work experience because, in a variety of crucial ways, the internet has the edge on school: where else could I have learned how to defend myself against alien abduction, for instance, or how to use a live wasp as a pickpocketing aid on the New York subway?

To my surprise the door to the drugs office was unlocked. Cool as an Eskimo's danglers.

I knew this particular office was a spare. It functioned partly as a store room and partly as a hang-out and chat room for staff. I shone my torch around and saw several sets of scales of the kind the Divette uses to weigh kids. Again I say kids, but she still didn't seem to be restricting herself in that department. Recently I'd clocked her weighing more odd stuff around the house. The previous Sunday afternoon I'd spotted her in her bedroom weighing an aromatherapy candle and Tuesday teatime I saw her in the kitchen weighing a bag of the Div's Chicken Dippers, alongside a can of Pledge (neither of which we were having for tea). As soon as she senses there's someone around she whips the stuff off the scales smartish and makes believe she hasn't been doing anything. Is that normal?

Apart from scales there were bags of other stuff in the spare office. There were gadgets used for measuring height and doing hearing tests, together with electronic equipment I didn't recognize. Stacked high on shelving along one wall were boxes and boxes of everything from rubber under-crackers to verruca socks. There were loads of books too – massive medical dictionaries, drug listings and lines of journals on things like childcare and 101 ways to muck out geriatrics. I knew that none of this stuff was worth yoinking. In fact, there was nothing in the entire clinic worth yoinking. Even the computers were ancient ming-crates. All still used Windows 95 and there wasn't a single processor faster than an Intel Pentium 2. Dark ages.

To my satisfaction, I saw that their means of storing 'dangerous' drugs hadn't become any more sophisticated recently. I used my foot to shift the heavy metal iron that kept the fridge door shut. No light came on when I opened it, so I shone my torch into the interior. On the top shelf were a couple of boxes bearing the name of a drug I've never heard of, alongside a dagger-bladed knuckleduster. The latter had almost certainly been confiscated from a Jerome Estate toddler. On the lowest shelf were several dozen ampoules of adrenaline, together with an amber pill bottle. There was a printed prescription label on the latter dated 1985. Obviously this was the stuff.

I positioned the pen torch on the top of the fridge so that it shone out into the room a little and then unscrewed the cap of the bottle. It was full to the brim with at least a hundred small capsules. In the half-light it was difficult to make out their colour but they seemed to be red and grey. I know nothing about uppers but the Divette told Tiffany it was speed and that was good enough for me. It was eighteen-year-old speed, of course, but I figured this wouldn't matter. Either way it would buy me some time with Blubbs.

The degus' commotion had ceased now and the office was thick with quiet. I listened to it for a second or two and was a bit spooked by its eeriness. In the process of replacing the pill-jar lid, however, I became aware of a noise – not from reception this time, but closer. A rustling? A skittering? I froze and, almost immediately, the noise stopped. My heart kicked me in the throat as my ears trawled the silence. After ten or so seconds of stillness, my pulse was just beginning to decelerate when the noise started again, coming from the direction of the fridge. The degus were out.

Given that they're sold as pets, I assume some people find degus attractive, but I can't fathom that. The thought of them being free in such close proximity made the hairs on the back of my neck bristle. The base of my skull seemed to want to descend into my ribcage. It reminded me of the time I was watching an amateur showjumping event and a passing horse hoofed a cowpat on to my head. I'd been about seven at the time. Had it been a dry cowpat it wouldn't have been so bad, but this thing was semi-sloppy and boiling with flies. It landed like an obscene beret on my head and began running down my face. Whenever I recall it I shudder the way I do when I think of eating spiders or licking the underside of a slug. This is a slightly different shudder from the one I experience when I think of Simon Cowell's bitch-tits.

I forced myself to be calm – degus are only small furry things, after all.

Another noise.

My eyes followed it and beheld a sight that – I'm ashamed to say – made me squeal with terror.

It was the image of a degu, projected huge on to the wall of the office. I'm not sure if it was Ant or Dec, but there it was. The creature was on top of the fridge and the pen torch shining beneath cast its terrifying shadow, like the vampire ascending the stair in *Nosferatu*. It took only half a second before I realized the source of the image but this was long enough for my cool to boil. Frankly, it swivelled my giblets. The jolt of fear had me dropping the bottle and losing half a dozen caps on the floor as the degu skittered away into the darkness.

For a while I could do nothing but tremble.

When I'd eventually chilled, I grabbed the pen torch, retrieved the bottle and made for the door. I didn't bother to collect the caps I'd dropped or, for that matter, close the fridge. Conscious that the other degu would also be loose, I hurried through reception and out the front door. I couldn't reset the alarm with the degus roaming free of course – they'd trigger it before I was far enough away. But I did take the trouble to lock the door. Then I had a dilemma. In the morning it would be clear that someone had been in and, if the door was locked, it would be obvious it was someone with a key. As far as I knew only five or six people had keys to the place so this would incriminate the Divette and, by association, me.

Thinking on my feet, I took a chance. I turned the key just one revolution so that the bolt was only half on, then I gave the door a running boot. Sure enough it flew open, the bolt tearing easily through the door frame. Instead of scarpering after the kick I crouched down in a corner of the car park, letting the noise settle. It was agony, but the most sensible thing to do. Nothing stirred so I crept up to the door and pulled it to – disgusting as they were, I didn't want the degus to escape into the street and get run over; or, more likely, to start savaging the local wildlife.

Then I scooted, retracing my earlier route and inspecting my booty as I went. There were half a dozen caps less than I thought I'd have but it was a decent haul. I suppose

I should have been pleased but, as experiences go, this one blew. I'd been scared out of my mind and I'd become a burglar. I think I was feeling something close to shame: is there anything lower than robbing a clinic?

14

Weight (*n*)

HAZEL

'Morning, sweet cheeks,' said Minty, when he showed his face at breakfast. He was being excessively chirpy with me, testing me out to see if he was still in the doghouse. He was.

'Mm,' I said.

'Don't speak, then, Miss Snooty,' he said.

'OK.'

Minty sighed heavily. It was clear to me – someone who'd known him twenty years – that with this sigh he was changing his tactics. He was about to become the hard-done-by innocent, oppressed by a nagging wife – i.e. one opposed to her husband violently assaulting toddlers.

Minty felt the teapot, tutted, opened the breadbin and tutted again. He opened the cupboard, saw we were out of Pop-Tarts and tutted. He looked in the fridge, tutted, shook his head, tutted, shook his head some more and tutted again. Still gazing into the fridge, he sighed. He then sighed again: a longer, deeper sigh. Then another, and another. You'd think he was gazing at a locust-ravaged field. I've no idea why the interior of our fridge should surprise him seeing as he does all the family shopping and cooking. Eventually he selected a probiotic yoghurt, holding it the way you'd hold a bronchitic's sputum pot.

Sitting at the kitchen table he began to eat it, grimacing with every mouthful.

I'd been up early. I'd weighed two towels and a tube of pump-action Colgate on the bathroom scales before showering. Later, on the kitchen scales, I weighed the wok. Now I was busy with the day-planner section of my diary, checking my schedule of afternoon visits.

Minty finished his yoghurt, managing not to vomit. He rose, walked to the bin, then flung in the pot. The force was excessive and petulant.

'Now,' I said, in my calmest voice, 'could you go back to the bin, take the teaspoon out and put it in the washing-up bowl.'

'Wha?'

'You've thrown the spoon away with the empty yoghurt pot.'

'Stroll on,' he said, pained. You'd've thought I'd asked him to treat the spoon to a mini-break in Milan.

Wearily he returned to the bin, retrieved the teaspoon and tossed it in the direction of the sink.

I continued with my diary and he sat and sulked. I knew he'd be the one to break the silence, though, because he always does. He can't stand silences. They unnerve him. He's the opposite of his son in this respect. Where Minty needs to fill the air with talk, Nigel resents every word he's forced to utter.

'OK, OK, OK. What have I done *this* time?' he said at last.

'The same thing as every time, Minty. You've been you.'

'Is it the accident, sorry, the *event* at the barbecue?'

He groaned as I set aside my diary and produced my *Mini Oxford* from my skirt pocket. I was turning to the word 'irresponsible' when he plucked it from my grasp and tossed it into the bin. I stood and coolly retrieved it from among the spent tea bags. Now I'd decided to read the word 'juvenile' instead.

'Juvenile,' I said, 'sense two: childish –'

He snatched the book and flung it back into the bin. I went to rescue it again but Minty sat on the lid. I walked into the hall, lifted Minty's lolly hat from the coat stand and returned to the kitchen. From the fridge I took a bottle of squirty tomato sauce and, flicking off the plastic cap, held it over the hat.

'Get Mo out of the bin, dry her off with some kitchen roll and place her in my work-bag.'

Minty followed my instructions then backed away to the corner of the kitchen with his palms up. I squirted a big dollop of sauce into his hat and frisbeed it towards him.

'Never get married,' I told Tiffany as we drove to the clinic.

She widened her eyes. 'Not even to Nigel?'

I was about to say, especially not to him, when I checked myself. I suppose he *has* got time to grow up. He might eventually disprove the old adage that men never do.

'Don't take any notice of me, love. The morning didn't start well.'

'Maybe things can only get better, Mrs Trebor?'

'You've got the right attitude, Tiffany. With that sort of optimism you might be the perfect wife for Nigel. And the perfect health visitor.'

It was silly making references to marriage of course. She and Nigel were only sixteen. Though I'd lots of married sixteen-year-olds on my caseload, I felt sure it wouldn't happen to Tiffany and Nigel. They had more options than the teenagers I saw; they were lucky enough to have been born into a different world. And yet, was it luck? I knew that Tiffany was raised by a single mom and was, by necessity I suppose, something of a latchkey kid. In fact, Nancy Valentine once told me that she'd heard Tiffany had been left to her own devices as a child, even to the point of neglect. It was difficult to see what harm this had done her. She was quiet and a bit serious, perhaps, but she was also one of the most sensible, polite and selfless teenagers I've ever met. It was embarrassing to compare her to Nigel who, of course, had had the full-time attention of his father throughout his formative years. Maybe Tiffany's good nature was just that: *nature*, as opposed to nurture.

We'd been driving for five minutes before I spoke again. 'Don't take this the wrong way, Tiffany, but I've often wondered: what *do* you see in Nigel?'

'Seriously?'

'Seriously.'

She thought for a moment. 'Well, he's good looking.'

'*Is he?*' I said, sounding so amazed that I made myself laugh out loud.

As ever Tiffany remained straight-faced. 'He's not bad. He'd be better if he shaved that goatee off and stopped wearing his beanie all the time.'

'Don't you think he's a bit . . . immature? When I was your age I always hankered after older men.'

She was quiet for a bit and I was worried I'd embarrassed her. Tiffany was pondering her reply, though, and at last she said, 'He doesn't mean to be rude all the time. He's a nice person underneath.'

'Yes, but *how far* underneath?' I asked, laughing again.

Still there wasn't even the flicker of a smile from Tiffany. 'He needs to grow up, I admit,' she said, earnestly, 'but he's much more sensitive than he admits to being. It's difficult for men to be sensitive, isn't it?'

'I suppose so,' I said, thinking of the times I'd seen

Minty openly weeping through *Animal Hospital*, *Children in Need* and, more bizarrely, *Columbo*.

'Trebbo doesn't say much most of the time, but I think he has a lot locked up inside him . . . Perhaps he doesn't feel I'm the right person to open up to.'

'Blimey, love, don't say that. I'm banking on you to redeem him!' Again, though I said this with a jocular inflexion, I failed to elicit a smile. Tiffany just nodded solemnly, as if contemplating her potential role as my son's moral adviser.

I'm ashamed to say that I questioned Tiffany's judgement. I love my son, obviously, in the 'attachment' and 'affection' senses of the word, but I'm not sure he *is* a particularly nice person. It is hard to see him as anything other than an adolescent misanthrope who is only interested in himself. OK, he's never been nasty or malicious, like some kids: I could never imagine him shooting a cat with an air gun, for instance, which is a commonplace activity on Jerome. And when he was young I'd seen him be kind to other children, which seemed to indicate a good nature. But these days he appeared to be determinedly antisocial and it was difficult to think of him as nice, even at the deepest, most well-concealed level; he was a bad-mannered, selfish wanker. I suppose I should have been grateful that he wasn't *literally* a criminal.

The traffic was very light and we made such good time that we were the first to arrive at the clinic. As soon as we reached the door I could see something was amiss.

'Funny,' I said, 'the door is open.'

'Maybe someone's already here?' said Tiffany.

'No, love. No cars on the car park.'

I pushed lightly at the door and it swung open. I could see that the lock had been forced.

'You stay here a sec, Tiffany,' I said, moving cautiously through the door to reception. The green light on the alarm keypad told me the system had been deactivated.

I noticed the door to the degus' cage was unfastened. This wasn't particularly unusual because they are adept at unravelling the steel wire we use to keep it shut. We store a pair of gardening gloves under the reception counter for retrieving the beasts. It's usually just a matter of scooping them up and popping them back in.

But where were they?

'Ant . . . Dec . . . ?' I called loudly into the building. I did this, not because I expected the degus to scamper up to me like a couple of puppies, but just in case the intruder was still around.

Was it possible the degus had been stolen? I felt a mixture of sadness and anger at the thought. It wouldn't be the first time unlikely things had been purloined from the clinic. One year someone made off with our Christmas tree, complete with a collection of marzipan dwarves.

I made a move for the phone but stopped myself: I didn't want to mess up any fingerprints. I called the local police on my mobile and then rejoined Tiffany in the car park.

Eunice arrived before the police and treated us to a protracted account of the time her caravan in Colwyn Bay had been vandalized by Welsh Nationalists. By the time the coppers turned up, the receptionist, Wendy, and the manager, Joe, had also joined us.

The two policemen could've been twins they looked so alike. They both had blond hair, very pale complexions and, I guessed, a combined weight of no more than twenty-two stone. They're too light to be policemen, I thought: if I was their mother I'd worry.

The five of us followed them from room to room,

gazing over their shoulders as they opened each office door in turn. Nothing seemed to have been stolen, or even disturbed until we reached the spare office.

'My God,' said Joe, immediately putting his hand to his nose, 'what in the name of Christ has happened here?'

The scene was bizarre and, even for a nurse, bile-inducing. The dangerous-drugs fridge door was open and prostrate before it were Ant and Dec. The degus were dragging themselves around by their front legs; their hind legs having apparently been paralysed. Snaking behind each of them was a reeking trail of liquid faeces. It was a pathetic and repulsive sight. Each had lost all its fur: shed hairs and whiskers criss-crossed the area. More alarming from my point of view were the split and semi-chewed remnants of red and grey capsules that lay at the centre of the scene. The evidence suggested that Ant and Dec had gorged themselves on eighteen-year-old speed. Inevitably my thoughts went back to Sharon Clackett's story of the Rottweiler.

Wendy collapsed sobbing into Joe's arms and Tiffany also began to cry. I comforted her as best I could but I also felt unsteady. I hated that feeling, the weightlessness, the take-off terror, not only because it made me light-headed and queasy, but because I was experiencing it more and more. Was gravity denying me, or were my bones becoming hollow with age?

I spent the morning explaining to Joe and the police what had been stolen and why it had been on the premises. Joe was lovely about it. He went out of his way to assure me I'd done the right thing in removing the drugs and the police agreed. They insisted I give them Sharon's name and address, however, because they'd need to speak to her.

I ate my lunch alone again that day. My excuse was that

I needed quiet in order to prepare a witness statement for a child abuse case.

I set up the Salter desktop once more and weighed a box file, a marker pen and a sample pack of Dermol anti-microbial creams. I then cleared the scales, opened the Dermol sample pack and weighed a single tube of cream. I added another tube to the scales. Heavier. I added another. Heavier still. I added my left shoe to the pile, observed the weight, added the right and observed again. Heavier, heavier.

I began to feel a bit better so I sent a text message to Kelvin. We had a rendezvous later that afternoon. I felt better still when he replied within two minutes.

By 2 p.m. Ant and Dec's condition seemed slightly improved: they were no longer – to use NHS parlance – 'circling the plughole'. They needed a vet, though, and Eunice offered to drive them.

'Do you think this shoebox will hold them?' she asked.

I looked in the box. The degus lay like a pair of spooning lovers with their little teeth chattering. 'I think escape is the last thing on their minds, Eunice.'

For some reason the break-in hit Tiffany very hard. She was subdued and often tearful for the rest of the day. I wasn't sure why – maybe it was her fondness for dumb animals. Tiffany could see good things in everything after all, so why not degus? Her distraction was useful for me, though: it meant she was less likely to notice my own.

15

'This Beautiful Day'

Solomon King (Columbia)

MINTY

I soaked up the sauce with a sponge, scrubbed the interior of my hat with a damp cloth, and then dried it with Hazel's hairdryer. My wife's outburst had been worth it – it shook the strop from her system. By the time she left for work she seemed to be pretty much over it. She gave me a dry kiss at the door, which meant I was at least half forgiven.

Despite being worried about Danny, I was feeling pretty chipper. Today I was going to collect my records.

My first stop after my morning lolly shift was the post office, where I signed for the foot-square brown box. I took it round to McDonald's, ordered an Egg McMuffin and sat with my booty.

Having only had a bloody yoghurt for breakfast I was famished, so I devoured the McMuffin before opening the box. I could, I thought, put off the bliss of seeing my vinyl for another few minutes. I needed to milk every second of anticipation from this treat. After all, it would take yonks to pay for it.

I finished the McMuffin, wiped the grease from my mouth and fingers and then carefully, oh so carefully, began to remove the packaging. I peeled the brown masking tape from the flaps at the top and opened the box. The discs were packed in polystyrene and folded around this was an invoice from Scarce Soul Supplies. I lifted the packing out of the box and separated its two halves. The discs were individually sleeved in cardboard and separated from each other by inch-thick polystyrene blocks. I slipped out the first sleeve and, careful not to touch the grooves of the disc, slowly removed 'This Beautiful Day' by Solomon King. It was a tune I'd owned in my youth, back in my days as a serious collector. It's very rare on its original Columbia release. Not only that, it's a sensational, life-affirming song – one that helps you feel better about paying three figures for it. I examined the vinyl under the bright lights of McDonald's and it was shiny black and scratch-free. They'd play Solomon King in Mr M's oldies room at Wigan – a tiny dance hall away from the main room which specialized in classics from the past. I loved it in there. In my stash of old photos I have a brilliant one of me and Nipper Kid in Mr M's. We're arm in arm and I'm holding up a copy of Solomon King for the camera. Nipper had just lent me the money to buy it. We're both sporting tank tops, perms and weird Freddie Mercury-style moustaches. I remember the occasion well: it was a Friday and, later that night, I copped off with a girl from Warrington called Kathy. I spent the rest of the weekend with her, sleeping at her flat on Saturday night and taking the late train back to the Midlands on Sunday. We stayed friends for as long as I was on the scene and I'd run into her and her mates at most events north of Knutsford. She'd always approach me from behind, put her hands over my eyes and say: 'Can I fondle your seven inches?' I'd always answer with the words: 'Is that you, Keith?' Great times; great people.

I removed each record in turn and inspected them. Nearly a thousand pounds' worth of plastic. I knew Haze would pop her stopper if she ever found out; I'd need to keep the records hidden. I'd be like one of those billionaires who buy stolen masterpieces on the black market. I'd certainly never play them; no need, I was aware that all the songs I'd bought were available on cheap CD compilations. The thrill is knowing that you have the original; it's knowing you own an item that other people can't buy even if they want it. These songs, ignored when they were released thirty or forty years earlier, are like rare orchids that no one gets to see, unless they go out of their way. And to appreciate them you need to be a connoisseur, aware of their preciousness – that awareness is itself a rare and special thing. Few people in that McDonald's restaurant would have even heard of the tunes in my box. In this sense I half resented the KFC advert. It broadcast 'Do I Love You' – the daddy of all rarities – to the masses and cheapened it the way you cheapen Van Gogh by putting him on a tea towel.

I repackaged the records and left the restaurant. As I slid the remnants of my breakfast into the 'Thank You' bin, I thought about putting the records receipt in there too as a way of hiding the evidence. I decided against it, remembering that my credit card details were on the document.

My next port of call was a little junkshop in George Street where I purchased a second-hand record box that could accommodate 7-inch singles. It was designed to hold fifty and was made of red plastic. It wasn't in good condition: the metal fittings were rusty and its seams were beginning to split, but I needed something for my new sides.

Carrying the singles box through Walsall town centre gave me a strong sense of *déjà vu*. In my youth I'd had numerous similar cases and I felt almost like a teenager as I made my way through the thickening crowds of pensioners arriving in town by the bus-load now that their off-peak passes were valid. The person I was on my way to meet would often have seen me with such a case in the seventies. That person was Dave McVane.

Mac was one of the few people from the Northern days I'd stayed in touch with. In the seventies he was a leather-worker who made everything from saddles to S&M equipment. Then he went to college, got a degree and became a journalist. He worked for the *Walsall Reflector* and even wrote a book. Now he's back in the leather. His problem was booze. The guy spent the 1990s arseholed every night until something exploded in his guts and he had to give it up. Since then he's become a bit of a hermit.

I entered the Leather Museum to be greeted by a plump, grinning receptionist.

'Are you here for a guided tour, darling?'

'I'm just here to have a word with Mac. Er, Dave . . . Dave McVane?'

'Oh, David.' She giggled. 'He's part of the exhibition. He's on our Working Craftsman Stand. He won't be able to see you until the tour is over, but you can join the tour party; they've only just started. Through those double doors and turn left.'

I followed her directions and quickly found the tour party: a group of thirty children from Jerome Juniors. You could tell they were from Jerome Juniors because they were wearing the unofficial school uniform: hooded sweatshirts and tracksuit bottoms for the boys; evening gowns and tiaras for the girls. Several of both sexes proudly sported electronic tagging devices on their ankles.

They were rowdy. Their teacher – a powerfully built skinhead with a 'Karate is Life' tattoo – was doing his best to keep them under control. Sadly his best wasn't really good enough. They kept interrupting the museum guide, a guy with the unfortunate name of Mr Beckham, with cries of 'Show us your golden balls' and 'Bend it, bollock-face.' He never seemed to get beyond, 'Walsall is famous for the production of leather goods, because –'

I hung back, pretending to look at the exhibits and information boards. The exhibition started with the basics: a stuffed cow. It took the Jerome crowd ten minutes just to get past this. The boys started a game of hoopla, tossing the girls' tiaras over the cow's horns. They ignored the information about leather cutting and tanning but were extremely taken by a display of bullwhips. A sensible curator would have placed these in a glass case, but here they wanted to provide a 'hands-on, interactive experience'. What followed was a vicious whipping contest between two of the larger boys which resulted in their teacher getting a nasty lick as he attempted to disarm them. It flared like a lipstick stripe on his cheek.

By the time the party reached the living exhibition, the museum guide was semi-tearful and even their battle-calloused teacher looked wan and, frankly, frightened.

Mac was standing at a board, hammering tacks into a saddle seat. He was surrounded by the tools of his trade together with rolls of leather and examples of saddles in various stages of completion. Above his head was a large sign which said: LIVING EXHIBIT: A SADDLEMAKER AT WORK. When the tour group arrived Mac glanced up, nervously, from his work. He didn't spot me.

'This, children, is a saddlemaker in action,' said the guide, in the manner of a lame antelope addressing a pack of hyenas. 'Does anyone want to ask him a question before the tour concludes?' I saw Mac grimace at the prospect.

Immediately, a hand went up. It was a red-headed kid with sweat stains under the arms of his hoodie. 'Hey, mate, where's your fucking hair gone?'

'Oi!' said the teacher. 'He means questions about saddles.'

'Do yow mek saddles fer race osses?' asked a boy with a fistful of sovereign rings on both hands.

Mac cleared his throat. 'Sometimes, son, yes.'

'Gorra tip fer the two-thirty at Newmarket?' asked the kid, taking out his mobile as if in readiness to buzz his bookie.

'Sorry, no.'

'Cunt,' said the kid, who then vented his frustration by putting his elbow through the glass of the fire alarm. There followed a deafening clatter of bells.

'Right, everyone out!' bellowed the teacher, shepherding the horde towards the exit sign. 'Why does it always have to end this way?'

Why indeed? My exposure to these devils made me conscious of the easy ride I had with Nigel when he was their age. His transformation into the Demon from the Dustbin was recent and seemed to parallel the emergence of his wispy goatee. It made me shudder to think what these Jerome kids might be like when *they* hit puberty. How will they ever become socialized? How will Nigel? Come to think of it, how did I?

Mac was chuffed to see me. When the alarm was silenced, we were able to repair to the Leather Museum café where I filled him in on my week. I'd been looking forward to talking to him because I knew he'd be interested. I told him about Petey and Muncher, and about the intensity with which my old passion seemed to be swelling within me.

'I know, I know,' Mac said. 'I'd not thought about rare soul music for years, but my hair nearly grew back when I saw that KFC ad.'

I placed my record box on the table. 'Take a look in there.'

Mac flicked swiftly through. 'Blimey, Mint. I was never much of a collector but even I know you must have two hundred quid's worth there.'

'Try a grand's worth.'

Mac, who was taking a sip of cappuccino, sprayed it back into his cup. 'You what?'

'I paid nine hundred and ninety nicker for these babies. Prices have gone up, mate.'

'So have lollipop men's wages by the look of it.'

'Well, no. These are between you and me, Mac. For fuck's sake don't mention them to Haze.'

'Bit of a rash purchase?'

'She'd think so.'

'I can imagine. So are you going to get back into the scene; start collecting again?'

'I can't really say. I just wanted some of the old tunes; some rare stuff.'

'To remind you of your lamentably distant youth?'

'Perhaps. Mostly I think I want them because they represent something that isn't to do with being a lollipop man, a hacked off father and a frustrated husband.'

'Frustrated? Is Hazel still taking her dictionary to bed?'

I laughed, hoping that my expression wouldn't betray the fact that she actually *did* take her dictionary to bed; indeed, it *had* featured in our sex life (although we hadn't played the 'naming of parts' game for months). I tended to keep my sex life with Hazel to myself, partly out of decorum, but mostly because Mac's sexual exploits always appeared much more interesting and varied than mine. He'd had lots of affairs with women, some of whom seemed tormentingly exotic to me – women from the southern counties, for instance, and even one from Guernsey. His horizons were broader than those of the average Walsall man. He once even had a shot at chatting up Gladys

Knight on the occasion she and the Pips appeared live at Wigan Casino. He followed her backstage and was apparently doing well until one of the Pips took exception to his presence in the dressing room. Still, when Mac returned to the dancefloor he had Gladys's autograph spiralling around his navel.

Even as a bald semi-recluse Mac still did all right, plundering the surprisingly rich vein of women who were impressed by his status as an author. When they actually got around to reading his kinky book they tended to pack him in; but still, he pulled with impressive ease. I suppose it didn't hurt that he was rich – he supplemented his income as a Living Exhibit by flogging leather goods from his website, www.fleshofthebeast.co.uk. He made everything from lap dancers' thongs to gun holsters. I've always envied his way with women. In my days as a bachelor I was crap at chatting them up. I was forever treading on their platforms or elbowing their Cherry Bs over. Indeed, the last time I had sex with my first girlfriend – Mandy Tapper – we did it in her parents' shower and we ended up slipping on the tiles and breaking her clavicle. Besides Hazel, Kathy from Warrington was one of my few successes and she'd chatted *me* up.

I gave Mac the details of Fanny's and asked him if he fancied it. It's a question I could have asked by phone, of course, but I wanted it to be face to face because I knew that way there'd be more chance of talking him into it.

'I don't know, mate. I don't go out much now I'm off the booze; I get the jitters.'

'But the Northern scene was never about drinking, you know that.'

'It was about getting off your shed on speed, as I recall.'

'Partly. And talking of which, Muncher's Preene's promised to get hold of some gear for the night.'

'Just like old times.'

'Did your quack say you had to lay off dancing powder as well as alcohol?'

Mac thought for a moment before cracking a grin. 'What time are we meeting?'

Me and my old mate continued to flap our jaws for the next half-hour. I told him about the cops' visit and he told me about the latest antidepressants his quack had prescribed. I don't know why he needed antidepressants given his new relationship with a double-jointed Pilates instructor from Perry Barr, but still. I was just about to split when he happened to ask me if I'd seen that week's *Walsall Reflector*. He said it contained an article that might 'fellate my fancy'. I hadn't, so I walked with him back to his work station where he'd left his copy.

'As soon as I saw this,' he said, handing me the paper, 'I thought about a certain lolly-jockey who'd be interested.'

The *Reflector* was open at the puzzle page and I couldn't help noticing that the word LAGER had been written in all the blanks of the crossword.

'It's on page six,' Mac said, ignoring my look of sympathy.

It was an article about Billy Peebles, the kid who'd been injured in the accident I had when I was little. Apparently he'd become a successful footwear designer and much, much more. Under the title, 'Billy, You Are a Hero' it opened:

Walsall-born boot boffin Billy Peebles, 44, is on top of the world after successfully climbing Mount Elbrus, one of Europe's premier peaks, in May this year. Billy – whose feet were severely crushed in an accident at the age of 7 – used special boots of his own design to make the ascent. Speaking from his luxury mock-Tudor home in Solihull, the mountaineering marvel said, 'I wanted to do the climb for charity but, if I was going to make it, I needed boots that would offset the curvature of my feet. None were available so I designed a pair myself. They were a success and I hope to use them to do other charity climbs in the future.' Now Billy's boots have kick-started his climbing career, who knows where his high-flying heroism will take him?

The article went on to explain how Billy Peebles, OBE, had sold his footwear design and manufacturing company in the mid-1990s for 'one point seven million' in order to devote more time to charity fundraising and to his hobbies: mountaineering, white-water rafting and conkers. The accompanying photograph showed Billy sitting on top of a child's climbing frame, balancing one of his special boots on the end of a hiking pole.

My mouth suddenly felt incredibly dry, despite the large mocha I'd just consumed. 'He's a millionaire,' I said, 'and he has an OBE.'

'Yep,' said Mac.

'And he's climbed one of the highest mountains in Europe – with boots he made himself.'

'Technically I think it's *the* highest. Good news, eh?'

'I thought Mont Blanc was the highest?'

'No, Elbrus. It's one of the Caucasian Mountains that form part of the border between Europe and Asia. Good news about Billy, though, eh?'

'Er . . . yes, yes. Of course. Fantastic. Absolutely . . . amazing.'

It seemed that Billy Peebles knew how to land after all. On his feet.

16

'School'

Nirvana, *Bleach* (Sub Pop)

TREBBO

'What are they, man?' asked Dicey, scratching his head through his baseball cap. I had my bag open and was giving him a glimpse of the red and grey caps. We were standing on the playing fields watching the rest of our class do PE. It was a rugby match and our games teacher, Hannibal, was busy breaking up a scuffle with excessive force. Hannibal is one reason Dicey and I never do PE. Another reason is that both of us are averse to the spirit of competition; another, admittedly the main one, is that neither of us can be arsed. I'd written us both excuse notes for the entire term on NHS headed notepaper yoinked from the Divette's clinic.

'Slimming caps from the eighties, dude,' I said. 'They were left over in some woman's cupboard Tiff visited as part of her work experience. I broke-and-entered the clinic last night and yoinked em.'

'Mental. But what use are slimming tablets, other than as another means to oppress women?'

'They're uppers, Dice. Speed. Slimming tablets is what people took before they had E. It's gimmers' whizz.'

He reached into the bag, pulled out the jar and inspected the label.

'Du-ro-mine,' he read.

'Right.'

'Blubber-T knows his gear, Trebbo. If you're trying to rip him off . . .'

'Dude, I'm *relying* on him knowing his gear. I'm banking on him knowing what these caps are capable of.'

'So, what time are you meeting him?'

'*You're* meeting him tonight at seven.'

'Me?'

'He's threatened to come round to mine but I don't want him at the house. I can't deal him the knocked-off caps on our doorstep, can I? *You* can wait for him at the bottom of Longwood Crescent and head him off. When he arrives, give us a bell on my mobile and I'll come and sort him.'

'Why can't *you* head him off? Blubber-T scares me; he reminds me of Hannibal.' Dicey nodded toward the PE teacher who was in the process of walking off the pitch with two kids. He had their necks clamped in the crook of each of his overdeveloped arms and was taking them behind the equipment shed so that he could smash their heads together. For this he needed to be out of sight of what he referred to as the 'politically correct ponce-merchants' who might frown on his 'unorthodox coaching strategies'. In all my years of schooling I've never met a PE teacher who wasn't like Hannibal. The Div said it was the same when he was a kid: he chalks it up to too much testosterone and too little talent. According to Minty they're the 'angriest and most frustrated examples of those who "can't do"'.

'I agree there's a similarity, dude, except that Blubbs can afford more expensive tracksuits than Hannibal. But you'll be doing me a favour if you meet him. I want to be at home when my old lady returns from work because I need to hear what she says about the break-in at the clinic.'

I thumbed a Juicy Fruit in Dicey's direction and we watched as Hannibal emerged from behind the equipment shed minus the two pupils. They materialized a minute later looking slightly dazed, but composed. As they followed the teacher they circled their thumbs and forefingers and made exaggerated 'wanker' gestures behind his back, as if stroking the necks of invisible cellos. The two synchronized their movements, much to the hilarity of everyone present. When Hannibal turned to look at them they stopped and, when he turned his back again, they resumed. They performed with aplomb and perfect timing, offering the most enlightening lesson of the afternoon: rebellion is inherently cool.

That evening when the Divette arrived home from work, she prattled non-stop about the break-in. *The Simpsons* was on and me and the Div had our feet up in front of the telly. I pretended not to give a shit, but was alive to every syllable she spoke.

'Someone kicked in the door,' she told us.

'Yeah?' went the Div, but he had one eye on Homer, who'd just entered a doughnut-eating contest.

'But how did they know we'd forgotten to set the alarm, that's what I can't fathom,' she said.

Cool: she was under the impression that someone cocked up. I was dying to ask what made her think it *wasn't* set, but it would look suspicious if I appeared interested. I was a bit worried about the degus – who'd have thought amphetamines could have such an effect on small animals? It must be powerful stuff. I wanted to ask her if she thought they'd be OK but, again, I thought it wise to stay mute. I kept in character and did what I normally do when the Divette yaps through *The Simpsons*. I reached for the remote and tweaked the volume up a shade.

The Divette sighed, shook her head and left the room. Before long I heard her running a bath.

Emmerdale had just started by the time she returned, flushed and flabby in her towelling dressing gown. The Div wasn't bothered about watching *Emmerdale* and so now was up for conversation.

'Did you phone Suze to ask how that nipper is doing?'

'Yes, I did. It wouldn't have hurt you to have shown some concern yourself, come to think of it.'

'I *am* concerned, that's why I'm asking you.'

The Divette seemed to spend a second assessing whether or not this was true, although I'm not sure why. The Div worries himself to death over kids. One of my earliest memories is of the time he'd spend double-checking the strapping on my car baby-seat. The Divette would always be gunning the engine impatiently, on the verge of a dickie; he'd be scrutinizing buckles, rivets and stitches: tugging them, rattling them, sniffing them. He's an embarrassment when he's out because he's always telling kids off for not using the zebra crossing. He cries through *Children in Need* too, for Christsake – mind you, I've never seen him pledge any money.

'You'll be pleased to hear that he's out of hospital and he's expected to be fine,' said the Divette.

'Brills McGills.'

I felt my mobile vibrating in my jeans and, straight away, I was up and out of the room. The gimmers didn't even look my way.

In the hall I checked the display. As expected it was Dicey and I clicked to answer.

'Dice?'

But it was Blubber-T's voice: 'Am yow cowing fucking wi me?'

'No, no, Blubbs. Stay cool – I'll be there in one minute.'

'Be ere cowing now, bitch,' he said.

I shouldered my bag of caps and opened the front door only to be greeted by a bald guy in his forties who was apparently about to ring the bell. He was wearing a tank top.

'Betterware catalogue please, son,' he said.

'The dog ate it,' I said, because I couldn't be arsed to reach behind me and pick it up off the mat.

'You must have a big dog, son.'

'As a shire horse,' I said, and closed the door. 'Just mind you don't tread in his droppings, dude,' I added, side-stepping him. I thought I heard him mutter the words 'ignorant scrag-bag' but I wasn't sure.

I felt bad that I'd cheeked him. When I reached the bottom of the drive I stopped and turned: 'I'm sorry, mate,' I said. 'I'm in a rush – if you ring the bell my mom will let you have it.' He shrugged and turned back to the door. Well, I supposed they *were* only trying to make a living and I guessed it was *possible* to own a tank top and still be a decent human being. Just about.

It took me less than a minute to jog to the corner of Long-wood Crescent where Blubber-T and Dicey were waiting.

'Blubbs, dude,' I said, 'chill. We're sorted.'

'Yow've got mi two hundred bones?'

'Better, dude.'

Blubber-T began advancing on me. He was looking ape, *very* ape. By the expression on his face you'd think I'd just stuffed my thumb up his mother's arse.

'Yowm fucking wi me!' he shouted. There were frag-ments of what appeared to be peanut brittle on his teeth.

'I'm not, Blubbs. I've just got drugs instead of bones. Genuine eighties uppers: you can't get them any more. Top quality, dude.'

I held my bag open in front of me and watched myself doing so in the reflection of his Ray-Bans. I looked pale and scrawny. Blubber-T snatched the bag from me and pulled out the bottle.

'What's this cowing crap?'

'Amphetamine, dude. High grade.' I just tossed the last phrase in for effect but it sounded good so I added, 'The highest.'

'Duromine,' he said, tipping a couple of caps into the palm of his hand.

'You've heard of it?' I tried not to sound too surprised.

'Ar.' He examined his palm the way you might examine a hankie that's been sneezed in by someone famous. 'These look sarned. I think theym the right colour.'

'They're the genuine article, Blubbs. A whole jar full. There's got to be two hundred quids' worth.'

Blubber-T produced a Walnut Whip from his pocket and bit the nut off the top. He pondered the offer as he chomped. After about ten seconds he posted the rest of the Walnut Whip into his mouth and continued to chomp and ponder.

At last he swallowed and said, 'Fifty bones. Yow still owe me one fifty. I'll gi yow a wik.'

This was actually better than I'd hoped. I expected to be going home with my nads in my pocket. I was thankful to see the fat man pop the bottle under his rodent-skin hat and waddle away, content.

'What are we up to now?' asked Dicey, when Blubber-T had gone.

'I don't know about you, dude, but I'm going to see Tiff. We're spending the night round hers.'

'Mental – you're a lucky man, Trebbs.'

'Maybe.' Then I told Dicey about my continued lack of sexual success with Tiff. 'She really is a Poppins, dude,' I moaned.

'You should have more respect for her feelings, man,' he said. 'She'll lose respect for *you* if you keep pestering her for sex. She's a righteous woman. You're lucky to have her.'

'Have your freaking nads retracted, dude? You're supposed to be on my side!'

Dicey shrugged.

'If Tiff *does* lose respect for me, it's more likely to be because she hears I've robbed the clinic, so keep schtum about that, dude.'

'Safe,' said Dicey.

As it turned out, Tiff *did* lose respect for me, but it had nothing to do with either sex or robbery.

17

Satisfaction (*n*)

HAZEL

All through *EastEnders* I'd been thinking about Kelvin. I'd seen him again late that afternoon and, again, he'd worked his magic. Our liaisons were invariably brief: an hour here, a half-hour there, as little as twenty minutes sometimes – but it was always good. I'd only been seeing him a month but the extent to which I'd begun to depend on him staggered me. I was feeling grounded and calm.

'Mac,' said Minty.

'Eh?'

'I knew you weren't listening. I said I saw Dave McVane today. He's all set for Fanny's.'

'Really?' This was one of the many things I couldn't have cared less about.

'Yep. It's going to be quite a night. Why don't I knock the telly off and put my CD on instead? It'll help remind you of some of the old Northern tunes. Nigel's out so we won't have to bother about his moaning.'

'What joy,' I said, grabbing the *TV Times* and scanning it for something I could convincingly claim to want to watch. I wasn't quick enough, though, and the telly was off before I had a chance to complain.

'You didn't get around to hearing the rest of this CD,' he said. 'It has "You Got Me Where You Want Me" on it.'

'Get away.'

'By Larry Santos. You'll remember it.'

I couldn't imagine what he meant as I never really listened to his music even when I first met him. Though he'd dragged me round some of the soul venues, I'd tolerated rather than enjoyed them.

'I don't think I *will* remember it, Minty.'

'You used to claim it was your favourite.'

'Asking me about my favourite Northern Soul song is like asking me which childhood disease I enjoyed the most.'

He played the track and it did sound familiar*ish*. It wasn't something I'd listen to willingly, of course. I'd have to be in traction with the off switch out of reach. But, yes: some distant, half-forgotten bell seemed on the verge of ringing.

'Remember it?'

'Sort of.'

'It's brillo, isn't it? Don't you think it's spine-tingling?'

'No, Minty, a lumbar puncture is spine-tingling. This is just another soul song.'

When I met Minty the music I enjoyed most was the stuff they played in the Giddy Kitten, Walsall's only nightclub. I can't really remember the names of the groups but it was songs like 'Don't You Want Me' and 'Tainted Love'. In fact, the latter was playing the night Minty chatted me up. He said he knew a better version of the song recorded by the woman who was married to Marc Bolan. When he played it to me four times in a row a few days later, it *wasn't* better. It was just faster and more old-fashioned.

I was relieved when the phone rang. 'I'll get it,' I said.

It was Suze and the sound of her voice made my heart race. Danny might have suffered a brain haemorrhage. I was conscious of my pulse beating in my ear and, once again, the ground seemed set to disappear from beneath me.

'It's about this Northern Soul thing the blokes are going to tomorrow, Haze.'

'God, don't remind me,' I said, relieved. 'Listen to this.' I briefly pointed the phone towards the living room.

'They all sound the same to me,' said Suze. 'Are you still going?'

'Unless fate intervenes and I get run over or murdered. One can only hope.'

'I'm coming too. My mom's looking after the kids.'

'That's fantastic! We can be "soul sisters"!'

'To be honest, Haze, and don't take this the wrong way, I'm only going so that I can keep an eye on Mike.'

'Oh?'

Suze's voice dropped, 'I haven't told you this before, Haze, but Mike used to do drugs.'

'Really? Well, most people experiment, Suze, I wouldn't worry abou–'

'He sold them too.'

'Oh.' This was something I already knew, of course, but I didn't want to let on.

'Don't be too shocked, it was nothing heavy. Just minor stuff, or so he says. But still. It was when he started going to Northern Soul clubs that he got involved with it.'

'But he gave it up when he stopped going?'

'More or less. He carried on buying and selling a little – cannabis mostly, I think. I turned a blind eye until the kids arrived, then I made him quit.'

'So why are you worried? Has he started again?' I noticed that the song currently playing in the front room had the refrain, 'You've been cheating'.

'He's been on the phone to people and he won't tell me who. He's been out and he won't tell me where. And he's swiped the hundred quid in cash I've just withdrawn from the Halifax. I was going to put it in me mom and dad's wedding anniversary card. It's their golden next week.'

'He stole it?'

'He's borrowed it, apparently. He said he'd been hoping to get it back before I noticed. I wouldn't have missed it but I went to borrow a tenner out of it myself to get a tube of VO5 Hair Putty. And there it was. Gone.'

'Does he have an explanation?'

'He just said he owes a mate but he won't tell me who or why. It's exactly the sort of thing he used to do when I first met him. I wonder if he'll ever bloody grow up?'

I could hear Minty clapping, singing and stamping about on the carpet. 'You may as well ask that question about Peter Pan, Suze. And at least *he* looks good in shorts!'

Suze chuckled and I was pleased to hear it – her anxiety seemed to be lifting.

'I just think that, if I'm there, he might think twice about doing something stupid.'

'I'm sure everything will be fine.'

In the bathroom I quickly weighed a bar of Imperial Leather and a tub of foundation powder. Then I weighed myself and found that I was a pound heavier than the last time. For some reason this cheered me, doubly so when I took my clothes, watch and earrings off and it made no difference to the reading.

When I rejoined Minty in the living room he was dancing. His Doc Martens were making scuff marks in the pile of the carpet and his stomping was vibrating the ornaments on the Welsh dresser.

'Eh?' he said. 'Eh?' He was nodding in the direction of his feet. 'I've still got it, have I not?' He clapped his hands, kicked his left leg out and dropped into a semi-splits.

'Careful.'

'My neck feels back to normal,' he said, still in the splits position. 'I'm going to leave the brace off tomorrow.'

He scrambled uneasily to his feet and continued dancing. He's not a particularly good dancer. He always looks too tight and awkward, as if his underpants are troubling him, and he tends to have a stupid look on his face, like he's concentrating too hard on getting his steps right. Sometimes his tongue protrudes from his mouth and curls over his top lip and you can tell he's thinking really hard about it. I consider this dancing's equivalent of moving your lips when you read. Actually, he's pretty graceless in everything he does – I suppose this is the case with most accident-prone people. When we first started making love, for instance, he was useless. He had no sense of rhythm and was forever elbowing my boobs and dead-legging me with his bony knees. He used to mutter instructions to himself, as if he was reading *The Joy of Sex* from the back of his eyelids. I soon put a stop to that and after some coaching from me he's become quite an adept lover. There's no hope for his dancing, though.

'Suze is coming to Fanny's tomorrow,' I told him. 'She says she wants to keep an eye on Mike . . . Muncher.'

'Oh yeah, what's she think he's going to do?'

'Drugs.'

Though he continued dancing, I noticed straight away that Minty was interested.

'Oh yeah. What makes her think that?'

'You should know: you told me yourself that Muncher was a dealer.'

'Er . . . well, you know; he wasn't much of one.'

'But he used to deal drugs.'

'Well . . .' Minty stopped dancing. He can't concentrate on two things simultaneously. 'I think *deal* is too strong a word. Sell is maybe a better one. Never for profit; he wasn't that type.'

'When you mentioned him the other day you said he used to be "the main dealer" in this area. You didn't ask him to get you anything for tomorrow night, I hope.'

'Haze, what do you take me for?'

'I take you for someone who's seen an advert on the telly that's made him think he's eighteen again. I hope you're not going to do anything stupid – if I catch you taking drugs, Minty, I'll brain you – and that's a promise.'

'Oi, you're not fucking talking to Nigel now,' he said, with genuine emotion. 'I'm looking forward to tomorrow night. You'd better not ruin it for me . . . Stroll on, I wish I'd never asked you to come. What was I thinking of?'

He stomped out of the room. Ten seconds later he stomped back in, took his CD from the stereo and stomped out again. I heard him climb the stairs to our bedroom, slam the door and toss himself down on the bed.

Now I was guilty. I *was* treating him like a child and I was spoiling things for him. He was so excited about this reunion. OK, I thought it was midlife-crisis-style nonsense, but I didn't want to be a bitch about it.

After a few minutes I took my *Mini Oxford* from my bag and followed him upstairs. He was lying on our bed with his Northern Soul album playing on the little Sanyo CD unit that doubles as our radio alarm. I read him the definition of 'sorry'.

'It's OK.'

I could tell he was still annoyed, so I sat down beside him on the bed.

'You're looking forward to tomorrow, aren't you?'

'I s'pose,' he said, sounding so much like a sulking Nigel that I had to stop myself from laughing.

'Look, I don't want to put a damper on it, Minty, I'm

just a bit stressed at the moment.' We were both silent for a while and I watched my husband stare thoughtfully at the ceiling. This was out of character for Minty; unlike Nigel he's seldom pensive or introspective. It's what my mum loves about him. Despite the fact that he always shows himself up at family events, she thinks he's the life and soul. She calls him 'my mad Minty'. And though he's often embarrassing, I prefer him this way too. He can be a Charlie, but he's usually fun. I didn't like seeing him brooding.

'I'm a lollipop man,' he said, after several minutes of meditation.

'Erm . . . yes, Minty.'

'I've done nothing with my life.'

Blimey, I'd never heard him say that before. 'Don't be silly, Minty,' I said, 'you've achieved a lot.'

'Like what?'

'A house; a job; you've *raised a child*, for God's sake.'

'Yes, but everyone's done those things. Or most people. I've never really done anything apart from what everyone else does. And I haven't exactly done a wonderful job of that: you pay our mortgage, my occupation is menial and Nigel is Beelzebub's bastard spawn.'

'He's just going through a difficult phase,' I said, wishing I had a fiver for every time I'd said it.

'I don't seem to have done anything worthwhile, Haze. Compared to someone like Mac, for instance.'

'You mean Dave McVane, the single, alcoholic, childless, museum exhibit?'

'He's on the wagon. And what I mean is, at least he's *done* things. He's got a degree, tried different jobs, had his own business, travelled the world, written a book.'

'May I remind you that Dave McVane lives on his own and spends every day struggling not to stick his head in a bucket of brandy. He has no one to love and no one to love him. Give me your life any day.'

'He has lots of friends. *We're* his friends.'

'Being someone's friend is not the same as loving them.'

He stared at the ceiling for a few moments longer as if trying to make up his mind whether to tell me something. At last he told me about an article Mac had shown him on the kid who was injured in the car crash he'd caused when he was five. Billy Peebles. I'd already read the piece at work in Eunice's copy of the *Reflector*. I'd been in two minds whether to mention it but, given that I knew he'd see it eventually, I decided to let my husband discover it for himself.

'He's minted,' said Minty, 'and he has an OBE.'

'Excellent . . . They give OBEs to lollipop men too sometimes of course.'

'Don't patronize me, Hazel.'

'Sorry.'

'If that's not enough, he's climbed one of the highest mountains in bloody Europe, wearing shoes of his own bloody design. Can you believe it? Billy Peebles!'

'Actually, I think Elbrus is *the* highest mountain in Europe,' I said, immediately regretting it.

'The fucking highest then!'

'Well, Minty, surely this is *good* news?'

'Yes, yes, yes, but it's got me thinking, Haze. I mean, look at me: I've got two perfectly good feet – a pretty clear advantage over poor Billy Peebles – and I'm a penniless lollipop man who's *sat on his arse in Walsall all his life*!'

'Billy Peebles has made a success of his life, yes, but so have you in your own way. It depends how you define success. It doesn't necessarily have anything to do with money.'

'Or with receiving an OBE?'

'No.'

'Or with climbing Mount Elbrus, even though he's disabled?'

'*No*. You don't have to have done any of these things to be a worthwhile human being and to have made a useful contribution to society. That's *why* they give OBEs to lollipop men. If you're a conscientious lollipop man, who works hard to be the best lollipop man he can be, then you deserve an OBE as much as anyone else.' Even as I spoke these words, however, I wasn't sure I really believed them. If what I'd said was true then why was I so embarrassed about my husband's job?

'Millionaire,' said Minty, staring abstractedly at the ceiling.

Over the years we've often discussed the crash. It is my contention that it had affected my husband in ways he wouldn't admit. It's the reason he wound up as an accident investigator when he left school; it's the reason he's a bloody lollipop man, *obviously*.

But Minty always denies it. I often tease him about his denial but, to be honest, I don't think it's that funny. For me it implies a juvenile unwillingness to take responsibility for his actions.

'Just think, Minty,' I said, poking him mischievously in the ribs, 'there's no need to feel guilty any more. Maybe Billy wouldn't have been as driven and motivated if he'd grown up with regular feet. Far from ruining his life, your inadvertent handbrake turn might have *made* him the success he is today . . .'

This kind of banter would normally have Minty chuckling and taking the mickey out of my 'tuppenny-ha'penny psychoanalysing', but he remained stony-faced.

'Haze,' he said, 'I don't feel guilty about what happened to Billy Peebles and I never have. What I feel is inadequate.'

'Are you sure you don't mean unfulfilled?' I said.

Minty thought for a moment before taking Mo from my hand and thumbing through.

'The word "unfulfilled" doesn't occur in there, Minty,' I said. 'There's nothing between "unfrock" and "unfurl".'

I gave my husband a couple of seconds to ask me how I could possibly know that without looking, but he didn't. He doubtless imagined I knew the *Oxford English Mini Dictionary* by heart. He took my word for it and dropped the book on to the bed. Still on my mission to cheer him, I picked it up and read Minty a definition of the word 'worth'. He still looked glum so I repeated it, whispering sexily in his ear: '"Having value",' I purred, '"deserving a particular treatment". These words surely apply to Minty Trebor, in numerous departments. Particularly, perhaps, in the dinkle department . . .'

'You mean the humungous love-truncheon department, surely,' he said, a thin smile flickering.

'Of course.'

Encouraged, I set Mo on the bedside table and stretched out alongside him. He let me cuddle up to him. Lying on the top covers of the bed with Minty, listening to Northern Soul, reminded me strongly of when we first met. We'd lie in his bedroom together listening to tape recordings of his 'rare' records. He'd spend time telling me his top five 'current' Northern tracks, his top five 'oldies', his 'all-time' top five (which changed every week). I'd try to look interested. I had, however, considered his obsession adolescent, even alarming. When he was working for BR he was capable of spending his entire wage packet on a single record. To me this was an indication of how silly Minty could be. Particularly given that, when he eventually sold them to raise the deposit on our house, it turned out his 'rare' records weren't all that rare. Still, he *had* sold them and I know he hadn't wanted to. It was the first thing

Minty ever did that really impressed me. I didn't force him, or even suggest that he did it; he just did. It was a genuinely selfless gesture that, to me, proved how committed he was to our relationship. He *could* be mature, he *could* be serious and he *could* take responsibility.

I ran my fingers through my husband's thick, wiry hair. It wasn't always that easy to love him, but I did.

'I know something that you've got that Dave McVane hasn't.'

'Oh, yeah?'

'Hair. At least you've still got a full head of hair. He's been bald for twenty years.'

He smiled again, weakly. I'd made *some* headway, but I knew a sure-fire way to snap him out of his sulk. I nodded toward the CD player. 'What are your current top five Northern Soul sounds, Minty?'

He grinned: a big, lovely Minty-grin.

18

'It Really Hurts Me Girl'

The Carstairs (Red Coach)

MINTY

'Five: "Better Use Your Head", Little Anthony and the Imperials; Four: "I'm Gonna Change", the Velours; Three: "Cause You're Mine", the Vibrations; Two: "I Just Can't Live My Life", Linda Jones; One: "Do I Love You (Indeed I Do)", Frank Wilson. That's my *current* top five.'

Hazel smiled and nodded as I went on to list my top five from blue-eyed singers, my top five UK-only releases, my Wigan top five, my Blackpool Mecca top five, my Fanny's top five and, of course, my all-time top five.

'Frank Wilson is number one both in my current *and* my all-time top five,' I told her. She smiled and nodded some more.

Haze managed to get me right back in the mood, God bless her. She indulged me as I began singing along to the CD player and, when Edwin Starr's 'My Weakness is You' came on, I couldn't stop myself rolling off the bed and treating my wife to some comedy dancing. I'm lucky I suppose: I'm seldom long in the doldrums. Now I was in the mood to entertain.

'For one night only,' I said, 'live in Longwood Crescent, it's the man with the dancing love handles: Minty Trebor!'

Haze chuckled at my pelvic thrusts, executed with my

fingers interlocked at the back of the neck-brace. She laughed out loud as I began marching to the left and the right, high-kicking John Cleese-style and unbuckling my trousers. I let them drop to my ankles and then goose-stepped them off. I moonwalked backwards as I unbuttoned my shirt, waving it like a lasso above my head before sending it in Haze's direction. It covered her face and she pulled it off, laughing hard.

It was nice to see her laughing – she'd been very tense lately; more annoyed than usual by my 'immaturity'. She'd been preoccupied too, the way people are in soap operas when they're having an affair. She was using her dictionary more than ever. She's carried it ever since I've known her, of course, but she seemed to have her nose in it all the time lately and had even taken to reading it last thing at night. The John Grisham novel she started in March lay on the bedside table with the bookmark stuck at chapter two. When I asked what she was looking up she'd usually say 'everything'. I've always found Hazel's relationship with Mo endearing, but I was beginning to wonder if it wasn't becoming a bit . . . excessive? Still, now I had a chance to cheer her up.

'Look at these love handles go!' I cried, wobbling the flabby bulges of flesh above my waist. 'It's taken twenty years of Chicken Dippers to grow these babies!'

'More!' whooped Hazel.

I eased my boxers saucily over my thighs. Stepping out of them, I flicked them in the air with my foot, caught them and pulled them over my head. I sang along to the song through the flyhole and Haze rocked with glee.

I was feeling great now. Maybe I *was* better off than Dave McVane after all. He'd looked harassed and nervy today. And Haze was right: I *had* achieved things he hadn't. He'd spent his life spurning commitment, embracing good times rather than a family. The good times turned on him and now he had nothing in his life but a pickled liver. And as for Billy Peebles, it was selfish of me to think of his success in terms of my own comparative failure. I was always moaning about Nigel's self-centredness, but I was just as bad! Billy's success was fantastic news. OK, I did feel inadequate and I didn't need a dictionary definition to tell me that I felt unfulfilled too, but there was no point carping about it. I'd be better off *doing* something about it.

I turned my back on Hazel and wobbled my buttocks at her; she began screaming in mock disgust.

'One hundred and ten per cent British beef!' I bragged.

'Give us a nibble of your Yorkshire pudding!' cried Haze.

'Blowing Up My Mind' by the Exciters came on and I yelped with joy. Suddenly I was brimming with energy and, on an impulse, I leapt on to Hazel's exercise bike. For once it wasn't operating as a clothes horse. It's a pity because if it *had* been it might have saved me from yet another misfortune. Or do I mean accident?

I'm not sure why I was drawn to the exercise bike. I suppose I intended to cycle to the beat for a while, to continue the show. Grabbing the handlebars, I pressed myself high above the bike and let myself drop on to the moulded plastic saddle.

My dancing did for me again.

It wasn't my fault, it was the exercise bike. The height of the saddle is adjustable, you see: fixed to the end of a long rod which slides up and down inside a tube, in the manner of a telescope. The assemblage is held at the required height by a steel band that is tightened around the outer tube, like a jubilee clip. When I landed on the saddle it was at full height but the clip hadn't been tightened. The weight of my body brought it down hard and fast into the bike frame. It was an express, two-foot plummet and it drove the saddle into my coccyx with an appalling, nauseating crunch. My teeth clapped together and, as Hazel described it later, my head disappeared into my neck-brace.

Holy broken bones.

19

'Come As You Are'

Nirvana, *Nevermind* (Geffen)

TREBBO

Thursday had been a minger of a day. The only cool thing about it was that I'd managed to get Blubber-T off my back, at least temporarily. Tiffany had been a pain in the arse, though. I'd spent the rest of the evening round hers and the cheeky cat had the brass neck to ask if it had been me who broke into the clinic. The topper was that she threatened to pack me in if she found it *had* been me! I denied it, obviously, and in the end she gave me what she called 'the benefit of the doubt'. Maybe I was giving *her* the benefit of the doubt by not nixing our relationship!

By the time I got home it was five past midnight: Thursday was over at last and Friday was underway. The thirteenth! I wondered if things would take a turn for the better, or if this notorious date would live up to its reputation.

The gimmers had retired but, despite the hour, I could hear soul shite coming from their room. The beat was so strong it made the dust particles dance in the light of my bedside lamp. Shouldn't it be me playing loud music at midnight?

Instead of counting sheep I decided to read my copy of Kurt Cobain's *Journals*, picked up in a sale for £3.99. It's not one of those books you read all the way through – it's the size of a snooker table for one thing and you need to be Arnold Muscletits to hold it – but it's nice to dip in to. It has reproductions of handwritten extracts from his diaries and is full of the craziness and passion that you can hear in everything Cobain sings, even in his quieter vocals like on 'Heart-Shaped Box'. I love that song, the way he sings about 'eating cancer' and 'umbilical cord nooses' and still makes it sound like a love song. I put it on, thinking about his strange relationship with Courtney and how it was possible for love to be so full of contradictions. It made me think of Tiff. I wasn't sure if I loved her and I wondered what it meant that I'd never discuss my feelings about music with her. In a way it would feel wrong to admit to such passion with Tiffany; uncool. What does that say about us? She was a fellow Nirvana fan, of course, and she knew the lyrics to everything they ever recorded but, to my eye, she never seemed to actually enjoy their songs. She'd listen solemnly, occasionally saying something like: 'I think "Mr Moustache" is a critique of homophobia.' I'd reply by saying: '*What?*'

I got sleepy as I thumbed through the book and I began to think that I could get some kip. I set the volume on the bedside table, nixed the stero and the lamp and settled down. I was just drifting off, beginning to feel myself getting lighter, when a thunderous crunch came from the gimmers' room. It was as if someone had dropped an anvil through the floorboards and, had I not been wearing my beanie, my hair would have been standing on end. The crunch was followed by muffled shouting and swearing, the volume and tone of which implied the Div. Eventually the shouts were replaced by urgent talk and a great deal of banging about. The walls are pretty thick so I couldn't make out what was being said, but it was certainly a commotion.

The last time he made such a racket was when he dislocated his shoulder during a nightmare about arm-wrestling Dawn French. The Divette had had to drive him to Wesley at 3.30 a.m.

I banged my fist on the wall but, though someone killed the music, the loud yap continued. It was clear I wasn't going to be able to catch any zeds so I decided to seek my MP3. This meant getting out of bed and digging around for it in the computer room.

On my way I paused on the landing to listen in on the old folks: the Div was whining and the Divette seemed to be soothing him. Go figure.

In the computer room I found my player, still connected to the computer from the last time I downloaded some sound files. I switched it on to check the battery and noticed it was low. I needed the mains adaptor but couldn't remember where I'd put it. I tried the cupboard where we keep the paper for the printer. No joy. I scanned the shelves with their lines of CDs and computer mags. Ditto. As a last resort, I tried the deep drawer in the computer desk. I didn't imagine it'd be there because there's this unspoken rule that this is where the Div keeps *his* stuff. I opened it to find, not an adaptor, but an old timer's record case of the kind used to store 45s. I couldn't resist having a squint inside and, sure enough, there they were: his ten Northern Soul rarities, with their invoice. Most were American imports with the large round holes at the centre and all of them looked old. He'd hidden them here because the Divette avoids the computer room. She's convinced we use it for combing porn sites and says she's too afraid of what she might find. She must think we Blu-tack things to the walls. Of course a glimpse of Blubber-T's gangsta porn would freak her for the duration, but there was no chance of her finding this. Not even the Div was aware of the kind of surfing I did, before the coppers clued him in. This is because I have programs that untraceably delete my internet history, together with encrypted email. I like to stay one step ahead of the gimmers.

I replaced the sad 45s and continued my search for the adaptor. Eventually I found it in the eight-way trailing plug socket beneath the computer table. Penguin's nads.

On the way back to bed I was just in time to see the Div dart across the landing and disappear into the bathroom. I only caught a glimpse but he seemed to be holding a pillow to his arse. He was naked but for his neck-brace. Freakshow.

At breakfast the next morning the Div was white. He was more than white; he was the ghost of an albino Goth following a flour fight on a snowy day. He stood in the corner of the kitchen spooning yoghurt into his mouth. I noticed his legs were slightly bowed, as if he'd browned his strides.

'Piles?' I asked. I wouldn't normally speak, obviously, but I offered the comment on the off-chance it would nark him. In truth I'm not really sure what piles are. I just know it's an arse-related malady.

The Div, ignoring me, waddled over to the pedal bin and deposited his carton.

For some reason the Divette had a piss-taker's twinkle in her eye: 'Do you want me to run you over to the hospital just to be on the safe side?'

'No, I've told you already, no, no, NO!' He then left the kitchen with a horseshoe gait. I ignored them both from then on because I wasn't feeling on top form myself. I'd slept fitfully and the night had been punctuated by uneasy dreams. One featured a pack of Dobermann-sized degus within a weird, *Alice in Wonderland*-type world. I was the Mad Hatter and my mother and Tiffany, with the aid of the degus, were trying to hunt me down. They'd wanted to put me into a straitjacket.

I took two Anadins before I left for school.

The Div was still looking queer when, about an hour later, I clocked him at his lolly spot. I was with Dicey, crossing about a hundred yards up the road. He was in his crucifix, Angel of the North position as a line of mothers and kids trailed across.

'Your old man looks a bit weird,' said Dicey, squinting his eyes at him in the distance. 'Has he soiled his kegs?'

'I think it's piles,' I said.

'Freakshow.'

I noticed Collins and Jaybo across the way and gave them a wave. They're two of the coolest kids in our year.

'All right, Collo; Jaybo,' I called.

'Got any drugs?' replied Jaybo.

'Not today, Jay,' I said. 'Sorry, dude.'

'Later, then, Wankrag,' he answered.

I laughed. 'See you, dudes.' They didn't reply, just ambled in the direction of school, smoking and, every ten seconds or so, spitting.

'Twats,' said Dicey.

I didn't say anything – I was beginning to agree with him.

'They're real numpties, man,' he continued. 'They'll grow up to suckle the teat of the corporate whore. I don't know why you bother kissing their arses.'

Before I had a chance to reply I spotted Blubber-T about fifty yards away. He'd seen us too so there was no chance of giving him the slip. He pointed to our feet with what appeared to be a semi-devoured Mars bar – it was his way of saying we had to stay put. By the time he reached us the Mars was gone and he was mopping his lips with the tail of his raccoon-skin hat.

'It's about that gear,' he said, producing an Aero, 'the caps yow gid me last night.'

'Problems?' I said, preparing to bolt.

'Na, na. I was wonderin if yow could scower any mower, like?'

'Sorry, Dude, it was a one-off.'

'Yoam not fucking wi me?'

'No, Blubbs, straight up.'

'Fuck it,' he said, 'there's mower demand than I'd thought. I flogged the lot after I left yow.'

'Nice one,' I said, watching him dispose of the Aero in two mouthfuls. 'It looks like someone's going to have a sleepless night or two.'

20

Hazardous (*adj*)

HAZEL

It was possible that Minty had cracked his coccyx and, despite the fact that I'd taken the mickey out of him that morning, I would have felt happier if he'd gone to A&E. It was funny though. I'm not one to laugh at other people's misfortunes, but in this instance it was difficult not to. The 'accident' had left him with a ridiculous target-shaped bruise on his rear – a variously shaded collection of concentric circles. In all my years of nursing I've never seen such an impeccably shaped contusion: perfect rings within rings centred by an immaculate bullseye.

As I nosed the car towards the sign for the Broadway Ring Road I began tittering again. Tiffany was sitting alongside me.

'What is it?'

'Nothing, love, sorry.' I wasn't sure her stomach would be up to a discussion of Minty's backside. Besides, I wasn't entirely certain she'd see the funny side. As likeable as she is, there doesn't seem to be a humorous facet to Tiffany's personality. She smiles politely whenever she recognizes comic intent, but that's as far as it goes. Nigel is a bit like that too, although he used to laugh a lot when he was younger and I'd heard him guffaw at comedy TV shows while alone in his bedroom. But around us he's a miserable sod. Still, you can't blame people for not finding life funny, I suppose. Minty accuses me of being po-faced sometimes, but I prefer the word mature. Indeed, comedy aside, it was hard for me not to be annoyed at last night's events.

My husband seems to have too much energy: not the kind that compels him to do sensible things like mow the lawn or retile the bathroom, but the wrong kind of energy: the kind that's always spilling over into puerile exuberance. Nigel had sapped much of this as a toddler, but these days there's nothing to take the edge off it. I suppose that energy is another thing that makes Minty loveable, in a way, but it unnerves me: its potential mischief frightens me. It needs to be corralled and directed, but I'm not always up to that job; I was feeling less and less willing to cope with it. I had problems of my own.

I needed to see Kelvin again. Soon.

Tiffany and I arrived at the clinic to find Eunice already there. She was in the process of changing the degus' water.

I sent Tiffany to make the coffee and joined my colleague at the cage.

'The vet couldn't say for certain if their fur would grow back,' said Eunice. 'He said he'd never seen anything like it. Twenty years he's been practising, too.'

Their taste of amphetamine had left them emaciated, like a pair of little toast racks. With the amount of fur they'd lost they looked newborn: pink with a cartography of blue veins pulsing weakly beneath the skin.

'At least it's good to see them walking around again,' I said. 'I was worried the paralysis might be permanent.'

We watched Dec crawl with much effort to a tomato slice. When he reached it he merely rested his head on it.

'They don't look *too* bad, do they?' I asked.

Eunice gave me an incredulous look. 'No? Well . . . No, perhaps not *too* bad.'

'At least they're alive.'

'Oh, yes. In that respect, yes.'

Tiffany arrived at our side with the coffees. When she saw the degus she immediately began retching. She set the tray down on reception and covered her mouth with her cupped hands.

'Better take Ant and Dec into the spare office before the children start arriving,' I told Eunice. I accompanied Tiffany to the toilet where she vomited profusely.

Hearing tests are always a pain in the bum and the one I did that morning was no exception. Tiffany was with me observing (and presumably considering an alternative career to health visiting). The patient's name was Detroit (three stone, six pounds).

'Do you hear that, Detroit?' I asked the obnoxious three-year-old as I activated the sound machine. It was unlikely because for some reason he felt the need to stick his fingers in his ears whenever I switched it on. 'Just say, "Yes, Hazel" when you hear a noise from the noise machine, OK, pet?'

Detroit kept his fingers in his ears.

'Detroit,' said his mother, who was eating a packet of crisps, 'stop acting like a cunt.'

'Do you think Detroit's brother could stop playing that penny whistle?' I asked. 'It's difficult to conduct hearing tests when there's quite this much noise in the room.'

'Leonardo! I'll shove that thing up your arse if you carry on!'

'And maybe if you could stop crunching those crisps?'

'Fucking hell, darling, you don't want much, do you?'

'Well, no, actually.'

'I've had no breakfast, apart from a Mars bar and an Egg McfuckinMuffin!'

That'll account for the split in your leggings, I was thinking, as the door knocked and Joe put his head round, apologetically.

'Sorry to interrupt,' he said, 'but the police are here and they want to have a few words. It's about the break-in. They've spoken to everyone else . . . Eunice can take over here. They want to talk to Tiffany too.'

I wasn't exactly broken-hearted to leave Detroit and Leonardo, but I couldn't help feeling anxious as I followed Joe into his office.

Because of Joe's reference to 'they' I was expecting to meet two policemen, but only one greeted me. I noticed from the three stripes that he was a sergeant. He was much heavier than the blond kids who appeared yesterday: sixteen stone, ten pounds, I'd say.

'We've been asking everyone if they have any information that might help us determine who burgled these premises the other day.'

Tiffany and I both told him that we didn't.

'Are you sure? We'd appreciate anything – even if it's something you feel is trivial. You see it's *vitally* important we locate the drugs that were stolen.'

I was puzzled – the phrase 'vitally important' was surely unwarranted. 'Excuse me if I'm being naïve, or perhaps cynical,' I said, 'but I didn't think a bottle of slimming capsules would cause such a fuss.'

The sergeant glanced up at Joe, cleared his throat uncomfortably and said, 'It appears they're not slimming capsules.'

'What? But it said so on the bottle.'

'When we questioned Mrs Clackett about them yesterday we established that the capsules originally dispensed in that bottle had been . . . consumed. The capsules that were *actually* in the bottle were . . . are . . . something else.'

'What?'

'We're reasonably certain that in 1985 Mr Warren Clackett was involved in a break-in that resulted in the theft of certain chemicals from the University of Birmingham's research labs.'

'And you think . . . ?'

'Most of the drugs were recovered – they were found dumped in a North Walsall wheelie bin. They'd probably been discarded as useless. But it appears that some, the ones you retrieved from Mrs Clackett's daughter, were retained by her deceased husband.'

'Why those?'

'According to his wife he planned to sell them as slimming pills because the red and grey capsules resembled them so closely. He intended to peddle them out of his wife's old Duromine capsule jar.'

'I see. And are they hazardous, these stolen drugs?'

'It appears so. We contacted the university yesterday and they were able to tell us exactly what went missing.'

I looked at him expectantly.

'They were working on a range of powerful . . . I think they called them "depilates"?'

'Hair removal drugs?'

'Very strong ones for use with agricultural livestock. To save farmers shearing their sheep, among other things.'

'It would explain the degus' fur,' I said.

'Indeed.'

At this Tiffany began weeping. Joe put his arm around her and I explained to the sergeant how upset she'd been about the animals. The sergeant excused her and Joe escorted her out. I was beginning to get the impression that she wasn't cut out for nursing. Although her reaction surprised me a bit – I thought she was made of stronger stuff. Was something else bothering her?

'Isn't capsules a funny form for the drug to be in?' I asked, when we were alone. 'Animals don't take capsules, do they?'

'The boffins had been testing various delivery modes: injections, pellets under the skin, powder in their feed. But the capsules were made up by mistake, apparently.'

'So it's dangerous to humans, is it?'

'It's dangerous to animals, let alone humans. They discontinued tests because it had lots of nasty side-effects.' The sergeant took a notebook from his pocket and started reading. 'Paralysis, profound colic, bloated-tongue, fits, double incontinence, abdominal distension and about half-a-dozen other things I can't pronounce. And hair loss, obviously.'

'Am I going to get into trouble for this?'

'No, no. If anything you're a heroine, Mrs Trebor. Imagine what might have happened if those children had taken the drug. But clearly we need to find the capsules, so, to repeat, *any* information you might have would be useful.'

I felt as if I was in an episode of *The Bill* as I said the words: 'If I think of anything I'll let you know.'

When he left I consulted my watch. Four hours to go before Kelvin.

21

'Take Away the Pain Stain'

Patti Austin (Coral)

MINTY

I hadn't had a chance to look at the bruising on my backside yet but, judging from Hazel's remarks, it was pretty spectacular. I was praying the pain would subside before Fanny's kicked off. It stung with every footfall and, as a result, it took me twice as long to walk home from my lolly stint. It didn't help that on the way I had a spat with a woman speeding in a Mini Cooper. I shouted at her to slow down and she jammed her brakes on, climbed out of her car and squared up to me. She was bloody aggressive, not unlike the mad mullet bitch from Muncher's barbie. She asked me who the fuck I thought I was shouting at. I can usually put reckless drivers in their place, no problem, but that morning I lacked conviction. I suppose I just wasn't in the mood to argue. She told me that I had no authority away from my patrol point and she accused me of hiding behind my uniform.

'Take that fucking hat off and I'll fucking clock you,' she said.

It didn't seem to matter to her that I was wearing a neck-brace. 'I have the law on my side whether I have my hat on or not,' I said, 'and regardless of where I'm standing.'

'You're a prick,' she said, giving the peak of my cap a provocative flick before returning to her car.

I made a big show of taking her number: 'You'll be the fiftieth driver I've reported this year, love!' I shouted. In reality I knew that, this time, I wouldn't be arsed to report her: my mind was elsewhere. Plus I was exaggerating – I'd only reported thirty-eight drivers so far.

It was 10.15 a.m. when I arrived home. The phone was ringing.

'Minty?'

'Heya, Muncher.' I went to sit down on the stool beside the phone table but had to stand up again almost straight away.

'Good news, Mint, I've scored.'

'Fantastic!' I couldn't believe he'd managed it. 'How much did you get?'

'Enough for everyone.'

'Not red and greys by any chance?' I was thinking about the caps that Hazel mentioned had been swiped from her clinic.

'Duromine? I don't think there's any such thing these days, Minty. No, it's powder. Sulphate. I scored it from a local guy who an old mate put me on to.'

'You've come through again, you loaf-headed old bastard. How much do I owe you?'

'Twenty quid a wrap.'

'Nice one.' I went to sit down again but the hard stool soon created a throb that corkscrewed up the lower third of my back. I stood once more.

'Where are we gathering?' asked Muncher.

I tried to recall potential meeting places in Wolverhampton. Last time I'd been there Nigel was a nipper and we'd taken him to see *Aladdin* at the Grand Theatre. Russ Abbott was Wishy Washy. Our son had guffawed and applauded all the way through – shame he can't summon up as much enthusiasm for things these days.

'How about meeting in KFC?' I asked. 'I wouldn't mind trying some Chicken Nuggets. I'm told they're like Chicken Dippers but they –'

'Are you kidding? What are we, a bunch of fucking Girl Guides? I was thinking of the Dog.'

'And Duck?'

'How many Dogs are there? Of *course* the Dog and Duck. Like old times.'

The Dog and Duck was the pub we used to meet in when we were young. We'd always neck our gear in there before the doors opened at Fanny's.

'I don't think Dave McVane likes going in pubs these days,' I said.

'He can stand it for an hour. If he doesn't like it he can meet us inside. But tell him, if he wants any gear, it's the Dog.'

As soon as Muncher was off the phone, I went upstairs and switched on the computer. As the machine went through its boot-up procedures, I took the opportunity to slide open my special drawer and have a look at my discs. It was like opening a drawer full of Fabergé eggs. I removed the case and inspected my purchases. I selected a disc and, lifting it out of the case, read and reread the label. I then sniffed it: it smelt old and rare and lovely. When the Windows tune chimed I reluctantly returned the record to the box and the box to the drawer.

Standing at the keyboard I began to compose an email for Nipper Kid. I typed the following:

Nipper: we'll be meeting in the Dog and Duck at 8 tonight.
Muncher has scored some sulphate. Can't wait to hear those old songs again. That CD you emailed me is brillo.
  Keep the faith, Minty

I then deleted the line about the sulphate because it was incriminating. Then I deleted the line about the old songs because it sounded a bit girly, then I deleted the sentence about the CD because it sounded a bit gay.

I clicked on send.

Our email software can send messages to mobiles too so I texted Mac's phone, and the mobile number from Petey's business card:

Meeting in Dog+Duck at 8 4 a quick 1 b4 Fannys.

While at the computer I decided to search 'Billy Peebles' through Google. The piece in the *Reflector* had made me curious and, given his achievements, I felt sure he'd feature on the web. I immediately found his personal homepage. His biography made interesting reading. On leaving Walsall the Peebles family had lived first in Leominster then Warwick and Billy had become something of a scholar. In 1984 he was awarded a PhD in Human Movement Studies from Sheffield Polytechnic and almost immediately went into partnership with a shoe designer called Murano Del Piero. The two began a business designing and manufacturing footwear, with an emphasis on sports shoes. Billy bought his partner out in 1990 and then sold the company to Nike five years later. That's what had made him the big bucks. I found myself saying the phrase, 'one point seven million pounds' out loud.

Billy Peebles had a wife, Amanda, who was a consultant paediatrician, and twin boys, Adam and James. The boys were both studying medicine, one at Durham, one at Cambridge. Billy had been awarded his OBE in 2002 for extensive charity work, which included founding a training centre for disabled athletes. There were several photographs of Billy during his recent ascent of Mount Elbrus and it pleased me a little to see that he hadn't, as I'd imagined, done the climb single-handed, but had been a member of a rather substantial team. The site also included links to pages that explained the design of Billy's climbing boots, but I didn't bother reading these. Instead I went to Billy's hobby page and tried to follow a link to a website called 'Bonkers about Conkers'. I was disappointed to find it broken.

I spent ten minutes debating whether to send Billy an email but decided against it. What could I say? We'd been neighbours as kids but we weren't mates. I never even bothered to visit him in hospital after the accident, despite the fact that my mom and dad kept asking if I wanted to go. There was no emotional link between us, just a connection created by dumb chance.

I logged off.

I still felt as if my arse was in the jaws of a crocodile, so I decided to have another bath in the hope that this might ease the pain. It did, a little. This done, I was keen to check the state of my bruise. I needed a good mirror, but the one in the door of the bathroom cabinet would only have been suitable had I been seven feet tall. Nigel had a mirror in his room but, reluctant to stray into that nightmare, I gingerly descended the stairs with my towel around my waist. First I tried the mirror that Haze uses to do her make-up but, after bending and twisting about with it for five minutes, I was forced to concede it was too small. Then I tried the reflection of the TV. This offered an acceptable angle, but not the necessary definition. The only other mirror was on the chimney breast in the dining room. I contemplated taking this down but figured that, if I knelt on the dining table, I could position myself so that my bum was roughly the same height. I'd then be able to examine myself on all fours by gazing backwards between my legs. I dropped the towel and climbed on. Sure enough,

with the sunlight streaming through the front bay window, I managed to get a good look at my backside. Haze
was right: the target-shaped bruise was amazing. It was
startlingly vivid: dark at the centre, where the bruising
was at its most intense, with rings of a lighter shade
radiating away from the middle, from black, to blue, to
light green. I stared at these for a while, captivated, despite
myself, by their strange, Saturnian symmetry.

There was a tap on the window.

Oddly I didn't think to move. I turned my head to the
side and saw that it was Inspector Smiles. He grinned and
gave me the thumbs up. It's difficult to be casual when
you've just been caught eyeballing your own anus but, as
nonchalantly as possible, I rolled myself off the drop-leaf,
reknotted the towel around my middle and answered the
door.

On my way my heart pounded, not just with humiliation, but with fear. What did he want? Had they found
something incriminating on our hard drive? I wished I'd
never given them permission to copy it. Smiles said it was
voluntary so I should've told them to shove off. Who knew
what filth Nigel had downloaded. They wouldn't be able
to press charges, though, would they? He was only a kid.

This time Smiles was on his own. I was certain this was
a good sign. 'Yes?' I asked nervously.

'Lost something up there, sir?' As before, his sarcasm
was completely devoid of humour.

'Look, I know it must've appeared a bit odd but –'

'There's no need to explain, Mr Trebor, I've seen it all
before.'

'I'll have to take your word for it. Now, could you tell
me what you want *this* time?'

'I'm merely reporting back, sir.'

'I trust you found nothing untoward on our hard drive?'

'No, no, sir. As I said, it was merely for research. If we'd suspected anything serious we'd've confiscated all your equipment.' He made no effort to move, just stood on the doorstep, with a slightly creepy half-smile on his face. I felt like a tit in my towel, but I didn't want to invite him in. I found him rather frightening.

'Is there anything else?'

'We *did* find some encrypted email.'

'What's that?'

'It's email that it's taken us two days to get into, and even now we don't fully understand it, but we're pretty certain it's your son's correspondence with someone called Blackcountrygangsta@hotmail.com. We're not absolutely certain but the exchanges seem to be making reference to drugs. The word mephitis kept cropping up.'

'Who? What?'

'Mephitis mephitis is the Latin term for the North American striped skunk.'

'So?'

'Skunk is what the young folks call pot, sir. We don't have enough evidence to charge your lad with anything, though. I really just wanted to reiterate the importance of you and your wife keeping an eye on him, before he gets into *serious* trouble.'

Were there any further humiliations I'd be experiencing thanks to that little shit?

'I'll be sure to have a word with him, inspector.'

'Very wise. I've got a son your age so I know all about it.'

'Does your son give you problems?'

'He doesn't get a chance, Mr Trebor; we keep him in line with a firm hand.'

'I see.'

'We never have any trouble from him. We've raised him to respect his parents and the Lord God.'

'Congratulations.'

'There's no need to be sarcastic, sir. All I'm saying is that discipline is key. It pays not to compromise when a young person's character is at stake. And you don't have to go further than the Good Book if you're looking for a moral code. You have to drill it into them from an early age. The world's full of crooks you see: drug dealers . . . perverts.' His face was reddening slightly and, like before, he seemed to be working himself up into a vexed state. He raised a fist uncomfortably close to my face. 'I don't like drug dealers almost as much as I don't like perverts,' he said. 'They're fucking bastards (Lord forgive me for swearing).'

He didn't move his fist and it felt as if he was pondering the implications of pushing it into my nose.

I swallowed. 'If I see any drug dealers or perverts I'll let you know.'

Smiles nodded slowly and took some deep swallows of air. I wasn't absolutely sure the guy was stable and I began to wonder if it might be an idea to report my concerns to his superiors. He tended to speak the word 'pervert' with a little too much rancour for my liking. I was reminded of a serial killer I once read about who'd spend his spare time beating his privates with a copy of Billy Graham's authorized biography.

At last Smiles lowered his fist and patted me on the bare arm with his large, hot hand. I couldn't help but shudder at this incongruous intimacy.

'*Have* you considered parenting classes? It's never too late, you know.'

When Smiles finally left I needed to calm myself down. To this end I cooked myself a snack-sized helping of Chicken Dippers and found a nice comfortable cushion to sit on while I watched the lunchtime local news. First there was an item about the mortality rate at Wesley-in-Tame hospital, then one about someone having eaten a chocolate exhibit at Walsall's New Art Gallery. These were followed by an announcement on behalf of West Midlands Police.

'Walsall police have issued a warning about a number of capsules stolen recently from South Walsall Health Centre. This potentially dangerous substance has been mislabelled and it's feared it could fall into the hands of drug users. Anyone being offered the red and grey capsules should contact the police immediately on the following number.'

Stroll on: fame at last for Hazel's clinic.

22

'Downer'

Nirvana, *Insecticide* (Geffen)

TREBBO

Me and Tiff were side by side on the settee as the gimmers dressed for their all-nighter.

I was shitting my strides.

The police warning about the capsules had been on *Midlands Today*. It was also broadcast on Heart FM, Beacon, Radio WM, BRMB and Saga. The Divette, meanwhile, had done nothing but yap about her interview with the cops. It seemed the drugs I'd yoinked were the plutonium of the medical world. I was terrified they'd nix someone – I couldn't bear the thought of anyone dying as a result of something I'd done. To be faced with that prospect was the biggest downer of my life.

I needed to contact Blubber-T but I was too scared. Dicey was on the case. I urgently wanted to know what he'd done with the gear. I'd be freaking until I knew that whoever he'd flogged it to could still steam a mirror.

For her part, Tiff appeared to have twigged that I'd got something to do with the missing caps. She seemed able to smell guilt on me. She kept looking at me the way the Divette used to when I went through my phase of yoinking money from her purse. She could never prove anything and there was no chance of me fessing up, but she'd always let me know she knew, just by giving me a look. It was like some kind of Vulcan guilt glare. Can all women do this, or is it just the Poppins Brigade?

The Div was also on my back. The coppers had sniffed my email. I wasn't too worried because, even if they'd managed to decode it, there was nothing they could pin on me. My online correspondence related merely to weights, prices and pick-up times. These were to Blubber-T, who accessed them at a cybercafé in Bloxwich. The Div had been whispering threats to me about it, telling me we would be 'having words', but I responded by singing, 'Nine hundred and ninety quid' at him. In truth it was more of a chant than a song, but it had the desired effect: it shut his mouth. Mind you, he'd perked right up again during the last hour. He was soaking his pants about the all-nighter. His hair seemed four inches taller.

'Eh? Eh?' said the Div.

His neck-brace was off and he stood before us in a pair of enormous brown flares. The legs were cone-shaped, like a couple of wigwams. With these he sported a red and white bowling shirt tucked in to the top of the trousers. The latter's tourniquet waistband looked agonizing.

'Eh? Eh?' he repeated. 'What do you think? They fit me like they did in the seventies!'

'Yeah? So you were a lardarse in the seventies too, were you?' I terminated my query with a yawn.

'Behave! They're just a bit snug, that's all.'

'Change,' said the Divette, who entered the room wearing a black canvas skirt, black T-shirt and flat black shoes.

'What's wrong with this gear?'

'Please let him wear it,' I said, flicking a Juicy Fruit into my mouth with my thumbnail, 'if only as a service to comedy.'

'Change,' went the Divette.

'I repeat, what's wrong with the clothes I'm wearing?'

'They make you look like a tit,' said the Divette.

The Div appealed to Tiffany: 'You'll tell me the truth, chick. Do I look that bad?'

Tiffany, straight-faced as always, nodded gently and the Div was forced to concede to popular opinion. He left the room and ascended the stairs muttering.

When he reappeared he was a wearing a Reebok polo shirt and a pair of black jeans. These were straight-cut, cigarette-leg Wranglers and, again, they were two sizes too small. From a distance they looked like Lycra tights.

'OK, Nigel,' went the Divette, 'we're going to be gone all night. We're trusting you to behave like an adult; so you're not going to let us down, I hope?'

'Please don't leave me home alone, Mommy,' I said. I'd've come up with something more sarcastic but my mind was on the drugs.

'And Tiffany,' she continued, 'don't let him talk you into staying the night.'

'Don't worry, Mrs Trebor.'

I tutted and concentrated on watching a *Midlands Today* feature about the increasing influx of handguns into the Black Country from Eastern Europe. I pretended to be fully engrossed and, when the gimmers left, I didn't bother to say goodbye.

'Have a nice time,' said Tiffany.

As soon as they split I repaired to the shitter and got Dicey on his mobile. It rang so many times that I thought it would switch to answerphone but, at last, he picked up.

'Trebbo?'

'Well, what's the score?'

'Blubber-T says he flogged them to a bloke he knows. He wanted the gear because a bunch of his mates are going to some kind of reunion in Wolverhampton.'

'Fanny's?'

'It might well be.'

'Christ, that's where my old folks are off to tonight.'

For a second I found myself worrying about them, until I remembered they'd seen the news and knew all about the warning not to take any red and grey caps.

'Blubber-T's lost his cobbler with you, man,' said Dicey.

'Bollocks to him.'

I heard the doorbell ringing and the doorknocker knocking simultaneously.

'What do you mean "bollocks to him", man? He's a mentalist!'

'Dude, Blubber-T's the least of my problems. If someone goes tits-up from those caps and they're traced back to me, I might spend the next five years being chased around the showers. *Someone might die because of me, Dice!*'

I heard Tiffany answer the door. There was a muffled conversation followed by a scream. I clicked Dicey off and exited the bathroom. As soon as I was on the landing I saw it was Blubber-T. He'd got Tiffany and was shaking her.

'Weer is e? Weer is e? Dow cowing fuck wi me, bitch.'

'Oi, you fat cunt, leave her alone!' I could hardly believe I'd said it.

Blubber-T immediately began crunching up the stairs, floorboards wailing with every step. Alternative courses of action zoomed through my head. I could run and lock myself in the shitter. That was my strongest impulse but the drawbacks occurred to me straight away: first, I'd look a coward in front of Tiffany; secondly, Blubber-T was unlikely to go away even if I *did* lock myself in the shitter; and thirdly, and this was the clincher, there's no lock on the shithouse door. The Divette removed it last year after Minty knocked himself out on the bath taps.

Instead I went to boot Blubber-T in the face.

He easily avoided my kick and it glanced ineffectively off his furry hat. He caught my foot and yanked my leg towards him, bringing my arse down on the top step of the stair with force. Still holding my leg, Blubber-T began walking backwards down the stairs. I was compelled to follow, my backside hitting the steps, followed by my shoulder blades and the back of my head. I was conscious of how uncool this must look but I couldn't worry too much about it because I had to concentrate on not biting my tongue off.

When we reached the bottom I was touched to see Tiffany start hammering her fists on my assailant's back, but it was like butterfly wings on a buffalo. I worried he'd hit her so I told her to jack it in.

'Tiffany,' I said, 'go into the living room.'

'I'm calling the police,' she said.

'No! I'll deal with this. You go into the living room and shut the door.'

'You'd better not hurt him, you bully,' said Tiff. This was the most insulting I'd ever heard her be to anyone.

'Do as yower girlfriend says, bitch,' he told her.

When she'd gone I instantly stopped acting hard.

'Dude,' I said, 'how was I to know?'

'Yow've cowing fucked with me,' he said, producing a palm-full of Maltesers and slapping them into his mouth. 'No one fucks with me in my yard.'

'Stay cool,' I said, 'no one's going to take those capsules. There've been warnings on every local news programme. They'll end up getting flushed down the shitter.'

'I broke the caps up and shifted the gear as sulphate, day I?'

'Wha?'

'I sold it as cowing powder, yow mutha!'

'If my mom and dad take any of that stuff I'll kill you!' I found myself saying.

'Yow wha? I'll fuck yow up, bitch,' he said, and he pocketed his Maltesers and made to hit me. I managed to evade the blow, though, and, forgetting my vow to avoid fights, I popped a punch in his face. It didn't hurt him, my fist just skimmed his sweat-slimed spots, but he was so startled I was able to give him the slip. I reached the kitchen in three bounds and pulled a carving knife out of the washing-up bowl.

Blubber-T continued to advance on me, albeit warily. He was an orange-suited giant, incongruously huge in our house, but I tried my best to keep my cool. It generally stands me in good stead.

'Listen, dude, this is doing no good,' I said, holding the carving knife at arm's length in front of me. It was dripping water and strawberry cheesecake topping on to our kitchen tiles. 'We've got to use our heads.'

'If yow pull a cowing knife on me, bitch, yow'd better mek sure yow kill me.'

I wondered if Blubbs really believed his corny dialogue. 'Look, man,' I said, 'you're an intelligent guy, right?'

'Wha?'

I dropped my arm to my side so that the blade of the knife was pointing at the floor. Something the Divette told me about dealing with bullies is that it's always worth flattering them. 'You're a smart person, dude. There's no point us losing it with each other. You know as well as I do what you've got to do. You have to go to Fanny's and warn the guy you sold the powder to.'

'Ay?'

'You need to stop them dropping the gear, man.'

'I cor. I've got business in Dudley tonight.' He retrieved his Maltesers, tipped another pile into his chocolate-stained palm and wolfed them.

'Listen, dude, if anyone dies from taking that stuff the

only person who'll be in more trouble than me will be you. You know it.'

I looked him in the Ray-Bans and tried to adopt my sincerest expression. I noticed that the muscles beneath the skin of his fat face were quivering slightly and it struck me that Blubber-T was scared. This unnerved me even more: if Blubbs was losing his cool, what chance had I of maintaining mine?

'Ar, I s'pose,' he said.

'I can put this knife down now, can't I, mate?' I called him mate instead of dude, hoping to win his trust. I wondered how many GCSEs you need to be a hostage negotiator.

'Yowm coming an all.'

'My parents are at that club, dude, how would I explain my being there to them?'

'Yowm cowing coming, or else I dow gew. Mutha.'

It didn't take me long to conclude that it *was* probably important I went. This was a serious business, after all, and I couldn't trust Blubbs to take care of it on his own. 'What's the quickest way of getting to Wolverhampton?'

'I've got wheels outside, a I?' he said, and, having polished off the Maltesers, began unwrapping a CD-sized Wagon Wheel.

At that stage I didn't bother asking how the porky sixteen-year-old managed to be driving a car. Too much was happening. And I needed to deal with Tiff.

I entered the living room with the intention of calming Tiffany down before I left. I was impressed to see that she was already pretty chill.

'I've got to go out for half an hour, Tiff.'

'I'm coming,' she said.

'No, Tiff. I've got a bit of business to take care of, just me and Blubber-T.'

'You're going to Fanny's to warn someone not to take the drugs you stole from your mother's clinic.'

'I er . . . er. Don't be silly.'

'I have ears, Trebbo.'

I don't know why I imagined she wouldn't be listening to us. That's what I'd've been doing, after all. Perhaps I thought that Tiffany would be too much of a Poppins to eavesdrop.

'Look, Tiff,' I said, 'I'll explain why I yoinked the caps later. Now I need you to stay cool while I –'

'I'm coming.'

23

Reunion (*n*)

HAZEL

By the time we hit Wolverhampton it occurred to me that it was a mistake bringing the car. Every car park in town appeared to be either closed or full. I had to leave it about half a mile out of the centre in a dodgy red-light area called the Royal. As a frequenter of Jerome I had all the available security devices fitted: alarm, immobilizer, steering lock, gearstick lock, reinforced security-coded windows, locking wheel-nuts, removable CD fascia and an intercontinental satellite tracing system. But I still worried about my trusty Micra.

I was on edge generally and take-off terror nagged at me like a vague nausea. I'd been due to see Kelvin earlier in the afternoon but in the end he couldn't make it. He'd left a message on my mobile which I'd replayed seven times at the clinic. My mobile weighs three ounces – two ounces heavier than me, or at least that's how it felt.

As we made our way towards the city centre a young girl approached us on a mountain bike and asked if Minty and I fancied a threesome for forty pounds. I declined on Minty's behalf and she shrugged and began adjusting the tension on her chain.

'Don't they stand on street corners any more?' I asked my husband.

'Hee hee,' he said. He hadn't been listening because his mind was firmly fixed on the night ahead. I could tell how preoccupied he was as several cars had roared past us and he didn't even comment, let alone shout at them.

We arrived at the pub to find Dave McVane pacing outside. He'd do two or three revolutions, take a look through the glass door of the bar, then do two or three more revolutions. He seemed to be undecided about entering.

'Mac, me old mucker!' said Minty, when we were close enough.

He looked up, spotted us and grinned. 'Minty, Haze,' he said, 'how are you both? I was just hanging around till someone else showed up.'

'Scared to be in a pub on your own, Mac?' said Minty. 'Not like the old days.'

'Ha ha, yes,' said Mac, with a laugh so hollow you could hide a rhinoceros in it.

Entering the Dog and Duck was like walking back into the seventies. The tables were Formica-topped and the seats were covered in padded red vinyl. There was a Space Invaders machine in the corner beside a tin advertisement sign saying 'Beer at Home Means Davenport'. The entire room was nicotine-lacquered and polka-dotted with cigarette burns. There were even cigarette burns in the ceiling. Despite it being a Friday night the clientele consisted solely of two elderly men, one or both of whom seemed to have been fitted with a leaking colostomy bag.

'Better grab a table before the rush,' said Minty, gesturing toward the empty room. 'What's everyone having?'

I asked for a vodka and Red Bull and Mac opted for an apple and mango J_2O. The barmaid, an enormous suicide blonde (sixteen stone to sixteen three) asked, 'Who is Red Bull and what the pigging hell is J_2O?'

You'd've thought we'd asked for a beaker of badger's

tears. We adjusted mine to vodka and orange and Mac's to Coke.

'Puffs, nonces and Judies drink Coke,' one of the old men told Mac. He then coughed a cough that to my trained ear said chronic emphysema.

'Puffs, nonces, Judies and alcoholics,' said Mac, who seemed to be in an aggressive mood. 'If you drank more of it yourself, twat-face, maybe you wouldn't be such a reeking half-wit. *OK?*'

'My daughter-in-law works in a cake shop,' said the old man.

Mac, realizing he'd overreacted, composed himself a little and the three of us sat down.

'A smidgeon on edge, are we?' I asked him with a smirk.

Mac smiled. 'How are things with you, Hazel?' he said. 'Still ferreting for nits in the pelts of the impecunious?'

'They all shave their heads these days, Mac,' I said. 'And how about you: still pissing the bed and choking on your own vomit?'

Mac and I have always enjoyed our banter.

'Chin, chin,' he said, raising his Coke.

'Cheers,' I said.

Minty handed round a packet of Planters.

Mac is the only one of Minty's old mates who kept in touch with him after we were married. He was best man at our wedding and godfather to Nigel. I like him a lot, despite our ritual insults, but there's also a sense in which I don't really approve of him. He's never properly grown up, in my view. He's spent his life avoiding responsibility and that doesn't sit well with me. I'd seen him with some lovely girlfriends but he'd always reject commitment. A man needs a family, in my opinion – I can't take them seriously otherwise. I also felt him to be a bad influence on

Minty. Whenever my husband went out on the town with Mac he used to come back legless: the following morning I'd find him unconscious on the sofa, wearing a traffic-cone hat. We don't see so much of Mac since he quit the sauce, though, and it was clear that he was finding sobriety difficult. Minty told me that a few months earlier Mac had had a fist fight with someone over whether or not Jim Morrison was a significant poet.

I'd only taken two sips of vodka when a guy in a cheap-looking two-piece suit arrived, carrying an executive brief-case. His thick brown hair was coiffured in a curious comb-back, centre-parted style which seemed to be held in place by a half-dozen cans of hair lacquer. It looked like someone had constructed a sculpture of an arse by gluing together ten thousand Twiglets.

'Petey Fleetwood! Over here, mate!' My husband bawled this, even though it would have been impossible for Petey to miss us in that practically empty hole. It was a sign Minty was becoming overexcited. That worried me: it's when he's overexcited that he's at his most juvenile. In this mood he doesn't need a lollipop to show me up.

Petey joined us after purchasing a Campari and soda and ignoring a disparaging remark from the old fellow at the bar.

'You and Petey remember each other, don't you?' Minty said to me.

'Of course, how are you these days, Petey?' In truth I didn't recall too much about the man. I'd scarcely spoken to him in my early days with Minty.

Petey gave me a nice smile as we shook hands.

'What's in the attaché case,' asked Mac, without for-mally greeting Petey, 'your hair-rollers?'

'My business papers and a few samples,' he said. 'I didn't want to take the chance of leaving them in the car. I've parked near the Royal. I was approached by a prostitute on a mountain bike.'

'Did you try and flog her some Amway?' asked Mac.

'No,' said Petey, as if this was a serious question.

A few minutes of listening to Petey made it obvious that he wasn't the sharpest arrow in the quiver. He was another classic example of a sad, single, childless man. Where Mac's problem had been created by sustained self-indulgence, I guessed that Petey's was a consequence of social ineptitude; that and stupid hair. Still, I knew that Minty and Mac both had a strong affection for him.

'Do you think those two blokes at the bar might be interested in taking advantage of the Amway enterprise initiative?' he wondered.

There was a pregnant moment before Mac said: 'Your mom still lets you walk around with hair like a Pygmy's hut, I see.'

'Muncho the Munch!' cried Minty, before Mac got the chance to get on a mickey-taking roll.

Muncher and Suze entered. I was somewhat relieved to see another woman.

'Hey, Minto,' said Muncher, slapping my husband on the back, 'you're sitting a bit lopsided on that stool, aren't you? What's the matter, got piles?'

'No, Munch; it's, wait for it, a cycling accident!'

'How's little Danny?' I asked, cutting Minty off before he could launch into a comedy account of his stupidity.

'Absolutely fine last time I checked,' said Suze, 'although I haven't been able to get a recent update because Julie was out when I phoned this evening.'

'Probably at a black mass,' said Minty.

I should've known mentioning Danny was a mistake. It gave my husband a chance to narrate the barbecue incident to Mac and Petey. He told it as if he were relating the plot of a *Police Academy* film and I could see this pissed Suze off. The four blokes laughed hysterically throughout, but Suze was dour. I didn't want her to get the wrong impression about my husband; she might assume that he wasn't worried about Danny, but that would be a mistake. What was lacking was his sense of propriety, not his capacity to care.

'I'd keep out of Julie's way if I were you, Minty,' Suze told him. 'The woman's gunning for you. She was trying to find out where you live but I managed to put her off.'

Minty began a pantomime of biting his fingernails in mock fear. This news worried me a little, though: I didn't like the thought of Danny's mom searching for our address. The last thing we needed was for her 'Me Mother' tendencies to get out of hand. I thought I'd better change the subject again, for the sake of my blood pressure: 'Who else is coming tonight?'

'Nipper Kid,' said Minty, 'and here he is!' He stood to shake the hand of a bloke who'd just entered. His face looked slightly familiar from my distant youth – another of Minty's old crowd who'd briefly entered my peripheral vision as a young woman.

There was a protracted period of backslapping and where-you-been-all-these-years-mating, followed by a lengthy discussion of what all their mutual acquaintances were doing these days: who'd married whom; who'd died of drugs overdoses; who was still 'on the scene', who'd lost his hair, who'd grown breasts and so on.

'I fancy the loo, Suze,' I said. 'You coming?'

As we passed the bar, Petey Fleetwood was there ordering himself another Campari and soda. I caught his conversation with one of the aged barflies and he actually *was* trying to sell him Amway.

'If you're not interested in becoming an Amway executive yourself,' he said, 'maybe you'd like to purchase some of our products? I have a couple of samples in my case: Amway Breath Spray, for halitosis; Amway Squirt-and-Play foot odour treatment –'

'How about some Amway Brown-Away skid-mark remover?' said Mac, popping up at his shoulder. 'It smells like the old git could use some.'

'I've got funny-shaped plumbing,' said the old man.

Suze and I hurried to the Ladies. Inside there was only one cubicle so Suze went first.

'Anything suspicious so far from Mike?' I asked, to cover the embarrassing sound her wee made as it hit the water.

'Actually, no,' she said. 'I confronted him about it earlier on. I gave him a warning not to do anything daft and he was quite reassuring. He told me he'd do nothing to mess up what he has with me and the kids – he says his dealing days are long gone.'

'Well, there you go.'

There was a pause. 'What are you searching for in your dictionary?'

Suze's phrase 'searching for' was interesting. Kelvin had used it when he commented on my habit the day before. He thinks my dictionary is a search for simplicity of the kind that comes from the plainest, *Mini Oxford*-style definitions. I looked up and laughed to see that the loo door was still closed. Was I that predictable?

'"Porcelain" and "tap",' I said, dropping the book back into my handbag. 'I think we should try to relax and make the most of the night.'

'Sounds like a plan,' she said. 'What's the worst that could happen?'

24

'Be Young, Be Foolish, Be Happy'

The Tams (ABC Paramount)

MINTY

'Right,' said Muncher, as soon as the women were out of the way, 'I've got sulphate for those that want it. I've split it into twenty-pound wraps. A wrap should do you for the night.'

'I'm having slight cash-flow problems,' said Petey, returning from the bar with his Campari. 'You wouldn't consider taking some domestic hygiene products in lieu of cash?'

'Fuck off,' said Muncher, not unreasonably.

'It's a problem you have to face when you have your own business,' said Petey. 'All my capital is currently tied up.'

'In the meantime what are you doing for cash?' asked Mac. 'Do you still hire your hair out to "Ripley's Believe It or Not" museum?' This kind of mickey-taking might sound hostile to the uninitiated, but it wasn't really. It was light-hearted banter; it was the way we'd always been with each other.

'Do you think that old bloke at the bar has pooed his pants?' Petey asked, changing the subject.

'Fuck that,' said Muncher. 'I want to know who's up for a wrap before the birds get back.'

We all handed over our twenties, including Petey, who managed to dig out a note despite his cash-flow problems. Muncher had split his entire stash five ways and I could see he was relieved to get rid of the lot.

'What time should we do this stuff?' asked Nipper, who, despite being a regular on the scene, hadn't dropped any gear since the 1980s. 'I've forgotten the drill.'

'I'm taking mine before we get in,' said Muncher. 'I can't afford to get collared with any gear if the DS happen to be searching people.'

'Nor me,' I said, 'as a council worker.'

'Would the mayor snap your lolly over his knee?' asked Mac.

'Well, hardee har,' I said. I thought about mentioning the fact that, that very afternoon, I'd actually taken a step closer to a better job. My manager had phoned to return my enquiry about a supervisor's post that was about to be advertised. He said I had an excellent chance of getting it, if I applied. I'd known for a couple of months that the post might become vacant but, initially, I'd been ambivalent. It was nine to five for one thing, so my free time would be as good as gone. It was office-based too, which I wasn't keen on. Plus my duties would be purely related to budget and man-management, rather than accident prevention. Worst of all it meant change, which – pathetic as it sounds – was daunting after so many years. But the pros undeniably outweighed the cons: more money, a foothold on the local government promotion ladder and, above all, a humiliation factor of zero! I didn't say anything to Mac, though, because I hadn't mentioned it to Haze yet.

The women returned and killed our drug-chat. We began grilling Nipper Kid about the nature of Northern Soul in the twenty-first century and he told us about his trips to modern all-nighters, all-dayers and even weekenders around the country.

'I think I'm too old for all that malarkey,' said Mac. 'I don't even know if I'll be able to stay the course tonight. I'm forty; I once spoke to an insurance salesman who told me that's a bad decade for men. Elvis Presley was forty-two when he exploded on the shitter!'

'Oh, I'm sure you'll last the night,' said Muncher, giving him a knowing wink that made both of the women glare. Luckily Nipper pulled out a packet of old photos which distracted us. There was a great one of Petey taken after his hair caught fire at the Mecca in 1979 – he is sitting with four wet beer towels wrapped around his head, looking glum. Mac's standing behind pretending to warm his hands on the freshly doused coiffure. There was another of Muncher being chased down a Wigan backstreet by an irate milkman. It was early morning and Munch had just purloined a bottle of pasteurized from his float. He's running towards the camera and there is a cartoon look of terror on his face. There was also one of me and Mac having a mock fight, using our Adidas bags as clubs. I remember that occasion well. Mac accidentally caught me under the chin with his bag and it almost knocked me out. I'd angrily unzipped it to find that it contained sixteen cans of Banks's bitter.

We had another round and I began to get a nice lift from the beer. It had a welcome anaesthetic effect on my arse bruise and my neck felt pretty free too. Mac, however, didn't look comfortable. Within twenty minutes he'd torn every beer mat in the vicinity to shreds and he kept staring at the optics like Oliver Reed after a fortnight in the Sahara. Every time he sipped his Coke he grimaced. Another slight annoyance was Petey, who kept trying to turn the subject around to Amway. We all took the piss but he wouldn't shut up. Mac tried again.

'For fuck's sake, grow up, you ponce. Amway survives because daft tits like you buy their business packs and the dream that you're going to recruit other Amway "business" people. It's a pyramid scam. Admit it, if you've sold anything at all it will have been to your mother!'

This was like water off a duck's back to Petey. 'OK, Mac, OK. We know that none of us have been as successful as you. After all, you're the one who wrote the book that the *Walsall Reflector* called "mildly diverting"!'

Everyone guffawed but Mac. His eyes seemed to bulge with the effort of controlling himself. In the old days he would've laughed this off and then wisecracked Petey into a gibbering heap, but in his current condition (sober) it wasn't so easy. I could see the muscles in his jaw tightening. I could see his colour rising. I could almost hear his hands sweating.

'FUCK IT!' he yelled, rushing to the bar and almost knocking one of the old codgers off his stool. 'Give me ten triple fucking brandies!' He was panting as the gormless barmaid tried to assess whether or not he was serious. 'In a straight glass!' he added.

'I think it's time we went round to the club,' I said.

It took Muncher and me all our strength to wrestle Mac away from the bar. At one stage he climbed over it and almost managed to lock his mouth on to one of the optics. I had to stick my finger in his eye in order to force his compliance. Once we'd subdued him we dragged him out into the street while Hazel talked the barmaid out of phoning the police.

Usefully, after the commotion, Haze and Suze decided to use the Dog's bog again, which left us time to neck our gear. The sulphate provided a valuable distraction for Mac. He tipped the contents of his wrap into his palm and half snorted, half ate the lot. He resembled a clown I once saw who smashed a custard pie into his own face.

I poured mine into two piles and snorted them off the back of my hand like snuff. Nipper opened his wrap and licked away at it like the lid of a yoghurt pot. Petey was the least discreet. He rolled up one of his business cards, sprinkled a line of powder across his briefcase and snorted it up cocaine-style. This made me nervous.

'That looks a bit obvious, Petey,' I said. 'Try to remember you're in a public place!' It wouldn't do much for my new career plans if I got busted and it began to occur to me that perhaps this wasn't the most sensible thing to be doing, at my age. I glanced around for CCTV cameras and prayed that Haze wouldn't suddenly appear while the tit was re-enacting the closing scenes of *Scarface*.

Fortunately, by the time the women emerged arm in arm from the pub we'd dropped all the gear. The only sign of it I could see was a barely discernible fleck of powder beneath Mac's twitching left eye.

I had forgotten my concerns by the time we reached Fanny's and there was a knot of excitement in my stomach as we approached the door. It looked much the same as it had twenty years before. It still bore the old sign – the name, 'Fantasy Rooms', written in black calligraphy on red perspex; the bulb behind it unlit as it always seemed to be in the old days. Along the kerb outside was a line of motor-scooters, many of which were adorned with multiple mirrors.

The Fantasy Rooms occupied the second storey of the building, while the ground floor had been used for various things over the years. In our day it functioned as a greasy spoon café called Bangerlicious. We'd drop in first thing after the all-nighter for a coffee. Our stomachs would be shrunken from slimming pills and the whiff of bacon would turn us shamrock green. Since then it had been a record shop, a video rental shop and a shop selling iron collars for Staffordshire bull terriers. These days, however, the bottom floor seemed unused and empty.

'What's going to happen to this place anyway?' I asked Nipper.

'They're demolishing the whole row of buildings to make way for an extension to Wolverhampton City College – it's going to be a hairdressing academy.'

'Hey, Petey,' said Mac, still twitching, 'here's a chance for your barber to retrain. They might teach him to use scissors instead of a fucking hay-baler.'

'Baldy,' said Petey.

'*Touché.*'

You need to ascend a flight of stairs to get to the club and, as we climbed, they seemed a bit narrower than they used to. In fact the whole building felt smaller – a bit like returning to your old infants school with its tiny desks and bogs the size of teapots. At the top of the stairs sat a woman behind a table, taking money. We each handed over our tenners and she slid them into her metal security box, before stamping the backs of our hands.

'Blimey,' said Petey, 'the last time I had the back of my hand stamped I was writing love letters to Valerie Singleton.'

'Don't you mean John Noakes?' I quipped.

'More like fucking Shep,' said Mac, slapping something invisible away from his left shoulder.

The music was audible even before we entered. The muted thumping of the beat gave way to a roar of sound as Nipper pushed through the double doors that led inside.

The dancefloor was already packed despite the early hour: it was only nine o'clock and all-nighters don't usually get going till later. In my day many of them didn't open their doors till midnight, but Fanny's differed, running from eight till eight. It was only fitting that this closing-down event should run the same course.

A hundred heads bobbed to the beat of 'Nothing Can Help You Now' by Lenny Curtis.

Looking around, I saw that the average age of the dancers must've been forty. Certainly there weren't too many people under thirty. However, as coincidence would have it, one group of younger folks I did spot included the student nurse I'd met, Kylie. I led our party towards them – they were clustered together in a recess off the main room where, away from the speakers, it was possible to converse. Kylie greeted me like an old friend, saluting and planting a Bovril-scented kiss on my cheek. This made me feel great and reminded me of what the scene used to be like. People you hardly knew would treat you like long-lost siblings.

Fanny's didn't have an alcohol licence so Mac began to relax a bit. When he got the round in it consisted of seven bottles of Coke. I drained half of mine in one go: the fluid would be useful because amphetamines really dehydrate you. I could barely wait for my buzz to kick in.

25

'Dumb'

Nirvana, *In Utero* (Geffen)

TREBBO

I was shocked to see that Blubber-T was driving a smart car. I don't mean smart car as in attractive car; I mean a smart car as in the size of a rollerskate car. It's difficult to conceive of a vehicle less appropriate for him save, possibly, a unicycle. Not only was it pint-sized, it was a colour I've since seen described as 'peach puff'.

'It's me old lady's,' he said.

'You mean it's your woman's car?' I was surprised. I found it impossible to entertain the notion that Blubber-T had a girlfriend. In fact it was difficult to imagine what kind of girlfriend it would be physically feasible for him to have. Even J. K. Rowling doesn't have *that* kind of imagination.

'It's me old woman's car.'

'Your bitch's car?'

'Watch yower mouth, mutha, it's me mutha's!'

'It's your *mother's* car?'

'Ar, it's me cowing mutha's, mutha. Get over it!'

He went on to explain, between nibbles of Wagon Wheel, that his parents were out for the evening in his dad's car and he was making illicit use of his mother's wheels. Later he planned to take a trip to Dudley, though his reasons for doing so weren't forthcoming.

Watching him climb into the tiny two-seater was like watching a brontosaurus mount a midget's clog.

I got in alongside Blubbs while Tiff squeezed into the impossibly tiny space between the seats. Chocolate wrappers littered the interior and there was a box of Liquorice Allsorts on the dashboard. He popped a pink and white Allsort and gunned the engine. A gangsta rap tune immediately started up at full volume: 'Livin' in a Hoe House' by Hoez with Attitude. He wound down the side window and, with his right arm hanging out of the car, pulled sedately away. As we travelled, Blubber-T tapped out the beat on the outside of the driver's door, giving other motorists the finger whenever they sounded their horns at him. This was a regular occurrence, particularly on narrow roads, as his speed never exceeded twenty miles per hour.

'Maybe we should go a bit faster?' I suggested, but Blubber-T ignored me. He hearsed along as if he was cruising the hood, on the verge of perpetrating a drive-by.

'What are we going to do when we get to the club?' asked Tiffany, speaking from behind her knees.

'Look for the guy Blubbs sold the powder to.'

'What about your mom and dad?'

'I'll try and keep a low profile; with any luck they won't see me.'

'I'm coming in too.'

Of course she was. Just as I was keeping an eye on Blubber-T, so it felt like Tiff was keeping an eye on me. It was as if she didn't trust me to get this done. Mind you, at the speed we were going the all-nighter would be over and the dancefloor littered with corpses before we even made it out of Walsall. We crawled along Treece Street with a line of traffic behind us a hundred yards long – parked cars on each side of us meant that overtaking was virtually impossible. It doesn't take much to turn a motorist into a mad farmer and, whenever one *did* manage to overtake, we'd be treated to a bawling face full of blood vessels. It wasn't until we reached the dual carriageway that the huge tailback had a chance to pass. We attracted some incredulous looks as it did so: the sight of Blubber-T's huge form hunched in this confined interior must've had them glancing around for the Guinness Book of Records' inspectors.

When we reached Wolverhampton we combed the streets for ten minutes before finding somewhere to park. We settled on a badly run-down area called the Royal. Even as a veteran of Walsall's chav alleys I'd be wary of walking around this place on my own.

On our way towards the city centre an old bag approached us on a mountain bike and asked if we were 'looking for business'. Tiff and me ignored her but a curious expression came over Blubber-T. He waddled to the gimmer and, after looking her up and down, asked for her business card. He told her he was thinking of going into the gangsta porn racket and wondered if she fancied joining his 'stable of bitches'. She told him that she'd given her last business card to 'Donald pigging Trump' and left, wheeling her bike at her side. I caught a glimpse of a leopardskin thong as she swung her leg over the crossbar and began pedalling away.

'Does anyone take that idiot seriously?' asked Tiff.

Though we were walking some distance ahead of him, I still felt the need to shush her: 'Keep it down, Tiff,' I hissed. 'He's dangerous.'

It was the closest I've seen Tiffany come to laughing out loud: 'He's wearing a bright orange tracksuit and a raccoon-skin hat!'

'I know, I know. But he commands respect.'

'From who?'

'Me for one.'

'*He* commands your respect and your parents don't? How come you're so smart and yet you act so dumb?'

'Perhaps I'm not so smart.'

Tiffany shook her head. 'You're a funny guy, Trebbo.'

If I'm that funny, how come you never laugh, I thought.

26

Maturity (*n*)

HAZEL

Fanny's was pretty much as I expected: full of middle-aged people who've never managed to mature. Mostly in their forties, the patrons reminded me of those ex-Teddy Boy pensioners who still wear drape jackets and grease their hair with chip-fat. They are saddos trapped in that one period when their lives seemed to mean something. I've never been able to understand this. Is it the badge of belonging they crave, or youth? Are they subculture sheep, or deluded Norma Desmonds? It made me want to scream! What the hell is wrong with people growing up?

There *were* young people around – Minty was giddy with excitement as he introduced us to Kylie and her mates. But many of the other youngsters seemed to have come by mistake. There was an obvious irony about them. They were dressed in a self-consciously retro style: blokes in three-button suits and winklepickers; girls in Mary Quant miniskirts and false eyelashes. They looked as if they'd been expecting a sixties disco and they regarded the older dancers with a sarcastic twinkle in their eyes. It was my guess they'd be gone before midnight.

It was a fifty-fifty gender mix on the dancefloor, but the blokes didn't dance with the women. Dancing here was a private affair not a mating ritual. When for me that's one of the best reasons to dance, a prelude to sex. Everyone seemed to be wearing badges. Pin badges, patch badges, iron-on logos. They said things like: Wigan Casino: The Spirit is Still Alive; Wigan Casino: Keep the Faith; Wigan Casino: The Dream Lives On. And if they weren't wearing badges they had tattoos: Northern Soul: A State of Mind and a Way of Life; Northern Soul: Keeps on Burning; Northern Soul: The Eternal Beat. Why, I wondered, did they feel the need to wear these words? Were they telling the world who they were, or were they reassuring themselves? Mind you, I couldn't help feeling a bit hypocritical – who was I to criticize this fetish for words, with Mo in my handbag?

I became aware that I was scowling at the dancers and made a conscious effort to pull myself out of my bad mood. It was hard, though. For one thing, I'd found a set of scales in Fanny's ladies toilet and, given that on this occasion I wasn't accompanied by Suze, I weighed myself. The pound I thought I'd gained according to my own bathroom scales (which I'd confirmed that morning on a set of clinic scales) didn't register. In fact on the Fanny's scales I was two pounds lighter than I expected. I knew the Fanny's scales must have been inaccurate, but it still irritated me. And this wasn't the only thing.

It was pretty clear the blokes had taken something. When me and Suze joined them outside the pub, Mac looked as if he'd had his face in a bag of flour. I'm not sure if Suze noticed, though, and for her sake I didn't mention it. Mind you, I guessed it would become pretty evident when they started yapping like Eunice after too many cappuccinos.

At one point nurse Kylie joined Suze and me at our table. I'd been watching her dance and had to admit that she moved well. I envied her her energy. She seemed to know a lot of people and every time she spotted an acquaintance, she'd salute them. She was damp with sweat, which wasn't surprising because, along with her cotton circle skirt, she wore a denim jacket. Also, under her sandals, she sported white ankle socks. As if this wasn't enough, she was drinking hot Bovril from a vacuum flask.

'Did *you* ever go to Wigan Casino with your husbands?' Kylie asked, still panting slightly from her dancing.

Suze shook her head, but I admitted to having been once.

'Wow,' said Kylie, 'I wish I could have seen it.'

I noticed that she too wore lots of badges. Hers mainly advertised the all-nighters of the past: Wigan Casino, the Twisted Wheel, the Torch and the Catacombs. I knew from Minty that all of these places closed down years ago. Once more I couldn't help wondering why this young girl would want to wear such badges.

'You're a nurse, aren't you, Kylie?'

'A student nurse, yes,' she said, beaming.

'Have you ever seen a case of septic haemorrhoids?'

'Well . . . no, I don't think so. Not *septic* haemorrhoids.'

'When you do, pay close attention: it will give you some idea of what Wigan Casino was like.'

'Ha ha ha,' said Kylie, 'I don't believe that.' She drained her cup of Bovril and hurriedly rescrewed it to her flask as a record she liked started up. 'See ya,' she trilled, and hopped and skipped back to the dancefloor. I instantly felt like a bitch for patronizing her. She seemed a decent enough girl. But she hacked me off slightly and I'm not sure why. For a moment it occurred to me that I might be jealous.

And not just of her youth. Tiffany must be a couple of years younger than Kylie but somehow she seems more mature. Or perhaps serious is a better word. (More like me?) She's not overenthusiastic about silly things. You wouldn't see her wearing as many badges. You wouldn't see her salute anyone. It's difficult to imagine her even dancing – she's far too reserved. Reserved is the very last word you could apply to Kylie. It was my guess that Kylie would grow up to fall into the 'Fun Mother' category and Tiffany the 'Exacting Mother'. The former let their kids get away with everything; the latter have unbending moral codes. I'm not sure which is the best kind; neither guarantees that kids will turn out the way you want. As parents go, I suppose Minty was the fun one and I was the exacting one – and Nigel despised us both.

'I've just seen your Nigel's girlfriend over there,' said Mac, returning to our table after fetching himself another Coke.

'What?'

'Tiffany, isn't it?'

'Yes, but you couldn't have seen her – we left the two of them watching telly. This is the last place on earth you'd see either her or Nigel, I can assure you.'

'I'm pretty certain, Haze.'

'You must be mistaken.'

'I'm always sober these days, remember.'

'Perhaps you were temporarily "mildly diverted"?'

'Hey, Petey,' Mac called towards the dancefloor, 'Haze wants to buy some Amway Fanny Spray. If she uses plenty of it she hopes the graffiti in the men's bogs will become less insulting. Given time.'

Petey looked in our direction but wasn't able to make out what Mac was saying. He grinned and gave him the finger on the assumption that he was taking the piss.

Mac smiled and winked at me and I returned both before watching him head off towards the dancefloor. Knowing Mac made me aware that it *was* possible for people to be nice underneath. Beneath his arch and occasionally toxic exterior I knew him to be a decent bloke. Still, sobriety didn't seem to have helped him with his hallucinations.

27

'There's a Pain in My Heart'

The Poppies (Epic)

MINTY

I recalled from the old days that the more you move around, the quicker the speed takes effect. I'd danced to half a dozen numbers, though, and still no joy. Nevertheless I was enjoying myself. Kylie was dancing nearby and kept smiling at me and shouting jokes. She was full of beans; a bit eccentric, perhaps, but likeable. You'd meet a lot like her on the *old* Northern scene: people who had enthusiasm for the music and weren't afraid to show it. They weren't bothered about looking cool or self-conscious about enjoying themselves.

Because my buzz still felt a way off I decided to check out the record bar. As I walked around the perimeter of the dancefloor, I clocked Muncher and Petey among the dancers. Petey had taken his suit jacket off and looked less of a dick in his shirt sleeves and tie. In fact, because the tie was quite narrow, he had something of a mod look which would have been a respectable image in such a club twenty-five years ago and wasn't entirely out of place now. If only his hair was less stupid he'd look pretty good. As it was he resembled a hedgehog impaled on a chopstick. Idiot that he was, however, I felt a strong surge of fondness for him, and for Muncher too. They were both real characters and it was brilliant to seem them again.

Northern Soul dress style has always been a difficult thing to pin down. In the early seventies all the blokes wore flares on the scene but, when I got into it in the late seventies, the fashion for flares was being replaced by piped-peg trousers, particularly among modern soul and funk fans. Like lots of people, though, I'd still wear ultra-flared Spencer's Soul Bags because it was a sign of allegiance: flares for traditional Northern fans; pegs for funksters. Besides, I liked the way flares flapped around my legs when I danced. These days there doesn't seem to be a single style – there were people in boot-leg, straight-cut and flared trousers. Some of the women wore trousers too but the majority wore skirts. For me, women always look better in skirts when they dance.

The bright, fluorescent light of the record bar was a stark contrast to the semi-dark of the main dance area. Record bars were always my favourite territory. As record bars go, this was quite modest, with only about half a dozen dealers present. Records were on display in boxes along a line of tables while elsewhere in the room people passed around smaller, portable boxes of singles. I inspected every box. There were several records I would've bought if I'd had the money. Still, there would be other all-nighters for me.

I turned my back on the last record box and absorbed the atmosphere of the room. A wave of euphoria began in the pit of my stomach; the speed kick must be on its way. This is how it would always start for me: with a surge of joy, a rush of anticipation about what I knew would follow. In a few more minutes, I thought, I'll start accelerating. Everything will speed up; I'll begin thinking more quickly, so much so that my mouth won't be able to keep up with my thoughts. Linford Christie won't be able to keep up with my thoughts. My body will feel too small for me and my spirit will reach beyond me to mingle, throb for throb, with the driving rhythm of the music.

Fuck it, I thought, I've got to get on the dancefloor.

I left the record bar and moved back out into the main room.

As I danced, my limbs moved fluently and my neck didn't feel as vulnerable as I thought it would, given that this was my first night without the brace. I *did* get the occasional shooting pain up my lower back, but even this wasn't too distracting.

They were playing a lovely old tune by the Poppies called 'There's a Pain in My Heart' and the dancefloor was jammed. Dancing near by me was a tough-looking skinhead in a muscle vest. He was massive and, because of his size, stood out. He stood out too because he sang loudly and unselfconsciously along with the lyrics. When he came to the line, 'there's a pain in my heart', he put his fist to his chest. I know the lyrics aren't profound, but they had this big guy close to tears. I'd seen it a million times in the old days: hard men sharing the pain in their heart. Despite his size, if he'd done this anywhere else in Wolverhampton then the pain in his heart would be literal, rather than metaphorical. But here he was free to be his big soppy self.

I noticed across the dancefloor that Mac and Nipper had joined Muncher and Petey. Mac spotted me and grinned. His bald head was glistening with sweat and it was then it occurred to me how hot I felt myself. It must have been over a hundred degrees in the club. I decided to dance the Poppies tune out and then return to our table for a swig of my Coke.

I could feel the sweat making my scalp itch, which sometimes happens to me when I get hot. I have dry skin and I suffer quite badly from dandruff. Hot and humid atmospheres make it worse. I remember when we were in Orlando my itching head almost drove me insane and, in the end, Haze went out and bought me some special medicated conditioner from a drug store. I'd pretended to be mad because it cost thirty dollars and, for that much, I'd said I'd be happy to shave my hair off. Haze knew I was lying: I love my hair like Jordan loves her jugs.

After a while the itching became so intense that I couldn't help but scratch my head. This is a difficult action to incorporate into one's dancing so I did it as swiftly and discreetly as possible. Lovely. There's something almost sexually satisfying about scratching an itch. A delicious quiver ran through my head and set it tingling. It was a strange but lovely feeling, like wearing a skullcap made of spiders. The drug was beginning to work its magic, it seemed, albeit in an unusual way.

Nevertheless I decided to take a breather and I began to weave my way through the dancers. Mac was pumping away energetically to the track. Every inch of his bald, Easter-egg head was beaded with sweat, as if bubble-wrapped. When the beads ran into his eyes he clamped them shut, squeezing and thumbing the moisture away.

When I reached our table it was empty but for Haze and Suze.

'Enjoying yourself?' asked Haze.

'Fantastic,' I said. 'Are you two not dancing?'

'We haven't got your energy, Minty,' she said.

'There's still plenty of peep in my whistle, even at my age.'

'Clearly.'

'What's that supposed to mean?' I hoped it wasn't too obvious I was kissing goodbye to my tits.

'Nothing. Except that you've got the whole night in front of you. You don't want to wear yourself out too early.'

'Don't you worry about me,' I said, swigging my Coke. It was warm, but it took the edge off my thirst.

As I swigged, Haze gave me what I call her 'mother' look. It's one of those looks she gives when she's inspecting people to assess whether or not she should be worried about them. It's the look she gives Nigel when he's moaning about being ill. She'll take the mick at first, because he's always trying it on, but if he keeps it up she'll give him this look. Her irony melts away and her inspection becomes penetrating and diagnostic. Depending on her conclusions she'll either continue taking the piss or book a trip to Lourdes.

'What?' I said.

'Are you all right?'

'Why shouldn't I be?'

'Why do you keep scratching your head?'

'I don't.' I took my hand away from my scalp, noticing several strands of hair spiralled around my sweaty fingers. This was another depressing sign of my advancing years. I wiped my hand on the arse of my trousers and returned to the dancefloor.

The best plan would be to keep out of Hazel's way while the speed rush was at its most intense. It made sense for me to stay on the dancefloor and work my energy off there. Mind you, the amphetamine high I'd thought was just around the corner a few minutes earlier hadn't really materialized. In fact I was beginning to feel a bit strange. The itching in my scalp seemed to be getting worse; also, my guts felt a bit weird.

'One Way Out' by Martha and the Vandellas came on and this lifted me a bit. It was one of my all-time favourites from the old days, but even this didn't get me going the way you'd think it would. I noticed that some of the lads were looking a bit off-colour too. Mac was ashen and Muncher had stopped dancing and was staring into his cupped palms. I danced over and gave him a cheery slap on the back.

'How's it going, loaf-head?' I shouted.

He turned to me with a look of incomprehension.

'Are you OK, mate?'

He didn't reply, just held his cupped palms out for me to see what he'd been looking at.

It was as if he'd been sifting through the sweepings from a hairdresser's floor.

'Christ, Munch!' I said, at the same time becoming conscious again of the intense itching in my own scalp. I gave it another scratch and then forked my fingers through my hair. I looked at my hand in incredulous horror: it was as though I was holding a toupee in my fist.

Stroll fucking on!

At that point a profound odour of shit assaulted my nostrils. Muncher noticed it too because he wrinkled his nose and glanced around for the source. It was the distress on Mac's face that gave it away. Inexplicably he'd been on his knees and was now struggling to his feet. He only managed to get halfway up before he dropped to one knee and clutched urgently at his stomach.

I put my fist of hair in my pocket and went to Mac's assistance. I'm not sure why I decided to keep the hair. Mac held out his arm for me to help him to his feet and I took it. When he tried to rise, though, his legs buckled and he dropped back to the floor. By now the stench was overpowering and an empty space began to form around us.

'I've shat my fucking strides!' Mac hissed.

'Jesus! What's up with your legs?'

'Fuck knows; they've gone. I've got no fucking strength in them!'

Then, above the closing bars of Martha Reeves, I heard a scream. I turned to see Nipper staggering towards the edge of the dancefloor; he'd collided with a female dancer and now he was moving like someone who'd been shot in the legs, yet who was still desperate to convince himself that everything was normal.

Within seconds I felt a clench in my own stomach – as if someone had it in their fist and was milking it like a cow's teat.

28

'Smells Like Teen Spirit'

Nirvana, *Nevermind* (Geffen)

TREBBO

It wasn't till we actually reached Fanny's that it occurred to us that we'd have to pay to get in. Conveniently, though, we climbed the stairs to find the door guarded by nothing more than a snoozing gimmer at a table. She was sitting with her chin on her chest and a steel money box open in front of her. As we passed, Blubbs went to yoink a fistful of takings but Tiffany jabbed him in the flab and gave him a warning stare. The look on his face could've killed a pigeon but Tiff just glared right back at him. She's got guts, I'll give her that.

Inside Fanny's it was a trip to Sadsville via Div City. There were so many old gimmers dancing you'd've thought we were at a wedding reception. There were beer-bellied blokes with their shirts tucked into their trousers! Many dancers had beer towels hanging from their belts, which they used to mop up sweat. There were people dressed as skinheads and people dressed as mods. There were old blokes in cap-sleeves and old women in sandals with, wait for it, ankle socks. There *were* a few slightly younger people around but these were either retros dressed like Austin Powers or clueless young fogeys with no discernible sense of fashion.

And yet.

There was something about the place that interested me. We stood back from the action, observing the dancers and, as I watched, one girl in particular caught my eye. I'd say she was only a couple of years older than me but she was right in the thick of the dancing. She was dressed like a geek but, in an odd way, she looked OK. At certain points during a song she'd do these spins, a bit like the Div's. Her circle skirt would fly out and up to reveal her white knickers; she'd spin and spin, hopping in circles on her toes until suddenly stopping dead. This would coincide with a point in the song where there was a drum-break or a shift in pace or rhythm. Everyone would clap once and the geek's skirt would snap shut around her legs. Her timing was flawless. She was fascinating and impressive. The beat seemed to shape her movements, and yet it was clear she was in control. It was sexy – her dancing made the music sound good.

When the tune finished she left the dancefloor and walked in my direction. Several people called to her and she'd respond by saluting. Her name was Kylie. This suited her, perhaps because of her smile. She had a lovely smile. Smiley Kylie. There was something about this girl.

At first I couldn't spot the gimmers but, after scanning for a while from the shadows, I caught sight of the Div. He kept scratching his scalp so much you'd think his nads were on his head. He'd probably washed his hair in Domestos again. At one point my 'uncle' Mac walked past us and I slipped behind a conveniently placed column. Tiffany wasn't quick enough, though, and I saw him do a double-take.

'Can you see the bloke you sold the powdered caps to?' I asked Blubber-T. He stared gormlessly across the expanse of the dancefloor.

'I cor,' he said, folding a knot of liquorice lace into his mouth.

'Why don't you have a wander round, dude, see if you can clock him?'

Blubbs nodded the way a tortoise might if asked to do something it found only partially agreeable and he lumbered away. Surprisingly the spotty twenty-stoner in the orange tracksuit attracted only a couple of second glances and these came from the fashion-conscious retros. The gimmers were tuned exclusively to the beat.

'Hey,' said a very thin gimmer who, seemingly out of nowhere, appeared beside me and Tiff, 'how's it going?'

'Wha?'

The gimmer had spiky blond hair and a face that glowed white in the dark. He was so thin he could have been made out of drinking straws – a look that was hardly complemented by the fact that he wore a muscle-vest. He twitched furiously and chewed as if trying to kill a wasp with his tongue. His mouth made a smacking noise that was clearly audible over the music: kerchersmick, kerchersmick.

'I'm Chalky,' he said, sticking out his hand. Kerchersmick, kerchersmick.

I ignored him but Tiffany took it. 'Hello,' she said, 'I'm Tiffany, and this is Trebbo.'

'It's good to see some young folks on the, kerchersmick, scene,' said Chalky. 'Do I know your mom or, kerchersmick, dad?'

'Well, I –'

'Cause I've been on the scene years, see, kerchersmick, kerchersmick. I was there at the start, see. The Wheel, the Torch, the Catacombs, Va Va's, kerchersmick, kerchersmick. Wigan, Cleethorpes, the Mecca, kerchersmick, the Locarno, St Ives, the Ritz, kerchersmick. Stafford, Keele, Hundred Club, kerchersmick, kerchersmick.'

'Well, we're not really –'

'Kerchersmick. I've known all the jocks in my time too.' After listing all the Northern Soul DJs he'd met, he gave us an account of all the soul singers he'd seen and where; he then listed the varieties of slimming pills he'd taken. There were many. He went on to inform us, rather incongruously, that he'd had the same toothbrush since 1976.

'Please leave us alone,' I said.

'No, kerchersmick, problem,' he said. 'I'm off me fucking shed tonight as it goes. Kerchersmick. Have a good one.'

And he slipped away as swiftly as he'd appeared. I noticed that the badge on the back of his muscle-vest said 'Soul Survivor'. Barely, I thought.

'Do you think that man is on drugs?' asked Tiff.

'Da*haa*.'

Dahaa, indeed. Chalky was something of an eye-opener. He offered a glimpse of how drugs – which had always appeared rather glamorous to me – can turn you into a gibbering wanker. It was sad that there was probably a time when Chalky wasn't a wanker and even sadder to think that he probably didn't realize he'd become one.

I turned again to the dancefloor. I looked for the girl, but she was out of sight, hidden among the throng. The floor was packed and I was struck by how much people seemed to be enjoying themselves. Whenever I dance I have to adopt a stupid expression to let everyone know that I'm not being serious. The only people doing that here, though, were some of the young retros. They weren't dancing like the others but were poncing about, taking the piss. The people who seemed to be having the best time were those who'd given themselves up to the music. They were tragically uncool, and yet they impressed me. They seemed to get as much or more from their music as I did from mine and they were twice my age. That had to be wrong!

Then I heard the scream. My first thought was that Blubber-T had punched someone, but he was nowhere to be seen. A commotion followed: a couple of shouts and more screams, only partially smothered by the music. Tiff and I strained to see what was going on, but couldn't.

'Come on,' I said, 'let's move a bit closer.'

We shoved up to the edge of the dancefloor, making sure we were still concealed by dancers. The Div and Mac seemed to be dancing in a way that was weird even for them. Both were crawling around the floor using only their arms. Another gimmer in a cap-sleeved shirt was also poleaxed – he looked to be in a state of shock and just kept pulling at his hair with his hands. Even from ten yards away I could see that great tufts of it were coming out with every pull. Alongside them was another bloke with a square head. He too was doubled up, seemingly in agony.

I noticed Blubber-T standing off to the right of the commotion, observing the square-headed dude. I caught his eye and he nodded, grimly.

'It's the fucking caps, Tiff,' I said. 'Me dad and his mates have taken the caps I stole from the clinic. We've got to get out of here.'

'What? *What?* We can't, we've got to help them. We've got to find your mom!'

'I . . . I can't! I could get put away for this and so could Blubbs.'

'But you've got to let them know what they've taken. There's surely a better chance of treating them if the doctors know what drugs they're dealing with.'

What she said made sense, I knew that. But I was scared.

'No.'

'You have to, Trebbo!'

I saw the Divette emerge from an alcove. She spotted the Div and rushed over to him.

'No,' I said, and I began dragging Tiffany away.

'What kind of selfish, stupid pig are you?'

'The kind that doesn't want to go down, Tiff!'

'People could die! Your *dad* could die. Don't you love him?' There were tears in Tiffany's eyes, together with a look of disgust. Was it that look that changed my mind? Something did, because, though my Evil Puppeteer yanked and yanked and yanked at my strings, I moved towards my parents.

29

Shit (*n*)

HAZEL

The look on Nigel's face when he approached me that night in Fanny's reminded me of the look on Minty's just after he'd kicked Danny on to the barbecue. A mixture of panic and shame, shot through with fear. In fact, it was almost like looking at the *same* face and, as had happened several times over recent weeks, I glimpsed the power of the pod that had shaped these Trebor peas. The shock of the similarity almost outweighed the shock of him being there at all.

'It wasn't my fault,' shouted Nigel, in a voice on the verge of cracking.

'It's the defleecing drugs, Mrs Trebor,' said Tiffany. 'We think Mr Trebor's taken the defleecing drugs.'

On hearing this Suze ran at Muncher and began kicking at his prostrate form. 'You promised, you bastard,' she cried. Kneeling, she grabbed him by the collar of his shirt and shook him. He was pale, limp and, as his square head bobbed, hair floated away from his scalp like the seeds of a dandelion clock. Eventually Suze collapsed, weeping on to his chest. She moved when Muncher projectile-vomited a mixture of lager and Coke four feet into the air.

'My God,' said Tiffany.

Minty was also in trouble. He lay in the foetal position, so buckled by spasms that he seemed to be kneeing himself repeatedly in the throat. I put my hand on his arm and called to him.

'Minty?'

The foetus turned towards me, still spasming, and I took his head in my hands. Instinctively I wiped a film of sweat from his forehead and managed to thumb half his left eyebrow clean from his face. He bucked again and I heard a rasping noise from his rear.

'Minty, how much did you take?'

'I've beshat myself,' he said, and started crying. He clenched his eyes tight and tears pearled from their creases.

'Minty, you've taken the defleecer haven't you? The capsules?'

'I didn't realize. It was an accident!'

He opened his eyes leaving most of his lashes stuck to the damp skin above and below their sockets. Momentarily this gave him a grotesque, wide-eyed expression, not dissimilar to Liza Minnelli in *Cabaret*.

'My skin!' he whimpered. 'My skin's on fire, Hazel!' He began pulling at his shirt. At first I tried to stop him but, when it was clear he was desperate to get it off, I helped him. I peeled it away from his body – it was soaked with sweat and thick with coils of matted hair from his chest and back. Looking around I noticed that Minty's mates were shedding their clothes too. Muncher had his shirt off, Mac was down to his *South Park* boxers and Petey Fleetwood to his Y-fronts. The latter was in a particularly bad way. He sat lean and white on the dancefloor clutching his stomach, sporadically vomiting and wailing. Beside him on the varnished boards lay his clothes and, perched on top of the pile, his hair: its style virtually intact, like a discarded bird's nest.

I looked around for Nigel and at first I thought he'd gone till I noticed him beyond the dancers, most of whom were completely oblivious to the chaos. I saw him take a swing at a huge boy in an orange tracksuit. Tiffany pulled him away and the boy departed, shouting something about having business in Dudley. I wasn't completely certain but he appeared to have a raccoon on his head.

Minty's screams rose again and I almost joined him when I saw what was happening to his stomach. It seemed to be inflating before my eyes. Absurdly I began rubbing his back as I would a baby with wind and Minty screamed at the contact of my palm on his skin. He began tugging at the top of his jeans and I helped him unbutton them.

'Do you need to take these off too?'

'My legs hurt,' he wailed. 'My skin *burns*!'

Minty's problem was compounded by the fact that his jeans were a size too small, another symptom of his reluctance to admit he's getting old. He tried to speak again but began retching, adding to the pool of semi-digested Chicken Dippers on the floor.

'Try to take them off, love.'

He bucked and retched some more.

Thankfully, just a matter of minutes after Tiffany phoned them, the paramedics arrived. Not even their appearance caused a discernible pause in the dancing and they moved with difficulty through the throng of muscle-vests, bowling shirts and naked, sweaty torsos. The dancers were totally lost in music. Could nothing stop them?

I briefed the ambulance men as quickly as I could and they immediately called for backup. By this time Minty's screams were frightening. His stomach was massively distended and he complained that his jeans were agony against the burning skin of his legs. The paramedics began trying to free him but it was hard – they were ridiculously tight.

When, after a considerable struggle, they finally managed to wrestle them down, his underpants came too; worse, the tug on his trousers coincided with one of Minty's violent spasms. I've never heard a medical professional scream with as much volume as when my husband's knees snapped up to his chest and a spume of liquid faeces fired into the air. It should've been me screaming – boiling excrement splattered my forehead, nose and cheeks.

Perfect, I thought. Now two people had shat in my face: the helpless child that was my son and the grown-up child that is Minty. It's not what you hope for from your loved ones.

The paramedic gave me an antiseptic wipe as, thankfully, Minty's convulsions became slightly less intense. But there was no let-up in the intensity of the music: the relentless thumping provided a bizarre, infuriating soundtrack to the proceedings. The diameter of the space around us increased by a yard but, as I mopped my nose and cheeks, most dancers danced on. One exception was a young girl in a black minidress that had the words Tamla Motown emblazoned on the breast. She gave me her boyfriend's beer towel to help mop up the mess. I thanked her, hoping she wouldn't notice the brown, Jackson Pollock-like pattern that peppered her silver tights.

Most people would assume that Minty could do nothing more to humiliate me that night. After all, spraying excrement in one's face is as far as most husbands need to go to ruin an evening. Only people unacquainted with Minty Trebor would make such an assumption. Though it's difficult to imagine how such a thing could be possible, the evening did, indeed, take a turn for the worse.

The turn for the worse came in the unexpected form of a woman. A few minutes before the chaos kicked off I'd glimpsed this familiar-looking female, but I hadn't been able to make her out too well in the dark. I'd noticed her watching while the ambulance men assisted Minty. She was standing near a semi-naked forty-year-old with the words IT WILL NEVER BE OVER FOR ME tattooed across his chest. She didn't seem to be with him, though; she was one of the few people not dancing and, the more she caught my eye, the more certain I was I knew her. As soon as the paramedics left us to attend to Petey, this woman approached. She had a driven, venomous look and she was upon us before I recognized her. The Aileen Wuornos lookalike: Danny's mother, Julie.

Minty saw her before I did and, despite his agony, he managed to clamber unsteadily to his feet. Except for his socks, he was now completely naked and he covered his balding privates with cupped hands.

'Keep her away from me!' he screamed. 'Tell her to leave me alone!'

As Danny's mother broke into a run Minty's legs seemed to want to take him a variety of places. After twisting and almost buckling to the left, and twisting and almost buckling to the right, they settled on the opposite direction to Julie. To say that he ran away from Julie would be to misrepresent it, however: he toppled away, driven, one could almost imagine, by the noxious blasts that still intermittently fired from his backside.

I tried to grab hold of Julie as she passed but she pushed me aside with so much force I staggered and fell into the path of an athletic-looking black dancer. He skipped over me, scarcely altering his rhythm.

My husband fled as best he could on his semi-paralysed legs, but Julie would have had him in an instant had her progress not been retarded by a large lake of vomit which had her running on the spot for long enough for Minty to gain a yard. Eventually she lost her balance completely and tumbled into the table we'd occupied earlier. Hissing and spitting, Julie seized Petey's executive briefcase and, in one hammer-throw movement, flung it at my husband. Was she aiming for the vivid, startlingly symmetrical target-shaped contusion on his buttocks? If so she missed by several feet and the case cracked open as it landed, spilling all manner of bottles and aerosols on to the dancefloor. A shaven-headed fifty-year-old in high-waister flares almost took a tumble on a bottle of Amway bath emollient. But he danced on: he and every other dancer in the vicinity seemed largely unruffled. Indeed, I was perhaps less astonished by the surreal farce in which I found myself, than by the fact that no one else seemed astonished at all. I'm not claiming that we didn't raise eyebrows – how could we not? Numerous people looked our way; some even appeared concerned – but most danced on. Amidst the naked men and mad women, they danced on; amidst the vomit and liquid shit, they danced on.

Julie scrambled to her feet and went for Minty again. She should have been at home with her son but she was a 'Me Mother' and 'Me Mothers' take things personally. I've seen them a hundred times: punching teachers at parents' evenings, refs at junior league football, me once or twice. There's only one way to deal with them: run.

But Minty couldn't run and Julie wouldn't stop. She was like the Terminator, relentless in her stride. And Minty was in a state. He was flagging and tottering, giddy with pain. He was hers for the taking.

She was four feet away when she dived. She landed on his back, donkey-ride-style, with a force that sent them both tumbling towards the stage and the DJ's double decks. My husband headbutted the leg of the frame on which the turntables stood. The decks collapsed with a gruesome, ear-splitting screech of stylus on vinyl. A second of silence framed the collision: a strange, pregnant moment in which the beat was gone but the crowd was still in motion. Then came the explosion: a brutal, piercing crack made more terrifying by the silence that preceded it and more terrifying still by the screams it elicited.

The dancers stopped dancing at last.

ONE WEEK LATER

30

'Seven Days Too Long'

Chuck Wood (Roulette)

MINTY

The *Walsall Reflector* made difficult reading the following week. They must have spent the entire weekend dreaming up the headline: 'Naked Lollipop Man Frustrates Fannies'. Though the paper is well known for its grammatical errors, I feel sure their misuse of the plural was deliberate.

> Friday 13th was certainly unlucky for soul fans in Wolves last week. Fanny's all-nighter climaxed well before midnight thanks to one over-eager punter. Dancers were left downcast when Walsall Lollipop Man, Terrance Trebor, brought their fun to a premature end. It's reported that the frantic forty-year-old stripped naked and jumped onto the DJ's equipment. The council worker's wildman antics caused a minor explosion and a major headache for event organisers: unable to restore power in the building they were forced to refund over three hundred saddened soulsters. Stunned Soul Jock, Whizzer Tilsley, commented that he was 'pigging disgusted' by the cock-up at Fanny's.

And on it went. Typically they'd missed the real story: there was no mention at all of the sheep defleecer. But it *had* been my collision with the DJ's decks that brought the evening to a 'premature' end. It caused a short which blasted the deck's circuitry. Luckily I got away with minor abrasions and the small fire that followed was quickly extinguished. It was that mad bitch Julie's fault. Apparently she'd been tipped off about my whereabouts from someone who'd overheard me and Muncher discussing Fanny's at the barbecue. The bloody psycho tracked me down. I'm told she too was briefly admitted to A&E, where she was treated for a scorched scalp and the trauma of having lost three quarters of her mullet.

The effects of the sheep defleecer were powerful and agonizing. My consultant – Mr Dunderdale – said it delivered all symptoms of old age as effectively as if I'd gained five decades in an hour: baldness and incontinence were the most obvious, of course. He reckoned I might suffer temporary colic, impotence and diminished eyesight too. I forget the other thing. Oh, yes: memory loss. But nothing permanent. It's ironic: my attempts to recapture my youth had turned me into a geriatric. Hazel sees it from the opposite perspective. She said that my 'juvenile' behaviour had transformed me into a hairless, incontinent baby. She had a point – for the last seven days I'd been wearing a nappy.

When I examined myself in my shaving mirror that Friday morning I still looked pale but amazingly, *incredibly*, I didn't feel too bad. In fact I felt pretty good. I had the full use of my limbs again and my skin had lost its ultra-sensitivity. I was in full control of my sphincter too. I'd been through two changes of nappy since 10 a.m. on Thursday and both were unsoiled. They'd removed my drip first thing and it was a great relief to have the needle taken from the back of my hand. My guts ached from vomiting and my ring felt like the barrel of Andy McNab's Uzi but, yes, I felt good. My hair was beginning to grow back too – stubble had turned my skin to sandpaper over my entire body.

The rest of the lads were on different wards, but word was that they were all on the verge of being discharged.

Mac was the only worry. He'd been transferred to a psychiatric hospital. When he was admitted on Friday he began having flashbacks to the DTs he suffered last time he was a patient in Wesley. The rumour was that he finally freaked when they stopped him trying to suck the alcohol out of a cotton swab. The staff were forced to administer a chemical cosh.

The principal cloud on *my* horizon was how the coppers were going to react to this. Hazel told me it was Nigel who'd stolen the drugs from the clinic. The police questioned him on the night but, as yet, they hadn't charged him. Despite everything he'd done over the past days, I hadn't realized my son was *quite* such a tit. Many parents would want to disown him but, as the tit's father, how could I? When it comes to behaving like a tit, I'm his role model! What a pair we are.

I was more upset that he hadn't visited me. I hadn't seen him in a week and, given the circumstances, that was seven days too long. Being a tit I can forgive, but a heartless, selfish tit . . .

And yet.

And *yet*. I was deeply anxious about what might happen to him. Not worrying about your son is like not worrying about your own testicles. I hated him on lots of levels; in fact I felt I hated him on every level but the one that counts: the fundamental level that's stitched into the DNA and winds inextricably around each twist of the double helix. On that level it was impossible to do anything but love him. The little fucker.

He'd been on my mind for much of the morning when, about eleven, I had a visit from Inspector Smiles. This was a surprise. I knew the drug squad had spoken to Muncher and I'd been expecting them to visit me, but Smiles was vice.

'Inspector?'

'I wanted to have a word with you, sir,' he said, lowering his giant frame into the visitor's chair at the side of my bed. 'I wanted to tell you that we've now interviewed all parties involved in the incident last Friday night.'

He seemed a lot less smart-arsed than usual. His manner was more subdued and his tone more respectful. He seemed very uncomfortable. I wasn't sure if this was good news or bad news.

'Your son has admitted breaking into South Walsall Health Centre,' he told me. I went to speak but he raised his hand. 'And *my* son has admitted selling the defleecer chemicals to your friend Michael Preene.'

'Your son?'

'Yes, sir, I'm afraid so.'

'*Your* son?'

'My son, Trevor, is also in this hospital at the moment, I'm sorry to say. He was admitted last week in the early hours of Saturday morning after having had an . . . accident.' Smiles paused and raised his eyes to the ceiling. He seemed to ponder the fluorescent light for a few seconds before emitting a resigned exhalation.

'I . . . er . . .' My scalp began to itch again and, as I'd already scratched it raw, I gently rubbed the tender skin with the heel of my hand. 'I'm a little confused.'

His gaze moved from the light to the ward television, which was switched off. 'I'm afraid my son has issues.'

'Issues?' That was a word Hazel often used about me. It would occasionally accompany a speech about my immaturity, or one about there being no such things as accidents.

'Trevor purchased an illegal firearm in Dudley last Friday evening,' he said, having trouble looking me in the eye. 'He accidentally shot himself.'

I thought I felt my eyebrows rising before it occurred to me that I didn't have any. 'Shot himself?'

'It was a blank cartridge but the explosion did a lot of damage. It was caused by a faulty holster apparently: there was a stray cord inside which looped around the trigger.' Smiles gave a hollow laugh. 'The gun came from Albania but the holster was made in Walsall, would you believe?'

I was still confused. 'Is he OK?'

'He's lost his right thumb. He lost a lot of blood too and has burns all over his face and arm. He's alive, though, so that's the main thing, I suppose.' Smiles paused and, for the first time since he arrived, he looked me in the eye. 'Trevor claimed that he only wanted the gun to use in a gangsta porn film . . . As if that mitigates it.'

Slowly I was beginning to realize what might have happened, but I was still wary about voicing it. 'Forgive me if I have this wrong, but is your son the person my Nigel has been supplying with gangsta porn?'

Smiles nodded: 'I suspected he had dealings with your son. That's why I came to your home and copied your computer files. I'd been following Trevor, you see, and watched them exchange parcels.'

'You mean it had nothing to do with paedophile sites?'

Smiles shook his head. 'I refused to have a computer in the house because I've seen what people do with them, but it hasn't made a blind bit of difference. Trevor is as sick as any of the freaks I've seen on vice. *Sicker!*' He spat the last word and it was evident, not just to me but to everyone in a twenty-yard radius, that he was on the verge of popping a vessel. 'I found his films Saturday morning, not that he'd gone out of his way to hide them. One was still in our DVD player! It's as if he wanted us to find them. They are repulsive. *Dirty! Evil!*' Smiles slammed the palm of his hand down on his knee. '*And now a gun!*' he shouted. By this time most of the people on the ward were staring. Realizing this, Smiles paused, put his hand over his eyes and swallowed hard.

'Well,' I said, struggling to find a response that was both apposite and positive, 'kids, eh?'

Smiles slumped back in his chair; there were tears in his eyes now. 'We sent him to elocution lessons, so what does he do? He starts speaking like Aynuck the Black Country Pimp. We enrolled him in a gym, so what does he do? He becomes a compulsive eater. His father is a copper, so what does he do? He becomes a gangster!'

'Didn't you tell me your son never gave you any trouble?' I asked.

'I lied,' he sniffed. 'Lord forgive me for lying, but I have to because I'm ashamed of what he is; of what he's become.'

'Well, I agree he sounds a little rebellious.'

'A little rebellious? He's a fucking deviant!' The big man was still throbbing with rage. 'Lord forgive me for swearing, but I've tried everything. I've screamed and shouted at him till I'm blue in the face. I've locked him away. I've starved him. I've threatened him with the law. I've read him the Bible over and over. And I've belted him and belted him and belted him!'

I'm no expert, but Smiles didn't sound like the ideal parent.

'My wife always says that there are no such things as accidents,' I offered, still struggling to find helpful words.

He knuckled the tears from his eyes. 'What?'

'Hazel, that's my wife, she'd say that your son shot himself as a cry for help. She'd say that subconsciously he doesn't really want to be a rebel, so he shot himself on purpose to get your attention and to create an opportunity to make up with you. She'd say he shot himself because he loves you.'

'That's rubbish, though, isn't it?'

'Probably.'

Smiles gave a hollow laugh. 'I know he hates me. He's . . . a bad apple, I suppose. And now it's the Lord's will that he go through life with one thumb.'

'Did you hear about the bloke with crushed feet who conquered Mount Elbrus?'

'I'm sorry, Mr Trebor, but I'm not very good with jokes and, though I appreciate you trying to cheer me up, I'm not really in the mood for one.'

'What? No, no, it's not a joke. A bloke called Billy Peebles with severely damaged feet climbed Mount Elbrus. The point is that he hasn't let the problem with his feet stop him from doing anything: he can't walk more than a few paces, but he's become a millionaire, he has an OBE – *and he's climbed one of the highest mountains in Europe*!'

'Oh, right. Actually I think Mount Elbrus is *the* highest, technically.'

'Yes, yes, well. He climbed it last month.' I spent some time telling Smiles the full story of Billy Peebles, the circumstances of his accident and his subsequent achievements. My point was that losing a thumb wasn't the end of the world, but I'm not sure Smiles got it.

It was clear Smiles was a bit of a nutter and I tried to imagine what it would be like to have him as a father. Pretty intimidating, I assume. I wouldn't like to cross him. But his son had dared to – and all of Smiles' authority, all his raving and beating couldn't prevent that. I guess I'd been the opposite kind of father to Nigel. I'd tried not to be too strict; I'd never dream of hitting him. But my son was a criminal too and, just as Smiles didn't feel loved by his son, I didn't feel loved by mine. Even the Kray twins loved their mother, but it seemed Nigel detested both his parents. He couldn't even take the trouble to visit me in hospital – and it was his fucking fault I was here!

It was time to change the subject.

'So, inspector,' I said, trying to be as tactful as possible, 'where do we stand from a legal point of view?'

Smiles, somewhat more composed, thought for a moment. He was clearly considering how best to frame his reply. 'This business is potentially embarrassing for all of us,' he told me. 'As a consequence, my friends, my colleagues, in drug squad feel it might be in everyone's interest not to pursue the matter.'

'You can do that? You can sweep it under the carpet?'

'I'm not sure that's a phrase I'd advise you to use too frequently but, erm . . . yes.'

'I'm relieved,' I said. 'I love my son despite what he's done, you see.'

'I love mine too,' he replied, '*fervently*.'

Perhaps zealously is a better word, I thought, but I just nodded.

Smiles left the ward, pausing briefly to honk into a handkerchief that seemed way too small for his massive face.

31

'Son of a Gun'

Nirvana, *Insecticide* (Geffen)

TREBBO

'Your goatee is looking a bit wispy, man,' said Dicey. We were crossing the car park of Wesley hospital, on our way towards the main entrance. We weren't going to see the Div. I hadn't bothered visiting him yet. I hadn't laid eyes on him since they carried him into the ambulance last week. We were there to visit Blubber-T who, apparently, had been admitted a few hours after the Div. The rumour – which had reached us via a cousin of Dicey's who worked in radiology – was that Blubbs was badly burned and had blown his right thumb off.

'I fiddle with it too much when I'm nervous, dude. It thins the hair out.'

'Mental.'

I had a lot on my mind. For one thing I was expecting to be charged with breaking into the clinic at any moment; for another, I needed to see where I stood with Blubber-T. When the cops asked me what I'd done with the caps I had to fess up. He wasn't going to be happy. Knowing my luck we'd end up in the same young offenders' institution.

Blubbs was on Budgerigar Ward. At the nurses' station we asked where his bed was and it took us a while to remember his proper name. Trevor. When we spotted him, he looked even more incongruous on a hospital ward than he had behind the wheel of his mother's smart car – the bed was barely big enough for his bulbous heap. And it was as clear as a Day-Glo beanie that he was bollocksed. The right side of his face and neck were raw with weeping burns and his closed right eyelid was black and shrivelled. He was missing his jewellery, his raccoon hat – his right arm and hand were covered in bandages and he was missing his right thumb.

'Fucking hell, dude, you look rough,' I couldn't help saying. I was, however, a little relieved to see that he was immobile – at least he was in no position to punch me.

'I dow need to be cowing toad, yow mutha,' he croaked.

'What's the score?' I asked him. 'What happened to you, dude?'

From beneath the bedclothes he produced a bag of M&Ms. He opened them with his teeth, tipped the contents on to his chest and, using his good left hand, began dropping them into his chops.

In between mouthfuls Blubbs gave us a detailed account of what happened after he left Fanny's. He'd arranged to purchase a gun that night from a contact in Dudley. He wanted it partly for respect, he said, but mostly to use in his own movies – a planned move into the gangsta porn business. The gun went off as he removed it from its holster. Blubber-T immediately blacked out and, twenty minutes later, the coppers found him unconscious in Dudley Zoo car park. Apparently an African pygmy goat gave birth prematurely as a result of the bang.

Though the blast had blown some of the force from his voice, Blubber-T's distinctive Yam-Yam-from-the-Hood jargon remained. I tried to count the times he said 'muthafucker', but I gave up after twenty-nine. His speech had never seemed quite so forced and affected and I had the impression that it was costing him considerable effort to stay in character. I came to realize, perhaps for the first time, just how much of an act it was. Neither the dialect nor the street slang were natural to him. His language had always sounded corny and weird to my ear, but till now I'd missed the degree to which it was performed and, I don't know . . . wrong. I had the impression that, if he forgot himself for a moment, he'd start speaking like a BBC news presenter.

'Couldn't you have used a replica gun?' I asked. 'Who'd tell the difference in a porn movie?'

Blubbs chuckled at this, wincing as he did so. 'Replicas a as cool, am they, yow yampy mutha? They dow demand the muthafuckin respect.'

This was true. The maths is easy: less rebellion equals less cool. And this is where it had led.

'What's yower cowing business ere, any road?' he asked.

I dropped my voice. 'I want to know where we stand, dude. You're not going to be in bed for ever. What happens when you get out? Are we cool?'

Blubber-T nodded his head, slowly. 'When I'm out I'm gewin down the cowing smoke, a I? I've got contacts down there – phat, bitchin brethren who'll help me get established. I might get an ook for me thumb. That could be me gangsta gimmick!' He held up his bandaged hand and chuckled once more. I caught a glimpse of his tongue, stained reddish brown from the M&Ms.

I tried to ignore the ludicrous yet unsettling image of Blubbs with a hook for a thumb; I wanted to focus on the here and now: 'What about the law, dude? I mean, aren't there questions to answer?'

'Me old man's heat, a e? He's pulled strings.'

'Heat?'

Blubber-T went on to explain his, and my, situation. It appeared I was completely in the clear, both with the law and with Blubbs. And it was all thanks to his dad – 'the Pig', 'the Heat', 'the Muthafucker' – who had saved him. He'd saved me too.

'You don't sound very grateful to your old man,' said Dicey.

'He's a cowing muthafucker,' said Blubbs, his voice still managing to convey what I was beginning to feel was an unsettling measure of revulsion. Certainly it was strange to hear him call his dad a muthafucker given that, in this case, it was literally true.

'Safe, dude, safe,' I said, mega relieved that things were squared. I felt like crying with gratitude.

'So are you going to carry on dealing down the smoke?' Dicey asked him.

He nodded and popped another handful of M&Ms.

'And what about the porn and stuff, Blubbs? Are you still looking to get into the business?'

'Ar,' he said, swallowing, 'gangsta porn's big bones. And I should be able to get sweeter accessories down the smoke, without the Muthafucker around.' He nodded to his bedside cabinet. 'Sin me souvenir?'

I looked to see a leather holster. It was bloodstained, partially charred and had a large hole blown out of the bottom. I could still make out the gold-blocked maker's name, however: Flesh of the Beast Leather Goods, D. McVane, Walsall, England.

'Aren't you gonna drop in and see your old man?' Dicey asked as we left Budgerigar Ward and paused to get Cokes from a drinks machine in the corridor.

'Just like Blubbs, dude,' I said, popping my can one-handed, 'I'm no daddy's boy. I'm going to stay away.'

'Yeah, mental,' he said, in a tone that suggested I was being a prick. He swigged, and continued: 'So where are you going to get your skunk from now Blubber's out of business?'

'I'll find somewhere, Dice, don't worry.' I was bull-shitting, though. I'd already made up my mind not to bother. My brush with the law had put the shits up me. It made it clear to me that I wasn't much of a rebel. I knew I was jammy to get off with doing the clinic. Like being dead, having a criminal record is cool – but it has a shit-load of negative consequences. In fact, the whole concept of cool was giving me more difficulties than ever before. It had been hard to maintain it since the night at Fanny's. Particularly concerning the Div. I hadn't visited but that didn't mean I hadn't wanted to, or that I wasn't crippled with guilt over what I'd done. I *wanted* to visit him, but I couldn't. If I *were* to visit him I was afraid I might break down, bury my head in his shoulder and sob for a week. How uncool would that be? Although, of course, the likelihood is that *wouldn't* happen. It's more likely that the Evil Puppeteer would take control and make me stand at the side of his bed grunting monosyllables. That's what cool does to you, or at least to me: it keeps your emotions in a cage.

I drained my Coke and set the can down on the floor beside the machine.

'Let's split,' I said.

Dicey shrugged and followed me out of the building. The urge I had to go back to my can and place it in the litter bin was almost overwhelming.

32

Revenge (*n*)

HAZEL

I dropped in on Minty for the second half of visiting on Friday afternoon. As I parked the Micra I was pleased to see Nigel and his tramp-friend leaving the hospital. I'd been disgusted with how little he cared for his father. Nigel had to go a long way to redeem himself for what he'd done, of course, but visiting his dad was the first important step in that direction.

It had been the worst of weeks for me. During that time I think I weighed just about everything in the house. My weightlessness was so bad that I'd almost resorted to sleeping under the bed. God knows what I'd have done if I hadn't been able to see Kelvin. But now, at last, there was some good news: at least Nigel had shown himself mature enough to see his dad.

And it got better. At Minty's bedside I received the best news so far.

'Nigel is going to get away with it?' I said, suppressing a desire to hug my husband. I had to remember that I was still angry with him too. But it was all I could do not to yodel with joy as Minty told me the story.

After a week of uncertainty this was magnificent news. A criminal conviction was the last thing my son needed at his age. He didn't deserve to escape scot-free, obviously, and I'd be making sure he didn't, but I was delighted for him.

'So what did Nigel have to say for himself?' I asked.

Minty looked confused: 'What?'

'Well, he's been to see you, hasn't he? I saw him leaving the hospital while I was parking the car.'

Minty's face fell. 'He hasn't been here.'

'*What?*' Anger tightened my chest. 'So what the hell was he doing here if he wasn't visiting you, for God's sake?'

Minty thought for a moment. 'He must have been to see Trevor. Smiles told me his son is on Budgerigar Ward.'

'What on earth for?'

Minty shrugged. 'Search me – I wouldn't have thought Trevor would be in the market for any more gangsta porn at the moment.'

'*I beg your pardon?*'

'Ah, erm . . . nothing Haze, nothing.' But it was clear Minty had let something slip.

It took me the best part of half an hour to get it all out of him. By the time I had the full story I was as close to murdering Nigel as I've ever been. I believe I actually spent time estimating the practical consequences of killing him. Given the provocation, I was sure the courts would be lenient. I'd probably be free in under a year; I might even get away with a suspended sentence. I couldn't help feeling I'd be doing the human race a service.

'It sounds worse than it is, Haze.'

'*Pornography? Fraud?* On top of drug dealing and burglary! How can it be any better than absolutely fucking terrible, Minty?'

'Well, compared to, say, Trevor, Nigel's behaviour isn't too bad . . . I suppose.'

'Compared to Trevor, Heinrich-fucking-Himmler's behaviour wasn't too bad!'

'It's all just kid's stuff, Haze. He always paid the credit card bill; the pornography is legal and the drug was just cannabis. Kids do stupid things. My mom and dad thought I'd grow up to be a wrong-un, but look how I've turned out.'

Yes, I thought, you're a half-dead lollipop man who refuses to grow up! But I didn't say it, because that wasn't what he'd meant by 'turned out'. He'd meant that he'd grown, in spite of everything, into a good man. I couldn't disagree with that.

'Why are you sticking up for him?' I sighed. 'He doesn't deserve to be stuck up for, Minty, least of all by you. You and your mates could have been killed at Fanny's.'

My husband shrugged. He was pallid and completely bald but for the tiny dots of new hair that seemed to cover every inch of his skin. It was as if he'd been rolled in iron filings. His eyes were puffy, his teeth were yellow and he smelt vaguely of excrement.

'How are you feeling anyway?' I asked him. I needed to change the subject for the sake of my sanity.

'Brillo, actually, Haze.'

'That's good.' I couldn't help smiling – Minty's resilience and irrepressible optimism were impressive traits. It reminded me again of why I loved him.

'I can feel my strength coming back by the second. I can't wait to get out of here. I'm the last one.'

'Really? They've discharged the others?' I knew that Mac had been sectioned. The poor bloke's battle with the booze was far from over. I'd send him a get well card with a pint of lager on the front as soon as I had time. I knew that Mac would appreciate this in his own weird way.

'Yep, I'm the last one. Nipper, Muncher and Petey were discharged together at lunchtime. They popped in an hour or so before you arrived. Look what Nipper bought me.'

He gestured to his locker where there was a copy of a magazine about Northern Soul called *Togetherness*.

All the way back from Wesley my anger built as I thought about Nigel. It affected my concentration and I nearly ran over a willowy blonde jogger on a zebra crossing. It's a good job Minty wasn't with me or he'd have had a stroke. I knew it was my fault, but I still sounded my horn at her. The cheeky bitch blew a kiss at me. It was all I could do not to stamp on the accelerator and put a tyre track up the back of her pink 'Fit for Life' sweatshirt. Just by looking at her I could tell that she'd fall into the 'Keen Mother' category. This is the irritatingly conscientious type. She'd raise her child on mung beans and mashed yeast and have a thermometer up its arse every five minutes. She'd buy it educational toys and she'd read it poetry. She'd explain the point of every fairy story, every film, every news item, every argument, every 'accident'. She'd encourage it to have conversations about ethics. Her offspring would grow to be urbane, diligent and moral. Unless, that is, they didn't.

I arrived home about four-thirty, ready to kill. The fact that I almost broke my neck on a reeking pair of Nigel's trainers in the hall didn't help. Nor did it help that music was booming loud enough to shake the fillings from my teeth. I could only just make out that the phone was ringing.

'*What?*' I screamed into the mouthpiece.

It was Nancy Valentine from next door. 'The music is very loud, Mrs Trebor,' she said.

'Sorry, I can't hear you because of the music,' I bawled, banging down the receiver.

I stamped upstairs and entered Nigel's room without knocking. The smell of sweaty socks hit me along with the heat. It must've been ninety degrees. I made my way to the stereo and, unsure how to switch it off, pulled the lead out from the back.

'Oi!' said Nigel, apparently noticing me for the first time.

'Why didn't you go and visit your father this afternoon?'

'Wha?'

'You heard me. You were at the hospital, I saw you. If you can bunk off school to see your drug-dealer friends, you can at least find time to visit your father!'

Nigel shrugged.

'What were you going to see him for anyway – were you looking to supply him with any more specialist pornography?'

Nigel's eyes widened.

'Oh, you needn't look so surprised, you disgusting little bleeder. Your father's filled me in on how you've been spending your free time. He told me all about how we can add pornography and fraud to your list of pastimes.'

'Yeah? What did he say exactly?'

So I told him, exactly. And he didn't backchat me. He sat there as I bawled the meaning of 'disgust' at him from my *Mini Oxford*. It was a good, clear, Mo-style definition with no room for ambiguity: '"Revulsion", that's what I feel for you at the moment, son.'

Usually he took the mickey when I did this kind of thing: he'd sing through my definitions, or pull his beanie down over his ears. Either that or he'd ask me to define the meaning of the synonym that described the word I'd defined and then, if I was daft enough to go along with him, he'd ask for a definition of the synonym of the synonym. Not this time. He could tell I meant business. It would have taken just one of his smart comments for me to have kicked him out, knocked him out, or both. He must have sensed this and, if not exactly apologetic, he capitulated with a sheepish look on his face and a slight tremor in his voice. He even agreed when I told him he had to go and visit his dad that night. Not that I gave him much choice. 'I'll drag you there by that goatee you imagine you've got. *Right?*'

'Right.'

'Do you understand me?'

'I do,' he said, 'but there's something you should see before you blow your cool at me.'

'My God, I don't believe it: you've just uttered a sentence of more than three words! And what is it I should see?'

'Go to the spare room and take a look in the deep drawer of the computer unit.'

'*What?*'

'Go on. You'll find something in there that will interest you.'

I had no idea what he was talking about but I decided not to look – at least not straight away. I was too mad to do anything other than attempt to calm down. I needed to compose myself urgently because I was feeling peculiar: take-off terror roared in my tummy – that strange, weightless feeling seemed set to float me away.

In the living room I unpacked my scales and weighed a DVD of *Gladiator*. Then I weighed a bottle of *Becherovka*, an undrinkable spirit Dave McVane brought us from his holiday in Prague. Heavier. Then I added a bottle of Dreadhead, the undrinkable rum Dave McVane brought us back from his holiday in Barbados. Heavier still. Better. Then I told myself I had to stop weighing things. I weighed another three or four items before I actually did stop.

Next I phoned Kelvin on his mobile: I immediately clicked off when I received his answer service.

*

I found the records, together with a bill for nine hundred and ninety pounds addressed to Mr Terrance Trebor. Looking back, what I did next seems bizarre and stupid. Like much of what I was doing at the time, it *was* bizarre and stupid. But I did it.

I sat for maybe twenty minutes breaking the records up into small fragments. Some were easier to break than others: a couple of discs had very brittle vinyl that snapped readily, while others were made of much more pliable plastic. These would bend rather than snap and I had to cut them up with scissors. It was difficult for me to handle them because my hands were trembling with fury. Eventually, though, I managed to break every record into enough small pieces to make my mosaic.

I went downstairs, out into the garden and, after rummaging around the shed for two or three minutes, I had what I wanted: a two-by-four piece of hardboard and a pot of glue. When I returned to the house I passed Nigel in the hall. He was on the phone to Tiffany, trying to persuade her to go with him to the hospital. Unlike him, she'd already taken the trouble to visit Minty twice.

'Don't force yourself,' he told her, 'do what you want. Whatever. Just call for me about six if you're coming.'

How could any girl resist?

Tiffany had confided in me at work that she was thinking of breaking things off with Nigel. I could understand it, of course, but I was sorry. I'd been hoping that some of her good sense and decency might rub off on him, in time. Fat chance. Even *she* was beginning to concede that she might have been wrong about him being 'nice underneath'.

I climbed the stairs with the hardboard and glue and set to work in the computer room. First I sketched out the words in pencil on the hardboard, then I coated the area with glue. Using shards of the ruined discs, I spelt out the following across the brown, dappled expanse of the board: GROW UP OR FUCK OFF!

I set my handiwork up in front of the computer so that I could admire it. Here and there I'd applied too much glue and white rivulets began descending from some of the letters. They'd crawl an inch or so down the board before stiffening to a standstill in the warm air.

What had I done?

I'm not sure how long I stared at the mosaic, transfixed. I was shocked at myself. I knew what I *should've* done, obviously: I should have made Minty return the records and get his money back. But something in me snapped. My message could have applied to either Minty or Nigel because I was sick of being a mother to them. Mothering adults shouldn't be my role, or anyone's. I needed a different one. I needed a role that made sense, one that gave me more significance, more worth, more weight in the world. It was floating away; *I* was floating away. Is that crazy, New-Age woman's talk? No, it's not. It had taken a while for me to be sure of my feelings, of my needs, but now I was. I understood. Soon I'd have to try and make Minty understand it too.

I reached for my mobile and called Kelvin again. Still no answer. I set it aside and continued to stare at the letters I'd made. Eventually they became blurred with tears.

I'm not sure how long it took the tears to subside but, gradually, they did. And so did my rage. I didn't want it to. I wanted to stay mad at Minty's deceit and his ridiculous, immature behaviour. I wanted to wallow in my own hurt.

My mind turned towards Minty in Wesley and how weak with worry I'd been when they admitted him. He calls me a hard-nosed 'puppy-drowning' nurse, but if he'd felt what I'd felt last Friday night he'd never joke that way again. I'd fussed and blithered at his bedside like a besotted schoolgirl.

Why? Because I love him. 'Love' is a word I've looked up countless times in my dictionary; in many dictionaries in fact. All definitions are inadequate. When it comes to things like love, words are the enemies of reality; no word, or combination of words, can express or contain it. In my own heart and in my own way, I love Minty Trebor and I know he loves me. Look what he's done for me, after all. He sold his records so that we could get married; he gave up his job so that I could keep mine; he raised our son. Yes, we loved each other, but something had gone wrong. What had I done in return for his love? I'd tried to make him something that he wasn't. I'd deceived him. I'd scissored his prize possessions.

My reverie was interrupted by the phone. At first I thought it might be Kelvin returning my call, but I'd asked him to be cautious and he wouldn't risk using the house number. I moved to answer it on the extension in our bedroom.

It was Minty. He'd been discharged.

33

'The Key to My Happiness'

The Charades (MGM)

MINTY

Hazel seemed a bit odd when she came to collect me from Wesley. Subdued and yet jittery. She had a little argument with the charge nurse at the desk because she felt I was being discharged too soon.

I was feeling fine. I could sense myself getting stronger by the minute. It was a surprise to be discharged at that late hour, but they needed the bed, and I was glad.

In the lift down to the ground floor Hazel didn't speak. I was occupied with my thoughts too. I'd spent much of that week assessing my situation and I'd reached some decisions. The disaster at Fanny's hadn't diminished my enthusiasm for re-embracing Northern Soul. For drugs, yes; but not for Northern. Far from it. I'd decided to spend my convalescence reacquainting myself still more with the scene. There were plenty of Northern websites I hadn't explored yet: on-line fanzines and record dealers. I planned to attend more Northern Soul events in the future too and get to know some people on the current scene. I wouldn't be going to all-nighters every week – that wouldn't be fair on Haze – but once in a while. Most important of all, I intended to re-build my collection of rare singles, using my recent purchases as a start. A new job would help with that: I'd definitely be applying for the supervisor's post at the council. It was way past time. I'd spent too long in the lolliman rut and this job could be the perfect way out. Hazel would be chuffed, of course, but I knew what she'd say. She'd rib me about it and claim that the news about Billy Peebles' success had eased my subconscious guilt. For the first time it occurred to me that she was right – that I'd been feeling guilty for years and using it as an excuse not to move on.

I'd decided to come clean about my records to Haze. If Fanny's had purged me of anything it was my appetite for deceit. I was a crap liar. It seemed it was impossible for me to hide my shit, literally. Besides, I owed it to Hazel. I'd seen how much she loved me. The woman loved me even though I'd shat in her face! How could I deceive such a woman and why would I even need to? Hazel, above everything, was the key to my happiness.

'Haze,' I said, as we inched our way off Wesley-in-Tame car park, 'there's something I have to tell you and you're going to be a bit angry with me.'

'Go on, Minty.'

And I told her about the records.

I was expecting a dickie, but she remained calm. When she spoke she seemed serious and a little downcast. 'Don't you think you could have found something more useful to spend a thousand pounds on?'

'Haze, I don't expect you to understand, but for ages now there's been something missing from my life. I know it sounds pathetic, but those records have *changed* my life. Every time I think about them I get a rush of a kind I haven't experienced in years.'

'Thanks,' she said.

'I don't mean . . . I can't explain it except to say that, just knowing those records are in my possession gives me a thrill and, I don't know, a purpose.'

274

'And what about me?' she said flatly. 'Don't I give you "a purpose"?'

'Of course, *of course*, but this is different. Maybe purpose is the wrong word.' My meaning rang eloquently in my head but I struggled for words. 'For instance,' I said, trying a different approach, 'I've decided to get a job. A *real* job, I mean. There's a supervisor's post going at the council. My manager says that with my O-levels and good record I should get it no problem. If that doesn't come off, I'll try for something else.'

I was hoping this would impress her but surprisingly Hazel's face remained set. 'I'm pleased to hear it. Maybe the job should have preceded the extravagance?'

'I know but I think my buying those records was partly a compensation for me *not* having a decent job; for not having something fulfilling in my life, the way *you* have your career. Does that sound crazy?'

'You're unfulfilled. Remember unfulfilled? It's a word that, even without looking, I knew didn't appear in my *Mini Oxford*. Do you recall that?'

'Er, yes. But it's more than that, Haze. The records mean . . . I don't know . . . They give me something to prize; something to cherish; something to love.'

Hazel widened her eyes.

'Well, perhaps love is the wrong word. Let's just say that it would be good for us both if I had another facet to my life.'

Hazel bristled at this – I could tell because her cheeks reddened and the tiny muscles beneath her skin began to vibrate.

'A new fucking facet to your life? And what are the chances of me having another fucking facet to mine?'

'Well, I've always thought that you –'

'How do you think I knew unfulfilled wasn't in my dictionary? Have a fucking guess, genius.'

275

'Er, well, I know you're well acquainted with the contents, Haze, because you –'

'I've looked it up.'

'Yes, but you look everything up, even words you already kn–'

'It's all about you, isn't it? You fucking bastard! What about me? You get all the good things in this relationship: you're the one who gets to be irresponsible; you're the one who gets to ponce around in a part-time job for twelve fucking years. *How dare you moan?*'

We were on a main road doing about forty in third gear: 'Haze,' I said, tentatively, 'you could probably do with changing into –'

'And you got to stay at home and look after Nigel. All those years you watched him grow; played with him, bonded with him!'

'*Bonded* with him? Are we talking about the same –'

'YOU'RE LUCKIER THAN ME!' She bawled this into the windscreen with a ferocity that scared me. My mind struggled to get a handle on what she was saying. What *was* she saying?

'I . . . I'm luckier than you?'

She still hadn't changed from third and the gearbox was like a buzz saw.

'*I* wanted to be with Nigel,' she said, tears welling in her eyes. '*I* wanted to bring him up. *I* missed out.'

'I don't know where this is coming from, Haze, but it's a bit late to be telling me now – sixteen years too late!'

'It's not too late!' she screamed; and then again, louder: 'IT'S NOT TOO LATE!'

She stamped her foot on the brake and the tyres roared against the tarmac. My seatbelt jammed into my abdomen with such force that I thought I might shit myself again. The wheels of the Micra locked, we skidded and the phrase that javelined into my head was: *we're going to have an accident*!

We didn't have an accident – Hazel was still in control, just. The car immediately behind had to brake very sharply, however, and the sound of his squealing brakes made me squeal too. It was a loud, shrill squeal that seemed to come from deep within me and which sounded so weird I couldn't help but laugh with surprise and embarrassment. As the driver behind eased his Fiat Punto around us, bawling silent oaths, I waved an apology at him with a trembling hand.

When Hazel took her foot off the clutch the engine was still running and the Micra lurched and stalled. She was trembling too and struggling to calm herself. She continued to grip the wheel with bone-white knuckles – as if releasing it would mean her being sucked away through the sunroof. Eventually she let it go, but her hands still shook.

'Fuck me, Hazel, what is it?'

'I've been seeing a psychiatrist,' she said simply.

'*What?*'

With that my wife began to sob. I tried to comfort her but she shrugged me away. She wept into her hands until the torrent subsided and she was able to calm herself enough to speak.

Her psychiatrist's name was Kelvin. He was based at the Walsall clinic and he'd been seeing her 'very informally' because she was a colleague; indeed, she'd seen so much of him in recent weeks, he was also a friend. They'd been meeting for just over a month and almost every working day for the last fortnight. She'd been depressed, she said, and she'd felt she was losing control.

'I've been feeling as if . . . as if my world is floating away. I don't want it to, Minty.'

'Floating away? I don't understand, Hazel, tell me.'

Then she told me. It took her thirty-seven minutes by the dashboard clock. Perhaps I should have guessed; in fact, a more attentive husband doubtless *would* have guessed; but not me. It stunned me. I hadn't been expecting that particular four-letter word, not again. Why is it that it's the four-letter words that are the most powerful? 'Love', 'soul' and, in this case, 'baby'. Yes, I was stunned. It had never been an issue before, but I was relieved – at least I could try to help her.

'Don't worry, Haze,' I said, desperate to cheer her, 'we can do something about it!'

'Really?'

'Of course.'

'But I didn't think you wanted any more children after Nigel. You said that given half a chance you'd have your tubes knotted and you'd put plutonium in your pants to make sure. It was the night you tried to force Mo into the shredder.'

'That was just me flapping my jaw, Haze, you know that. If you want to have another child, we'll try.'

'But what if it *is* too late? I've been feeling empty, I've been feeling light-headed, I've been feeling as if I*'m* about to float away along with everything else in my world – my mom told me that it's the way she felt before the meno-pause. I know I'm supposed to be too young but she wasn't much older than me and you can never be sure with these things!'

'Rubbish! Anyway, we can try, can't we? We can do whatever it takes. We'll adopt if you want to.' I held her head in my hands. 'Whatever you want, I want too. I love you.'

She brought her hands up and placed them on the back of mine and gazed at me with eyes full of what I can only describe as love. I thrilled to see it; it was better than sex, better than drugs and better than Northern Soul.

Then to my dismay tears filled her eyes again. 'There's something else I have to tell you, Minty,' she said, 'something that will make you hate me.'

34

'All Apologies'

Nirvana, *In Utero* (Geffen)

TREBBO

Tiffany arrived about seven. She had the sulks, as expected.

'Good news,' I said, when I answered the door, 'we don't have to go to the hospital to see the Div. He's been discharged.'

'Then I'm going home,' she said.

'Why? Come up to my room, I'll stick a CD on.'

'I don't think so, Trebbo.'

'Go on,' I said. 'You can see the old man when he gets back. The Divette has gone to pick him up.'

She considered this for a moment before, unenthusiastically, making her way up to my room. She'd barely spoken to me since last Friday. I'd been round to call on her twice but all we'd had were a couple of terse conversations on her doorstep. Even though I stayed to face the music at Fanny's, the look of disgust she'd given me that night hadn't left her eye.

Tiff sat on the bed but her body language made it clear that I needn't make any advances. Her legs were firmly together and she stared grimly in front of her. I'd seen her sitting on that bed many times over the past few months. Though she hadn't looked so hostile as she did now, she never really seemed happy there. Happy to be with me, I mean. Mind you, Tiff never seemed *entirely* happy anywhere. But I suppose I could say the same about myself: we were a pair of miserable sods. How different we both were from that girl I'd spotted at Fanny's. Smiley Kylie. I'd thought about her a lot over the past week, even though I didn't get to talk to her at Fanny's. She was a geek, but she knew how to have a good time. I wasn't sure Tiffany did, or me either.

I decided to put *Nevermind* on the CD player. It wasn't Tiffany's favourite, but I considered it Nirvana's best album. It's much more melodic than the rest. It's the first they recorded for a mainstream record label, after the hard-edged and punkie *Bleach*. Tiffany, being a very earnest and ethical person, disapproved of such commerce. She and Dicey were often scathing about *Nevermind*, referring to it as Nirvana's 'easy-listening' album. They seemed to feel that my preference for it revealed some kind of flaw in my character. To be frank, I thought that their relative unresponsiveness to it revealed a flaw in theirs. As much as I liked them both, neither seemed to have much passion for what they professed to enjoy; they seemed indifferent to . . . I don't know, its soul?

I heard the Divette's car on the drive. The doors opened and shut and the gimmers made their way into the house.

'The gimmers are back,' I said.

'I want to go down and say hello to your dad and then I'm going,' Tiff said, although she made no immediate attempt to move.

'I'd leave it a few minutes if I were you, Tiff.'

'What?'

'Trust me.'

Tiffany didn't question me and we continued to sit on the bed, listening to the album in silence. 'Polly' had just faded into 'Territorial Pissings' when the commotion began.

'NAAAAAA! NAAAAAA! NAAAAAA! NAAAAAA!'
The sound of the Div's screams filled the house.

'What's happening?' cried Tiffany, swinging her legs off the bed.

'*NAAAAAA! NAAAAAA! NAAAAAA! NAAAAAA!*' went the Div.

Tiffany made to go downstairs but I stopped her.

'He thinks my mother has smashed his records up and made them into a mosaic,' I told her.

'What?'

'But she didn't: she thought she was smashing his vinyl but I swapped it for mine. I replaced his Northern Soul records with my Nirvana vinyl, so that she'd smash mine instead of his.'

'Your rare Nirvana records?'

'My rare Nirvana records, yes. Uncool, but true. They were the only vinyl discs I had in the house. It was mine or his.'

All through 'Drain You' and 'Lounge Act' I explained to Tiffany how, as soon as I'd done it, I regretted shopping Minty to the Divette. I told her how I regretted *everything* I'd done to him. I'd heard her threaten to smash any records the Div brought into the house and I was certain she'd do it: I know what she's like when she has one of her dickie-fits. I didn't want to be responsible for that. I knew what his rare vinyl meant to him. I knew because I knew what mine meant to me. The collector's gene is one I seem to have inherited. So, while my mother was downstairs fiddling with her scales, I removed Dad's Northern and replaced them with my vinyl. I was betting my mom wouldn't know the difference between Northern Soul and grunge. A woman like my mother is useless when it comes to music: all she does is listen to it!

'You sacrificed your most prized possessions to save your father from being upset?'

I nodded. 'How much of a numpty does that make me?'

'A pretty big one, Trebbo. I mean, why didn't you just *hide* your dad's vinyl?'

'Dunno,' I shrugged. That was the easiest way to answer her, even though I felt I *did* know.

Tiffany was silent. All through 'Stay Away' and 'On a Plain' she studied me. I'm not really sure what I was hoping for. Perhaps I was hoping that her face would soften and that by the time we got to 'Endless, Nameless' she'd be looking at me in a way no one had ever looked at me before, regardless of how much cheap skunk I'd flogged them. I'd have cherished that look, had it come. It didn't. But I didn't really need it. It was enough to know I'd done something that neither she, nor I, had been expecting.

David McVane

Author

The story you've just read is based partly on my own personal experience and partly on a number of discussions (call them interviews if you like) I had with the Trebor family shortly after I was discharged from North Walsall Psychiatric Unit.

Several years have passed since the events described took place and, as a way of concluding and updating my narrative, I'd like to include the responses I had from the Trebors when I emailed them last week. I asked them each the following question, a favourite of all Northern Soul enthusiasts: 'Could you list your current top five songs and briefly explain your choices?'

POOKIE'S (AKA TREBBO'S) TOP FIVE SONGS

5

'Too Darn Soulful'. Morris Chestnut. Kylie bought me an original demo of it for my eighteenth birthday.

4

'This Beautiful Day'. Solomon King. This is one of my dad's favourites and it reminds me of the all-nighter I attended the day after I was accepted for university.

3

'I Was Born to Love You'. Herbert Hunter. This was playing as Kylie and I announced our engagement at a weekender in Scarborough.

2

'This Gets to Me'. Pookie Hudson. Because I'm named after the singer who, as it turns out, is brillo!

1

'Do I Love You (Indeed I Do)'. Frank Wilson. This is the song that changed my life.

5

That beautiful record by Will Young. I can't recall the title. It was the first song I heard after our youngest, Sophie Tamiko, was born. Weight: actually, I can't recall how much she weighed.

4

'About a Girl' by that group Nigel used to like. My health visitor Tiffany Price (née Milton) is forever humming it.

3

'Don't You Want Me?' by the good-looking bloke with the funny haircut and the two girls who look much better now that they've put on a bit of weight. It was a Giddy Kitten classic.

2

'Tainted Love', *not* the version by the woman who was married to Marc Bolan. It reminds me of when I first met Minty.

1

'Do I Love You? (Indeed I Do)'. The tune from the KFC adverts a few years back. It's the song that changed our lives.

5

'Walk Like a Man'. Johnny Moore. Because I purchased a mint-condition demo of this the day I landed my new job with the council.

4

'You're Gonna Make Me Love You'. Sandi Sheldon. Pookie bought me an original, Okeh demo of this the day when, aged forty-four, I passed my driving test.

3

'Spellbound'. Tamiko Jones. This reminds me of my beautiful daughter, Sophie Tamiko Trebor. Let's hope she's as thoughtful and kind as her brother, Pookie, grew up to be.

2

'Tainted Love'. Gloria Jones (*not* the Soft Cell version). It reminds me of when I first met Hazel.

1

'Do I Love You (Indeed I Do)'. Frank Wilson. Do I need to spell this out? Indeed I don't.

About the Author

PAUL MCDONALD is Senior Lecturer in English at the University of Wolverhampton, where he runs the Creative and Professional Writing programme. His published work includes several books of literary criticism, poetry and fiction. *Do I Love You?* is his third novel. His hobbies include Sudoku and supporting Walsall Football Club. He uses the former to take his mind off the latter.

Acknowledgements

A number of people helped in the development of this novel. I owe a substantial debt to all at Tindal Street Press: Alan Mahar, Emma Hargrave and Luke Brown; and to Penny Rendall for copyediting. I would also like to thank John and Jenny Cattell, John and Pam Causer, and Lynne (Dictionary Lady) Tildesley for their various insights and information. Most of all thanks, as always, to my partner Pam for helping in so many ways.

Acknowledgements

SURVIVING STING

Paul McDonald

'A voice from the Black Country
as authentic as Baltis and Bank's bitter'
Time Out

1970s Walsall: 'the ugliest town in the country'. Emerging from the concrete is one Dave 'Mac' McVane, an eighteen-year-old saddle-maker who has, on a balmy August night at the Walsall Town Hall disco, just managed to seduce the most shaggable girl around with a mixture of urbane charm and the odd fleck of spit.

This transcendental encounter with the luscious Joolz Cartright prompts a crazy week of sex, violence and betrayal as Mac is immersed in the surreal world of the Jerome K. Jerome estate.

Take a cast list that includes demented Billy Bob and his twizzler parents, the sociopathic Tezza, a boy named Sue, and Brainy Kev, red wine drinker and physics swot. Add a pet scorpion and an overdressed Yorkshire terrier to this Black Country brew, vintage 1979, and a pacy comic nightmare takes over.

'A hilarious, laugh-out-loud comedy
that will have tears running down your cheeks'
The Walsall Observer

'A wholly unpretentious, humorous and easy read'
The Times

ISBN: 0 9535 89 54 4

KISS ME SOFTLY, AMY TURTLE

Paul McDonald

'Funny, moreish and puts Walsall on the map
in the way that Dante's *Inferno* did with Hell'
Mil Millington

The will-sapping tedium of life as a *Walsall Reflector* hack
has given Dave 'Ichabod' McVane a serious thirst for the
devil's juice. Now, after years of debauchery, the booze has
bitten back. Cathetered, bed-bound – and with what feels
like a rhinoceros buffeting its way through his stomach –
Dave wakes among 'regulars' in a hospital notorious for its
high mortality rate. And if his darkest hour wasn't dark
enough, a sinister figure from his student days at the Walsall
Academy of New Knowledge reappears . . . to leave Dave
reeling with pain and paranoia as he faces a slap-happy
surgeon. Join our hero as he embarks on a savage and hilarious ride from S&M to the NHS.

'This is the most fun I've had all year –
fast-paced, witty and surprisingly moving.
A distinctive Midlands voice – Paul McDonald
has done the impossible: he's made Walsall funny'
Patrick Thompson

"His prose is refreshing, surprising and comfortable
in its own lucid, unpretentious skin'
TLS

ISBN: 0 954130 37 5

Are you a keen reader of contemporary fiction?

*Want to discover some more excellent writing
from the English regions?*

Become a Friend of Tindal Street Press

Ten of a total of 33 Tindal Street titles in eight years
have achieved national prize listings.

By becoming a Friend of Tindal Street Press for a year,
you can choose FOUR from a selection of titles that includes:

DISTINCTIVE LITERARY FICTION

Clare Morrall	*Astonishing Splashes of Colour*
Anthony Cartwright	*The Afterglow*
Austin Clarke	*The Polished Hoe*
Grace Jolliffe	*Piggy Monk Square*
Ed Trewavas	*Shawnie*
Jackie Gay	*Scapegrace*
	Wist
E. A. Markham	*Meet Me in Mozambique*
	At Home with Miss Vanesa
Will Buckingham	*Cargo Fever*
Daphne Glazer	*Goodbye, Hessle Road*
	By the Tide of Humber
Catherine O'Flynn	*What Was Lost*

SHORT STORY ANTHOLOGIES

Her Majesty
Mango Shake
Loffing Matters
Are You She?

NOIR CRIME FICTION

Mick Scully	*Little Moscow*
Alan Brayne	*Jakarta Shadows*
David Fine	*The Executioner's Art*
Nicholas Royle (ed)	*Dreams Never End*
John Dalton	*The City Trap*
	The Concrete Sea

As a Friend of Tindal Street Press, you will be supporting a unique publishing operation focused on literary fiction with a regional and contemporary edge. And you will enjoy special discounts on our varied fiction list.

For £25 you can enjoy a fine selection of original regional fiction. Send your cheque to Tindal Street Press, with a list of your preferences and interests, to 217 The Custard Factory, Gibb Street, Digbeth, Birmingham B9 4AA. We will then dispatch your choice of four titles (subject to availability).

By supporting Tindal Street in this way you will also join our **Friends of Tindal Street Press** mailing list, where we will keep you up to date with launch invitations, events, readings, forthcoming publications, prize listings and author information.

See our website *www.tindalstreet.co.uk* for our full range of titles

'If you want originality these days, look to the independent presses. Tindal Street Press is one of the best (and certainly has the best address – The Custard Factory, Birmingham) The Times

PRIZEWINNING FICTION

Hard Shoulder (eds Jackie Gay and Julia Bell) *Raymond Williams Community Publishing Prize 2000*; **The Pig Bin** (Michael Richardson) *Sagittarius Prize 2001*; **A Lone Walk** (Gul Y. Davis) *J. B. Priestley Fiction Award 2001*; **Whispers in the Walls** (eds Leone Ross and Yvonne Brissett) *World Book Day Top 10 2003*; **Astonishing Splashes of Colour** (Clare Morrall) *Shortlisted for Man Booker Prize 2003, British Book Awards Newcomer of the Year 2003*; **The Polished Hoe** (Austin Clarke) *Overall winner of Commonwealth Writers Prize 2003*; **The Afterglow** (Anthony Cartwright) *Betty Trask Award 2004; shortlisted for James Tait Black Memorial Prize 2004, John Llewellyn Rhys Prize 2004, Commonwealth Writers Prize (Eurasia) 2005*; **Piggy Monk Square** (Grace Jolliffe) *Shortlisted for Commonwealth Writers Prize (first novel) 2005*; **Meet Me in Mozambique** (E. A. Markham) *Longlisted for the Frank O'Connor International Short Story Award 2007* ; **What Was Lost** (Catherine O'Flynn) *Longlisted for the Orange Broadband Prize, Man Booker Prize and Guardian First Book Award 2007.*